THE CHRONICLES OF CRALLICK

By

Brad C. Baker

Dear Joe,

Let no challenge overcome you.

THE CHRONICLES OF CRALLICK

First published in 2017
by Wallace Publishing, United Kingdom
www.wallacepublishing.co.uk

ISBN-13: 978-1975867522
ISBN-10: 1975867521

All Rights Reserved
Copyright © Brad C. Baker, 2017

The right of Brad C. Baker to be identified as the author of this work has been asserted in accordance with section 77 and 78 of the Copyright Designs and Patents Act 1988.

This book is sold under condition that it shall not, by way of trade or otherwise, be lent, re-sold, hired out or otherwise circulated in any form of binding or cover other than that in which it is published and without a similar condition including this condition being imposed on the subsequent purchaser.

This is a work of fiction. Names, characters, businesses, places, events and incidents are either the products of the author's imagination or used in a fictitious manner. Any resemblance to actual persons, living or dead, or actual events is purely coincidental.

Typesetting courtesy of KGHH Publishing, United Kingdom
www.kensingtongorepublishing.com

Table of Contents

Dedication 4

About the Author 5

Prologue 6

Chapter One 12

Chapter Two 22

Chapter Three 42

Chapter Four 58

Chapter Five 78

Chapter Six.. 100

Chapter Seven.. 144

Chapter Eight 162

Chapter Nine 192

Chapter Ten.. 210

Chapter Eleven... 226

Chapter Twelve 250

Chapter Thirteen 282

Chapter Fourteen 317

Chapter Fifteen 347

Epilogue.. 367

Dedication

This novel is dedicated to the ones I love:

Hongying Xue and Shawn Yu, whose love and support got me through the darkest time of my life.

Graeme Huffman and Sheri Rhines, who always called me family and never ceased to have faith in me.

Mass Hoyte, who likewise had faith in me and stood by me when the chips were down. God bless!

My actual family... all of you; without you, I wouldn't be me.

And a warm wish to my departed grandma, Gloria. You too, always had faith in me. I miss you.

About the Author

By Shawn Yu

Brad Baker, a forty-five-year-old science fiction/fantasy writer, comes from Toronto and now lives in Kingston. When he was nine years old he got lost in the northern woods for a week, and obviously survived. Then, when he was in grade eight, he won a Canada-wide Science Fair. Starting at the age of twenty, he hitch-hiked across Canada and the US. He saw a couple of cool things, like the Rocky Mountains and the Grand Canyon.

At the age of twenty-seven, he was diagnosed with Stargardt's disease, which destroys the center of the eye. At thirty years of age he got married, and then got abused by his wife for ten years, which of course, he survived. During this time he had a son who passed away, and then another who survived.

After a while, he went through a messy divorce that resulted in his alienation from one of his sons. Now he's with his new girlfriend, who helped him through the toughest part of his life. He is living a happy life with his new girlfriend and his son, me, who wrote this "About the Author" section.

Prologue

*"Queen Bannathae heard of Amarallan menace,
King Corr hungered from his tundra for greener lands.
'stead of proposing marriage, two lands embrace,
Troops, not flowers, he sent to take us in his hands."
-Verse 1: Ballad of Ser Crallick Carnage-born.*

Verdant-tinged gold light spilled in through the panes of the roughly crafted front window. It bathed the hearth and mantle in its molten glow. Bronzed, corded muscles lifted a two-handed sword up to rest on several skewed pegs driven into the stone wall. The sword was blue-grey steel, serrated blade, humble guard, wraps of dusk panther hide, with a simple appearing ivory claw crowning the pommel. The man placing the sword upon the wall was equally unassuming. Salt began to streak his long brown hair, crow's feet tramped around his care-worn eyes, and his Vitani features lent angular and lean-predatory lines to his body. Around his neck hung an eclectic array of drying and pungent trophies. A shirt of rust-pitted ring mail tried to protect his torso, breeches of a reptile's leather hide of poor craftsmanship clad his legs, with a pair of metal-shod boots adorning his feet to complete the warrior's presence.

"By Chessintra's black bosom! Crallick, ye don't have to do this!"

The protest came from a disapproving dwarf standing in the doorway of the three-roomed farm hovel. He was clad in polished and bright silver plate armor and carried, along with a disapproving countenance, a wickedly curved battle-axe and shield.

"Actually, Tobin, I do," Crallick growled. "And I've had more than enough of that black goddess's whoring ways to last a lifetime. I'm done."

Tugging at his beard, Tobin scowled. Then he scoffed, "Humph, what the fuck are you going to do with yourself? Farm? You don't know the first thing about farming." He pointedly rocked a table standing uncertainly on four uneven legs. "Let alone anything at all to do with housekeeping."

Crallick turned to look at his friend. "Arrylae's dead," he simply said.

"From the buggering pox, Crallick! The pox! Crallick, there is nothing that would have changed had ye been here, save probably yer own buggering ailment and maybe death as well! Get yer shit together and get your ass back out there with the rest of us!" Tobin tried one other gambit. "Besides, leaving your neighbours to look over your daughter would be a might bit safer for her, considering how most domestic things you try your hand at turn out, well..." he pointedly looked at the construction of the windows, "lacking."

With cat-like reflexes Crallick had his discarded greatbow off the chair, nocked, and aimed at his friend's head. "Care to call my daughter lacking again, Cliffreaver?" snarled the half-elven man.

Both gauntleted hands rose defensively, "Peace! Your martial prowess is not in question here, Crallick! I'm not calling Amalae lacking. She's a kiss from Jyslin herself!" The dwarf turned his iron-shod hands face up, "But now you haven't exactly been around to raise her, have you?"

The gentle creak of the bowstring loosening was Crallick's only somber reply.

Undaunted, the dwarf dryly continued, "Besides, did ye see the speed in which you respond to a threat, perceived or imagined? What are ye going to do with all those reflexes, not to mention the martial might that goes with them? I pity the cow who kicks while yer milking her." The dwarf became animated, jumping to a combat-ready stance, legs bracing under his shoulders, then sweeping a hand to block an imaginary bovine leg, "Hah!" Then he made a thrusting lunge with his other hand, gutting the imaginary beast. "Udderly killed cow," Tobin concluded, crossing his arms.

For the first time since walking into the farmhold, Crallick's face creased into a smile. "Hunh," came his muffled mirth.

"There, see, I knew ye were still able to smile." The dwarf smiled under his bushy, rust coloured beard.

Suddenly sagging, as though the three years of war, the two years of adventuring and the weight of friends buried on the path had finally caught up with him, Crallick sat suddenly on the stone hearth of the fireplace, not even making it to a chair. This put him at a height from which he had to look up into the eyes of his dwarven companion. "Tobin, what in the Luminous Etherium do I think I'm doing here?"

Sighing, Tobin strolled over to stand by his friend. Looking deeply into his eyes, he said, "The right thing, Crallick my boy, the right thing." Tobin smiled encouragement to the openly weeping warrior, "As much as I may taunt and cajole ye to come along with us and to not pursue this folly," he gestured to the ramshackle home, "it is purely for the selfish reason that I would miss yer companionship. Ye need to stay. Yer daughter needs her father now that her mother is gone." Tobin lifted Crallick's unkempt chin to gaze into his watery green eyes. "And I dare say ye need her too."

"Thank you, my friend." Crallick hugged the dwarf.

"Whoa there!!! Let's not do anything to make me have to suffer jibes for the next tenday on the trail with that lot." Tobin gestured back out towards the door.

The door knocked, as if on cue, and a woman's voice drifted in around the seams. "I'm not interrupting anything, am I?"

"No Elandra, ye damnable gossip!" quipped Tobin. He gathered up his axe. "Crallick here is just suffering from some pre-domestication jitters, is all. I'm coming." Waving at Crallick, Tobin walked out the door without another word.

Elandra slid her lithe elven frame through the less than rectangular door. She tentatively eyed the inside environment with great suspicion, her practiced eye scanning every particular piece of furniture with great care.

"Just sit if you're gonna sit," growled Crallick.

"Just noticing how well trapped this place is. You sure it's safe for a little girl?"

"Don't start…" Crallick began.

"Don't worry," Elandra hushed him. "I don't intend to. You are doing the right thing by retiring. You've lasted at this game longer than most. Also, you're getting older and slower. There is no sense you risking leaving your daughter an orphan. That reminds me..." Elandra drew out a leather pouch and a wineskin. "Vitarran Red for you, and the gems for your share of the treasure in an easily portable form. Just in case the farming doesn't work out for you. May Aarison favour you, my dear," Elandra paused at the door. "My condolences on your loss, and my best wishes for your future."

As she left, a five-year-old slip of a girl rushed in to leap on Crallick's lap. "Daddy, daddy, daddy, daddy! I miss you! Where's mommy...?" underscoring his daughter's bubbling torrent of questions, Crallick could hear the cantering hoof-falls of his former life drifting further and further away.

Chapter One

*"Queens Kyliessa and Torganna took council.
Queens of day and night solved the plight of Bannathyr.
Ten knightly orders gathered their troops to marshal
defense of their queens, and homes, marching without fear."
-Verse 2: Ballad of Ser Crallick Carnage-born.*

The prolific stream of rich amber darkened the half-rotted timbers by the stable door at the side of the roadside inn. The hissing continued for long moments. A puddle formed in the moisture-saturated soil.

"Hummmh…" Crallick exhaled while leaning his forehead against his right forearm that acted as a cushion against the rough timbered wall.

A few more sporadic spurts, several drips, and then, with a shake, Crallick shoved himself unceremoniously into his britches. He wiped a few salt-smelling drops from his fingers onto his chin. Crallick then shakily took a few hesitant steps away from the wall. Once sure of his equilibrium, he strode meaningfully back towards the front doors. Crallick pushed one open with a bellow, "Vlados! Get me another pint of that rotgut swill you deign to call dwarven ale!"

"Hey now!" The strawberry-blond dwarf behind the bar chided. "You just mind your manners and don't go getting all racist on me!

You show proper respect to my family's label or I'll just pour you some Ogre piss, ye ungrateful lummox!"

"Ho, ho! I could tell the difference?" Crallick scoffed. Then through the incensed blur of his drink-addled mind, he sensed that he had perhaps strayed too far with his banter. Crashing his backside down hard on a chair by the fireplace, Crallick raised a surrendering hand. "Vlados, you know I jest. I only ever drink your label. It is truly the best ale in the land."

Shaking his heavily bearded face, Vlados poured a tankard full of beer. Waving off his younger daughter with a, "Clean the top and handle anyone who comes to the counter, I'll take this to Cral."

"Okay poppa," came her quiet reply.

It took Vlados only sixteen strides to get to Crallick's table. With a mock bowing flourish, Vlados presented the tankard upon the table. "One Ironforge Ale, at your service."

Wryly grinning, Crallick slurred. "Well thank you, good ser. You'll forgive if I don't bow back."

Sitting across from him, Vlados asked, "Crallick, you've been here since noon. It seems like you're bent on being here 'til Chessfall. Does Amalae know where you are?"

"I'm sure she does."

"Don't you have a farm to run?"

"It's growing." A smirking shrug, "I think."

"How many have you had to drink?" This question held genuine concern.

"Not as many as I'll have had at the end of the day," quipped Crallick.

Shaking his head, Vlados rose from his chair. "Just don't make me have to cut you off," he warned his friend.

Crallick raised the tankard with a toast for his answer.

Vlados kept track behind the bar of the number of refills he had given his friend. When the marker read fifteen, he called over his Ephemeron bouncer. The bouncer had gold-tinged skin covering heavy muscles that belied a kind heart under a fierce countenance. "I think it's time to cut off Crallick," conceded Vlados.

"His daughter may soon arrive to corral him back home," pleaded Alpar. "Could we just give him another half an hour?"

Sighing heavily, Vlados called to his own daughter. "Bekka! Can you run over to Amalae's to get her to bring her father home?"

"Okay poppa." Bekka wiped her hands on the bar towel in her apron string. She then untied the apron and left the whole kit behind the bar before skipping out the door swiftly to do her errand.

Crallick was gesturing for another round. He had been the only constant fixture in the bar, aside from the staff and the furniture. Even those choosing to stay at the inn remained in the bar portion for long enough to slake their thirsts, fill their bellies, and then amble back to rooms or to exercise behind the way-house.

"Try to slow him down." Vlados encouraged his bouncer.

Begrudgingly, the bouncer took over a hopefully final drink to the retired ranger. "Here you go, friend," Alpar said amiably.

Bleary-eyed, Crallick looked up at the gold face of Alpar. "How's your neck?"

Alpar swallowed. Crallick was referring to the last time Alpar had tried to force Crallick to leave before Crallick had wanted to. While Alpar was stronger than Crallick, it had turned out that Crallick was not only faster, but craftier – even when blind drunk. Alpar had found himself in a chokehold that had resulted in a trip to the healer's... after he had regained consciousness.

"Better, thank you." Alpar quietly said. "I trust we won't have that kind of misunderstanding again."

"Hmmph," Crallick snorted. "I trust not. I suspect you're smarter than that."

There came the din of at least a score of hoof beats thundering up the inn's drive. Mounted men calling, mail clanking, and metal-shod wheels creaking on wooden axels added to the chorus.

Alpar looked up with only slight concern, but then returned his focus to the drunken half-elven man in front of him.

Both doors burst open as mailed men began

flowing into the bar. Drink orders began drowning out all other sounds in the bar. Vlados cheerfully began doling out his family ale.

Around a dozen men caroused at the bar when their apparent ringleader and his retinue graced the grime of the door. A heavily furred cloak obscured the physique of the middle member of the group. There was a grey cowl that shielded his features from the room's welcome firelight. The figure was clad in metal greaves at the very least, as that could be seen running from the hem of his cloak down to the armored boots that carried him into the bar.

The figure to his left was like a prehistoric mockery of a man. Standing nearly seven feet tall, and towering over the much shorter middle figure, this lizard scaled creature demanded attention. From the yellow and black war paint adorning the brown scales on his face, to the sword fashioned from the jawbone of some massive creature. The apparent lack of care for armor was also disconcerting. This type of lizardman, known as a Komodoman, wore only britches with a hole rent through the backside to accommodate his massively whipping tail. This tail was adorned with a spiked bauble.

The third member of the group was a svelte womanly figure in black and silver robes. At first glance, she had black velvet gloves. Closer inspection would reveal that those were, in fact, her hands. The feline grace in which she took her seat belied her Nekomin heritage.

Vlados ran out to get their order. On his way back to the bar, he cursed his ill fortune of having sent his daughter to get Amalae. Damn, he could have used the help.

Just after pouring his round to take over to the trio at the door-side table, Amalae and Bekka came jogging in. Both looked a little winded. They had become good friends over the years and were good girls. Vlados looked on with a sense of fatherly pride. A smile cracked his haggard face.

"Sorry I took so long, poppa." Bekka picked up the tray he had prepared. "Where to?"

He pointed at the table in response.

As Bekka's four-foot shapely frame swished off to get the brews to their intended patrons, Amalae's lean, forest and farm sculpted frame propped against the bar. "Sorry Vlados, where is he? Also, do you want me to settle up with you now?"

"Damn girl, you are a sight. No, just get your daddy safely home," Vlados winked. "We'll come by tomorrow to settle up over some roast boar, how's that sound?"

Leaning across the bar, Amalae hugged the dwarf. "That sounds terrific. You're the best! Thank you."

Turning away, Amalae headed over to her father. "C'mon daddy, time to head home. You've done enough damage here today." She smiled warmly to let him know that everything was all right.

Sniffing, then blowing a wad of snot onto the floor, Crallick said, "All right. Just let me piss first."

"Eww. You go take care of that, then come get me. I'll wait here with Alpar." Amalae waved him off towards the door. She then sat and began to chat with the bouncer. "Thanks for watching out for him."

"It's my pleasure." Alpar smiled, half in relief, and half with a fondness for the young woman who sat with him, "He's lucky to have such an adoring and dutiful daughter. Most girls your age would be busying themselves with boys, dancing, and embroidery." Alpar looked thoughtful for a moment. "I'm guessing, of course."

Giving him a condescending look that only a girl in her mid-teens could inspire, Amalae chided, "Really Alpar, do I look like the kind of girl to embroider?"

The pair chuckled and began chatting about the farm and the bar.

***

When the doors swung open, Crallick's impaired senses were assailed by the cacophony of horses and a pair of jailor wagons. Four warriors, one with some goblin blood in him, guarded the caravan's belongings.

Staggering a bit, Crallick went around to the side of the stables. He never heard the commotion begin inside the bar.

Bekka had dropped the tray, and the lizardman had her by one arm, with her feet easily off the floor.

"She's a virgin," declared the Nekomin mage, "as is the girl over there." She gestured to Amalae.

"Excellent," came the quiet voice from under the hood. "Bring her as well."

Amalae shot a quick glance at Alpar.

Alpar positioned himself between her and the marauders. "I'm afraid I can't let you have her. I can't let you have any of them."

"By Chessintra's black ass! Let go of my daughter!" Vlados growled. Then to Alpar, he called, "Catch!"

Alpar grabbed the tossed mattock. He easily hafted the twenty-pound weight. Vlados leveled a crossbow at the reptile holding his daughter. "Now you let her go."

"This is boring me already," said the cowled figure. "Take her!"

A group of six men approached Alpar. One lantern-jawed warrior ventured, "C'mon, why don't you just give up the girl before someone gets hurt?"

"Honestly?" Alpar asked.

"Yeah." Came the curt reply as the half-dozen men drew their weapons.

"Because her father scares me more than the lot of you." Alpar began to spin the mattock back and forth in front of him. Amalae smiled in spite of herself.

The eruption of violence was terrible and sudden, and was over as quick as it had begun.

A crossbow bolt flew through the air. With serpentine reflexes, the Komodoman swatted the projectile from the air with his tail. His claws dug furrows into the wrist of the young dwarf. Bekka cried out as they headed for the door.

Six warriors dove in at once on Alpar. His mattock crushed one head, and stunned two more with one swipe. Three blades made it through his defense. Lung, kidney and thigh were all run through. He fell.

Amalae was grabbed, though not without her leaving red weeping furrows in her abductor's cheeks and arms.

Vlados began reloading through salty tears.

The host withdrew out the door.

"All you had to do was let us take the virgins. We'd have paid you well for them. Instead, your foolishness causes us to leave you with our retribution," the cowled figure chided.

Crallick finished shaking the urine off when he noticed the two unconscious men being tossed onto the backs of the horses. Two small figures now occupied one of the jailor wagons. A pricking sense of foreboding began to eat its way, rat-like, into his brain. Crallick began to take a step forward, "Wha…"

"Finish the judgment," commanded the fur-bundled figure, leaping up into his saddle.

With a spin and flourish that caused the robes to swirl up around the Nekomin's legs, revealing the black furred tail and haunches, she hissed out the spell, "Pyrreth Fortuna." A bolt of blue-black fire launched from her fingers towards the open mouth of the inn.

The bolt passed the crossbow quarrel flying in the other direction.

"Shit," said Vlados.

"Mrowr!!" cried the Nekomin in pain as the quarrel found its mark in her shoulder.

"What the fu…" began Crallick before the fireball overwhelmed him.

Blackness enveloped his world.

Alpar dove over the bar onto Vlados, driving him to the ground. At least he would meet his goddess on good terms.

The Nekomin leapt into her saddle and joined the retreating column as they headed westward into the dying sun.

Chapter Two

*"Jyslin's face graced the eastern skies to bless the day.
Her sister's storm clouds swiftly moved in from the north.
Cradle Knight Crallick was the only one in their way.
Twenty thousand Bannathyrran troops sallied forth."
-Verse 3: Ballad of Ser Crallick Carnage-born.*

Crallick's vision began to clear. At the very least, the blackness began to take on a reddening hue. *'Wait, no, that can't be good,'* he thought through the roaring, pounding, head-breaking hangover. No, he had opened his eyes; there were the stars creating a field of dewdrops upon a black tabard. The troubling thing was the reddish smear, like blood, flowing across that tabard. Was it a fellow warrior slain? Crallick's addled mind panicked as he tried to recount the haze of the last twelve drunken hours. He heard cries of Vitani and humans alike. How the sounds reminded him of a battle. But he hadn't been in one for so long now, had he? He was on his back. This realization pushed into his brain as he felt the pressures of dirt and gravel on his back. Dragging an elbow back under his shoulder, he lifted his head up delicately to survey the scene.

"Hey, there's one over here!" came a call from Erathyr, one of his neighbours.

Along with long draughts of horror that

threatened to drown him as assuredly as all the ale in Vlados's Rest could, the sight that Crallick registered chilled him to the bone. Vlados's Rest lay in rapidly charring timbers while flames roiled into the air. Gently reassuring hands held Crallick's shoulders and helped him sit fully upright.

"Are you alright?" Erathyr asked.

"Vlados?" Crallick shuddered thinking about the last patrons of the bar. "Bekka?" Then the thought hit him, his daughter had been talking to Alpar. "My goddess! My daughter! Alpar!?"

"I don't know." Erathyr tried to be consolatory. "They're trying to get the flames out and they're looking for survivors in the meantime."

Crallick felt a cool cloth touch the back of his head. Hauling himself up to his feet, Crallick ferally snarled, "There's no time for nursing here. They may not have that luxury! "

"You can't…" began Erathyr.

"Who's going to stop me?" cut off Crallick. Then he began deliberately marching towards the blazing ruins.

Erathyr quickly ran towards some other rescuers, unsure of how to deal with the stubborn man.

Roast boar. Hunger panged at the pit of the dehydrated and calorie starved dwarf. It smelt like roast boar. There was a heavy weight and a persistent heat, like sitting too close to the damned cooking fire. Vlados opened his eyes to see eyes staring back at him, only fingers away from his face. The gold and now sightless eyes were Alpar's. Vlados groaned and wept his dismay as he realized the roasting smell was his dear friend and bouncer, Alpar. Vlados looked to his left to see the guttering flames from the gutted tun of ale. To his right, bluer and hotter flames ran the length of the storage under his bar, where the stronger spirits had been kept until they had burst in their bottles from the heat. Vlados slid the cooking man over to his left. The main explosion had flash-cooked the entire back of the Ephemeron. "Jyslin keep you," Vlados silently rasped. He closed Alpar's eyelids as best he could.

Cautiously, Vlados rose to his knees over the other man's chest. He sobbed, while wracking coughs assaulted his heat-seared lungs. He knew his bearings but with his daughter gone and so much destruction, he just couldn't see any point to go on. No tears survived the heat to belie his feelings, but the gut-wrenching twisting of his mouth in agonized misery was unmistakable.

Crallick slid over the burning bar-top to land in a graceless crash beside Vlados. "Well, this is a shitty way to end the day!" he yelled over the crackling inferno.

They both involuntarily jumped when part of the second story fell to the timbers of the first-floor ceiling. The supports creaked ominously all around them.

"Where are the girls?!" Crallick was all sober business in an instant.

Vlados didn't know what to do or say. Now was not exactly the time to broach the sensitive subject of, 'Our daughters have been kidnapped'. But he had to tell Crallick something. "They're out!" he settled on.

"Best news I've heard all night," Crallick returned. "Let's get the hell out of here."

Defeated, Vlados simply nodded.

Crallick slid his arm under the armpits of Vlados, hoisting him up. Then, with more alertness than Vlados could ever remember the drunk farmer having had, he was propelled towards the exit.

There was a sundering roar as the upper story caved in in front of them. Pausing only for a heartbeat, Crallick shifted his pell-mell run thirty degrees to the right and began to pick up speed. He headed not for the blocked front door, but instead for the stone-glass window to the left of the door that let in natural light during the day.

"Wha, wha, what... *cough*... do you think..."

In answer to Vlados's unfinished question, Crallick bundled his red cloak around them and leapt at the window. There was a shudder, then a crash, but mostly a lot of screams from the two of them riding out the broken and glowing wrought iron frame from the sill of the window.

The horrified crowd gasped, then themselves screamed as the porch roof stove in upon the pair.

Crallick and Vlados stared at each other in the heated cocoon. "Why aren't we ashes yet?" began Vlados.

"I told you my cloak was a bit of wing from a dragon," Crallick said matter-of-factly. "Why didn't I see the girls? Outside I mean."

"Umm…" Vlados could tell that this wouldn't be avoided. "They were taken."

"What!?" came the explosive retort. It was accompanied by the stench of booze and accusatory glaring that would allow for no quarter. "How!?"

"The score of patrons that came in before you were to leave took them. They did all this…" Vlados began.

There was a sudden lightening of weight around their lower bodies. Erathyr had organized some brave volunteers to approach the blaze to try to dig the two of them out.

"Why didn't you stop them?" Crallick accused.

"Why didn't you!?" Vlados countered.

What followed was poignant and sobering to the dwarf. "Because I'm just a useless, drunk farmer now."

The two felt the sudden sensation of being dragged in their cocoon; they then cooled and quickly rolled apart, gasping in fresher air. They both staggered to their feet and helped each other away from the fire. Others offered cool water, salves, and herbs. All were accepted gratefully.

Vlados then took three deliberate steps to Crallick and punched him off of his feet.

"You aren't useless, you self-centered, miserable excuse for a ranger. You can go hold whatever pity is fashionable for yourself after our daughters are rescued. Are we clear?" Vlados shook out his charred fingers that wept at the force of the blow.

Crallick looked up from his back. He nodded slowly. "Agreed," he quietly said.

Farmers and villagers slaved fruitlessly to save the inn. They at least prevented the surrounding forest from catching alight. The two friends watched the cremation of Vlados's Rest well until the break of dawn. As light crested the eastern treeline, the friends got their first good look at each other.

Vlados's strawberry blond beard had been severely burned. So much so that he had to hack it off short. Tufts of hair burnt out of his head left visible bald patches. There was soot caking the Dwarf's careworn face.

Crallick was relatively unscathed. Caked in soot, sure, but nothing more than a serious sunburn over his arms and legs. The greatest injury to Crallick was a pair of goose-eggs that adorned the back of his head. Scrapes and cuts latticed his forearms and face.

The pair looked on at the inn's remains. After they had received treatments from the village healer and the well-meaning neighbours, Vlados found that tears could finally come to his eyes and grief shook his shoulders.

"I'm sorry, my friend," Crallick's soft, rough voice cut the dawn's silence. Crallick had been watching the innocent travellers' corpses being collected to a wagon for burial.

"Yeah? For what exactly?" came Vlados's choked reply.

"Hunh," Crallick grunted. "I suppose I deserved that... for my not being able to prevent this. For them." He gestured at two blackened and twisted figures that couldn't have been more than two feet in height each. "I'm sorry I wasn't able to keep our daughters and your livelihood from harm. I'm sorry I wasn't twelve years younger."

"Hah, you may as well apologize for not being a hot female dwarf while yer at it," Vlados mirthlessly offered. Then after an awkward silence, "So what are ye going to do about it?"

Shoulders rounded with the weight of resolve, Crallick slowly straightened his hunched back, then rose to his feet. "I'm going to go home, eat breakfast, rest for a bit, return here, then get them back," he defiantly declared.

"Horse shit," Vlados stated.

"What?" Crallick shot back.

"Horse shit. You can't cook." He grinned wanly, "We'll go back to your place, I'll make us breakfast, we'll rest, then return here and get the girls back."

Crallick smiled. It wasn't a particularly nice smile but it seemed to fit him better than the dour, crunk countenance that Vlados had come to know over the course of many years.

There was a fifteen-minute trek to Crallick's failing farm; the closest farm to the road and the inn felt much longer as the adrenaline wore off from their harrowing evening. They lumbered up the weed-choked lane to the ramshackle hovel-house, which was too good a word to describe the domicile. Cottage was too quaint, and cabin was too sturdy. Crallick glumly thought hovel was the only word to describe this building.

The front door slewed open with a groan of protest from the half-rusted iron hinges that did more to hold the door closed than they did to facilitate its opening. They cleared the threshold to a remarkably undusty living room. A testament to Amalae's housekeeping, not Crallick's. Noticing how Amalae had managed to balance all of their eating and cooking utensils on a seriously sloped shelf, Vlados couldn't help but wonder why she had never come to work for him. He busied himself with the kitchen area by the fireplace while Crallick wandered into a back room.

"Well, I never thought I'd ever be doing this again," Crallick whispered to no one in particular. He easily lifted the heavy timbered bedframe, mattress and all, and cast it aside. He pried up two loose boards, which ironically fit in with all the other loose boards of the house. *'No,'* Crallick thought grimly, *'with the amount of wealth in this home, manor is more fitting a word.'* With a grunt, Crallick hoisted out a long trunk; rectangular, and jointed, with rough iron-mongered edges. He slid it to the side.

"Under the bed? Really? Couldn't you find a better spot to hide your money?" laughed Vlados from the doorway.

"I did," Crallick nodded back the way Vlados had come in. "That's in the whiskey still out back. This is my adventuring gear."

"The still?" Vlados hung his mouth. "You mean you don't actually make your own?"

"No, you and everyone else should know by now that I'm useless at cooking," Crallick grinned, "but no one would think that a drunk farmer would use a still for anything other than whiskey."

Vlados shook his head with amazement, "You, my friend, are way too good at this sort of thing to be wasting that talent on whatever it is you do here."

"Farming," Crallick volunteered.

Scoffing, Vlados said, "Whatever, supper is ready."

They sat down to a welcome meal of bacon, eggs, and spiced potatoes. There was a wedge of cheese and a loaf of half stale bread between them as well. Two mugs of water completed their fare. After the meal, Crallick nodded towards the other door, "You can crash on Amalae's bed."

They each parted into their respective rooms.

As Crallick made ready to drop into his akimbo bedframe, he heard sobs raggedly leaking between the doorframes. Crallick started to rise to go and comfort his friend as a lump jammed his heart into his throat. His memory took him to a mourning child of seven, sobbing from that very room over the loss of her mother two years ealier. His warrior's hardening failed to console her. Crallick gritted his teeth. For his friend's sake, now was not the time to succeed. They would face far harder trials in the time ahead. If their daughters were to hold to any chance, Vlados would have to toughen up and Crallick would have to refine his temper. With a final shuddering breath of his own, Crallick went back to his own bed. Sleep overtook him before he could reach for his bottle of mash.

They slept.

***

Several hours later, Vlados awoke to the sound of crashing in the other room. Leaping to his feet, he grabbed a broom and rushed to see the source of the commotion. A belly laugh overtook him as he surveyed the scene. Half-naked, Crallick was reeling around the living room, his head stuck in the sleeve of a ring mail shirt, while an arm poked out of an offending head opening. The disfigured abomination stopped and oriented itself to his laughter. "Thanks for this," Vlados sobbed between guffaws. "I needed that more than I realized."

"It's been a while since I wore this, that's all," growled Crallick, "I sure as hell didn't do this for your amusement."

Still chuckling under his much shortened and bedraggled beard, Vlados offered, "C'mere and let me help you, you graceless oaf."

Crallick obliged the dwarf, getting down on his knees to accept his help. Ten minutes later, the mail shirt adorned Crallick's chest. Crude leather breeches clad his legs in dusky coal grey. Black lacquered metal-plated boots shod his feet. The ratty, rust red cloak wrapped his shoulders and hooded his long brown salted mane. Warrior braids kept the hair out of his eyes.

Vlados pointed at a brown leather cord around Crallick's neck. "What's that for?"

Walking to the pile of boulders that he called a mantle and chimney, Crallick reached up for his serrated greatsword. Glancing over his shoulder he grimly smiled, "Trophies."

Crallick lifted a ladder up and used it to grab a black leather scabbard from the rafters. He slid his sword into the sheath, cinched the strap over his shoulder, and then doubled his travelling pack to the same strap. He inhaled deeply, "All right, I'm ready. Let's get the money, and then we can get you set up and go."

Vlados followed him out to his still. Taking a splintery mallet, Crallick knocked the dented top off the copper pot. He reached in through the corn mash soup and pulled out an oiled leather pouch. Crallick opened it to reveal a fistful of gems.

"Whew," Vlados whistled lowly. Then he looked sharply at Crallick. "Are you kidding me?" he exclaimed.

"What?" puzzled Crallick, cinching the bag closed after taking six gems out.

"You mean to tell me you have all that money, and you can't hire some craftsmen and artisans to fix yer damned home?"

Crallick looked shocked and a little hurt. "What's wrong with my home? I did all the work myself."

"Fine, fine," Vlados soothed. Then under his breath, "Ye can tell."

"Huh?" Crallick looked up.

"I said let's get going, swell," Vlados lied.

Crallick saddled up a horse and a pony. He mounted the horse, then handed the reins of the pony to Vlados. "To the inn then," he invited.

***

Ten minutes later, the pair galloped up to the gutted and smoldering remains. Crallick dismounted and began pacing around the mauled landscape of the inn's yard. His attention was grabbed by first this rut, then that print, as he paced around mumbling to himself.

Vlados tentatively sifted through the ruins of his life. He carefully avoided hot spots. He gazed down the hole that had once been his brewery cellar. He picked up the lump of metal that had once been his coin box. He dolefully followed Crallick back to the road. On the signpost that cheerfully advertised, "Vlados's Rest Inn and Tavern; put your troubles and yourself to rest," were two markers that had been helpfully posted by the townsfolk. One said, "Closed for renovations." The other attended Vlados to come to the town hall.

"The slaver wagons head west down the royal road. That also runs through town. We can get you kitted out for the road, and you can see what they need at the town hall," Crallick observed dryly.

An hour later they cantered into the cluster of buildings at the heart of their Vitani community. Signs for a smithy, ferrier, and general store dotted the clustered buildings. The stone town hall and the Jyslinnic shrine stood slightly apart.

Crallick glanced at his friend. "What do you need? I'll pick it up for you while you touch base with the town council."

"All right," Vlados thought a moment. "You've done this longer than I have. I'll trust if I neglect something, you'll cover it. I am good at using a crossbow, and a hammer as well. I'm used to light armor though. Nothing heavier than cuir bouilli, please. I'll meet with the healer to pick through her apothecary for chemicals for mixing."

Crallick nodded his understanding, "I'll meet you back here after midday."

"All right." Vlados then turned his pony towards the path to the healer's cabin.

***

The healer met Vlados on her veranda. "Well met Vlados! I see you haven't heeded my advice to rest! I assume your delinquent friend is just as uncooperative?" She shook her head.

"Well, no. I guess we must make a pair of lousy patients," Vlados conceded. "We're setting out to hunt down the villains who did this and stole our daughters." His lower lip began to quiver, as though speaking these words aloud to any other than Crallick somehow made them more real. Somehow.

"Say no more," the elder woman said. "I see your resolve as clear as day. I shall put together for you a travelling kit to aid your wounds."

Vlados handed her a crumpled list, hurriedly scratched out along the path. "Can you add these reagents as well?"

She glanced over the list. Cackling, she laughed, "Why Vlados, your writing is getting as terrible as mine." When no mirth returned to her, she continued, "These shouldn't be a problem."

About half an hour later, she returned out of her cottage with a strapped wooden box. She offered the pair of leather straps to the dwarf.

"Thank you, Marte. How much do I owe you?"

"Now don't you dare insult me by asking me to charge you! You go get those sweet young girls back now, you hear me? When you return, you may settle up with me by telling me your tales. If you happen upon some interesting reagents along the way, I wouldn't object to a souvenir or two." Marte smiled warmly.

Vlados hugged her briefly, then quickly muttered, "Of course, thank you so very much."

As he went back to mount his pony, kit upon his back, he heard her call out, "You mind you watch over that no good drunkard!"

"You can rest assured I shall!" he called back over his shoulder as he rode away, back to town.

Crallick, meanwhile, had found a studded leather jacket in a green dappled colour, leather britches and hardened boots. He had found a passable hammer at the smithy's, but was unable to find anywhere with a crossbow. He figured that would have to wait until they got to the city. His old bow had rotted away, but he was undaunted. In this elven community, he knew of many who were talented in bowery and flecthery. Erathyn was among them. Walking across the Groveholme circle, he noticed Vlados jogging from the hitching post up to the town hall. Crallick took his finds and went to the Vitani Elm to wait for Vlados among the roots.

The cool interior of the town hall was refreshing for Vlados. He walked up to the table at the farthest point of the single room. Benches stretched out left and right of the aisle that he walked down. The three council members waited at a triangular table with rounded ends; this allowed each council member to sit effectively at an equal point from each other, while keeping the widest edge of the table to the town populous for meetings. For today, however, there was only Sathira, Goonderyn, and Fillantos. When the three were not ruling the council of Gladeholme, Sathira was the wife of the smithy, Goonderyn was an accomplished farmer, and Fillantos was the town constable.

Sathira was the first to speak, "By Jyslin's breath, we are so sorry for your loss."

Vlados held his tongue, lest his traitorous lower lip betray him again.

Fillantos nodded, "Worry not, my friend, we have discussed the matter at length already, and ascertained unanimously that you are not to be held at fault. There is no culpability or negligence related to the thirteen deaths, five of which were children, nor the arson that led to the destruction of the inn, tavern, and adjoining stables, nor the abduction of the two women."

As Vlados heard the matter-of-fact manner in which the constable addressed the damages, he felt his temper rise and rise, until beads of sweat broke his crown.

Goonderyn saw Vlados's peril and quickly spoke to salve his rising ire. "Now that unpleasantness is over with," pointedly he added, "permanently." Then he continued less at the council members, and more directed at Vlados, "We can get down to why we are really here. Whatever melted currency you have, take it to the smithy and he will slurry it, purify it, and cast coins for you. These will go towards rebuilding your inn while you're away."

"How do you know I'm going anywhere?" Vlados interrupted.

Sathira said, "My husband."

Goonderyn, overlapping, said, "Marte sent a bird."

Fillantos, likewise, quick with a source, "Erathyn made a bow for Crallick. Also, it was yours and Crallick's daughters that were taken."

All three said in harmony, "We know Crallick."

"Okay, so we're going to get our daughters back, and now maybe try to avenge ourselves upon them for thirteen others." Vlados conceded. "But I have no idea how to do any of this. And I know Crallick too. He's a drunken, failing farmer. I don't see how we're going to survive this. Sure, he has a temper and fights in barroom brawls like a man possessed. And sure, he boasts about having a dragon cloak from a wing of a great servant of Asha, but really, c'mon, we need to find our daughters and take on really well-trained men." Vlados shrugged, "I don't see how we do this and survive."

Sathira smiled sweetly, "Then why, good Vlados, are you going?"

"If the crazy gobhole wants to commit suicide, why should he do it alone? Besides, it's not like I have anything left to live for. And he is my gobhole friend, so I may as well commit suicide with him," Vlados confessed. No one needed to know the mind-set of his friend so shortly after the rescue. Not a single gods-be-damned soul.

"You've known him what, eight years now?" Goonderyn asked.

"Yeah, about that." Vlados couldn't see the relevance.

"What if I were to tell you that, knowing Crallick from the old days, I believe he has no intention of committing suicide? Would that make you feel better?" Fillantos asked.

"I'd assume ye were trying to shove sunshine up my ma's kilt," Vlados grunted, "or that you seriously overestimate Crallick's ability."

"Crallick used to be a great adventurer, then when the Vitani war of sedition happened, he fought as an elite elven ranger, in a demon hunting unit. He survived that until the war was won. Whether that fireproof coat is demonic or draconic hide, I don't know, but I'd promise you it's genuine. He may be a drunk, but he is skilled. You have a good chance of coming home Vlados. I'm sure of it."

"No shit?" Vlados said hesitantly.

"No shit." Crallick's voice echoed through the chamber. He had entered unseen during Fillantos' roll of Crallick's deeds. "I promise you Vlados, if I didn't feel I could keep your miserable self alive, I would never let you come along."

"Crallick, sorry…" Sathira began.

"If you say one Chessintra-be-damned word of apology, sympathy, or anything other than a lead, I'll kill you and let Vlados see how effective I can be against the town guard."

"Crallick," chided Fillantos in a soothing voice. "She only means well. She doesn't understand men like us."

"Few do," acknowledged Crallick.

"The only leads I was able to gather were some sightings as they galloped through town. Predominantly black attire, with a white hand motif. Fingers upwards, palm out. I couldn't get if it was the right or left hand. Most of the host were human or elven. One seemed to be a Nekomin wizard."

"That's the gob-child who torched my bar and killed the thirteen," Vlados confirmed.

Fillantos scribbled a note, then continued, "Thanks. There were a pair of reptilemen: one riding, and one driving one of the slave wagons. There were two wagons, with reports of captives ranging from one to three." Fillantos glanced up, "I know it's not much, but I hope it helps."

"Thanks, it'll do," growled Crallick.

The pair made their way back out to the hitching post, where Crallick had tied his mare beside the pony. Crallick passed the procured armor, hammer, and some travelling rations to Vlados. Vlados changed, and mounted up

On their way out of town, Vlados quickly ran into the general store. He emerged a few moments later with a wide-brimmed hat. "I have to do something about my hair," he grumbled. "The last thing I need is sunburn on the bald spots on my head."

Smiling, Crallick turned them towards the west route out of town. "Let's go get them," he growled.

Chapter Three

*"Jyslin's face graced the eastern skies to bless the day
Her sister's storm clouds swiftly moved in from the north.
Cradle Knight Crallick was only one on their way,
Twenty thousand Bannathyrran troops sallied forth."
-Verse 4: Ballad of Ser Crallick Carnage-born.*

Riding west on the Royal Road was short-lived on that first day. The pair had left Gladeholme just after midday, and the spring days had not yet lengthened to allow for more than five hours of riding. They camped that first night in a hollowed rain wash that ran the side of this part of the road. They slept uncomfortably among the deadfall, without the benefit of a fire, and awoke in the morning chilled with a teeth-chattering numbness.

Their second day's travels began with a hurried handful of oat porridge that would have tasted better with some honey, or sugar, or even if it had been cooked. After their wolfed down meal, the pair again hit the poorly cobbled road and headed westward. They rode twelve hours that day.

The next four days were much as the second; quick meals that punctuated three-hour stints of riding.

On the seventh day, they came to a fork with roads leading west, and northwest. A signpost indicated the Port City of Marahaven, and the other indicated the direction to Aurumhold in the north. The latter was where Vlados's family hailed from. The other was the city-state sized capital of the Bannathyr Kingdom. Crallick inspected the prolifically scarred road. There was some time of pacing back and forth, occasionally getting low to the ground or grabbing clumps of dirt. Then he remounted and declared, "This way," as he gestured and pointed his horse towards Marahaven.

Furrowing his blond brow, Vlados asked, "How can you be sure?"

"Do I ask you for your familly's ale recipe?" Crallick paused to glance at Vlados, reveling in the dwarf's horrified expression.

"No, and I'd never give it to you," Vlados glowered. "You'd only end up buggering it up anyways."

"Exactly, now let's get going," Crallick answered.

"But…" Vlados began.

"I'd bet my daughter's life on it."

That shut the dwarf up. They rode the next four hours in silence.

They came to a roadside inn. The Merry Gold Inn. The proprietor obviously took pride in their sense of humour, as the lane leading up to their yard was flanked by wide stone walls that had plants growing atop them. Vlados imagined that they were marigolds and later in the spring, there would be a ton of them around the place. There were large flower beds in front of the bay windows, and beds on the side of the stables.

"It's getting late in the day," suggested the hopeful dwarf.

"There may be clues," agreed the grim half-Vitani.

They dismounted and took their mounts up the drive to the stable doors. A cheerful, rotund man waved to them, "Welcome, let me take your steeds, good sers." The wobbly character held out his bulbous hands and grasped the reins in rubbery palms. He then turned his attention to the two animals he led into the stables. "Who are lovely and noble steeds? You are so deserving of comfort. I bet you're starving? Well, well, Yanni will take care of you right quick."

Crallick exchanged glances with Vlados. "They're in good hands I'm guessing."

Vlados harrumphed, "I'm just wanting a soft bed for my arse, and a warm meal for my arse."

"Don't you mean a warm meal for your belly?" Crallick opened the front door of the inn to let loose a puff of cumin and cinnamon air that mixed with the scent of burning maple.

"Nope, I mean arse. I haven't been able to have a good shite for three days now with all those oats ye been stuffing down my throat." Vlados walked in and inhaled deeply, "I should finally be able to pass a movement after a warm meal of venison and vegetables."

Crallick barked a short laugh then headed over to the innkeep.

The innkeep was behind a low desk with potted marigolds at either end. This was to the immediate left of the door. Midway along that wall rose a flight of stairs to an upper mezzanine that looked down on the dining area. Doors to rooms led off that floor. There was also a door on that side that led to a kitchen, Crallick mused from the traffic going in and out. Six circular tables, each with a potted plant in their center and holding eight chairs around them, accommodated the dining patrons. There was a hearth, and a mantle adorned with potted plants opposite the door; maple logs burned merrily in the fireplace. The right wall that adjoined the stables held a small stage for entertainers to ply their trade.

"I need two beds for the night, two meals, and two breakfasts." Crallick fished out a single small gem. "I hope you can make change." Then as an afterthought, he added, "I also have two mounts, a horse and a pony being stabled."

The ruddy-cheeked inkeep, whose eyes had widened greatly, said. "I'm sure we can come to an arrangement." He licked his lips, glistening eyes focusing brightly on the stone.

Crallick cynically grinned. "I'm sure we can."

"I will hold it in the cashbox until you are ready to leave ser. I am Harold Freeman, and my wife is Lara Freeman. We are honest folk you can trust." Harold began to assure Crallick.

"Ser, I assure you, I do trust you. I trust that you and your wife wish to continue to live. You won't cheat me." Crallick gave a predatory smile, "Actually I'm hunting someone. Perhaps you can help me. Please come and find me after I sup."

"Of course ser," Harold gulped.

That evening a passably pretty human woman played a passable performance of a passably cheerful song. An exquisitely spiced roast of venison neck was presented to both Crallick and Vlados by a buxom, blond-braided woman. Their meal was served accented by a side of carrots and bread. They had ale to wash it down with.

"Don't mind my asking ser, but what happened to your hair and beard?" asked their server with gentle concern.

"You get many dwarves in here, lady?" Vlados said, a little sensitively.

"Aye, we do," she smiled unabashedly. "That's why I have the compassion to ask and to offer to help fix it up for you."

"You are Lara?" asked Crallick.

"Aye. I am ser."

"Go with her Vlados, you're ugly enough without the help of the fire," Crallick said.

"Go bugger yerself," came the dwarf's acid reply. "Yer ugly from birth." But he got up and accompanied the human woman anyway.

Harold came over to the table and sat. The inn hadn't been particularly busy that eve, with only twelve patrons to scatter themselves among the dining room's six tables. "I can chat now with you if it pleases you, ser."

Crallick tapped his mug, "Come back with a full one of these and we can get going."

Harold rose up, disappeared into the kitchen, and then returned with a pair of mugs. He sat down, sliding one to Crallick and drawing a swig from the other. "Alright then ser, what, or who are you hunting?"

It was Crallick's turn to draw from his mug. "There was a caravan of marauders, driving two slave wagons. There were at least two girls prisoned in those wagons. They numbered about a score. Two were reptilemen. Others of whatever heritage. They were travelling west down the Royal Road. They may have stopped here, or passed by. I need to know all you know."

Harold gave a slow exhale of resignation. "Those were some dangerous customers to be sure. Now that's not to say you don't look capable enough, but you should make sure you have a good enough reason to follow that lot."

"They burned down my friend's inn, and took our daughters," Crallick growled.

"Those are good reasons," Harold admitted nervously into his mug. "I will help you in any way I can."

"Just tell me what you know," Crallick sipped again.

"They came through early yesterday. They refused the hospitality of the stablehand, Mr. Hobbs. This disappointed him greatly, as Yanni is quite fond of animals and he recognized some Talban plain blacks. They rather rudely said they would care for their own mounts and wagons. There were two elven looking girls, both Vitani, I think, and a dwarven maid. There were the two reptilemen of which you spoke of. The Nekomin she-cat was a practitioner of Chessintra's arts." Harold shuddered, thinking of the black and silver robed cat. "She seems to be the advisor to the leader. I think she answered to the name 'Ferran'. One reptile had a spiked weapon on his tail. The other never left the wagons. They bought enough meals for twenty-six breakfasts. They paid with gold minted coins. I'll get one for you." Harold got up and returned with a coin. He offered it across to Crallick.

Crallick took it and examined it. The one side held a profile of a human matriarch, the other side a dragon rising behind a shield with crossed blades. "An Amarol Dragon?" Crallick confirmed.

"That is what I thought too," confirmed Harold. "I've seen them before, but usually from lone travellers, or merchants who've travelled a long way indeed."

The men looked up at the approach of Vlados and Lara. The dwarf looked much improved. His strawberry blond hair had been shaved from either side of his pate, and cropped short, creating a wide and low mohawk. It fanned out at the base of his skull to flow into his shorter beard, which now was thickly braided into three short and full braids.

"Well, shite, don't you look a sight better?" Crallick greeted him.

Vlados snorted in reply.

The pair retired to their room. "Learn anything useful?" Vlados asked as they settled in for the night.

"Yeah," Crallick yawned. "See you in the morning."

***

Golden sunlight streamed in the Merry Gold Inn's windows, piercing the eyelids of the sleeping men. Crallick dragged himself up. Vlados stirred under a goose down duvet. Crallick threw a shoe at him with a thud.

"Get up."

"Bugger off," Vlados snarled.

"Is that what you want me to tell the girls?" Crallick smirked.

Vlados was up and donning his armor. No mirth showed on his face.

Wordlessly, the two descended to the dining hall. They walked up to Harold, who smiled. "Good morning, sers. I've had your stone appraised. I've removed the fees for the beds, meals, and stabling. There was a five percent commission to the money-changer." Two bags of coins were presented to Crallick. "There are seven-hundred and fifty crowns, and two-hundred and fifty dragons. I figured you may find those more useful than I would find them."

Crallick tossed the lighter bag to Vlados, then opened the larger bag, drawing out twenty-five coins. He proffered them back to Harold, "Give five to your wife, as I can stand to look at my friend again, and then divvy up the rest between yourself, Yanni, and the minstrel."

"Thank you ser Crallick," Harold gushed.

"I'll double your tip if your wife can fix his face," Vlados said.

Laughing into her hands, Lara said, "I'm sorry, master dwarf. I'm afraid that's a miracle for Jyslin's hands, not mine."

"Let's go," Crallick growled.

The eighth day progressed at a hurried pace. They had found that Harold, or Lara, or both, had put cinnamon buns in their packs, along with a rasher of bacon each. They were much better fed throughout the day, so they rode deeper into it.

The ninth day found them crossing the Bhanrigh River. There was a marble quarried bridge that married dwarven craftsmanship and Vitani magic. Tall spires anchored the corners with a white, smooth surface that could accommodate four horses abreast with room to spare. Low walls on either side lent a feeling of safety and security, with decorative reliefs adding artistic beauty to the bridge.

The companions took no notice of this beauty, their focus set solely on their objective somewhere out of sight, down the road.

The last day of the ten day trek should have been reserved for prayer, but the two determined travellers chose to ignore this as well. What didn't go ignored was when, close to evening, they were about to begin looking for a campsite when they heard guttural tongues in the dusk-light. Crallick swiftly dismounted his ride. Crouching low, he quickly moved into the brush. Vlados trailed him a little less certainly, and a might bit less silently.

"Goblins," Crallick hissed.

"How the blazes can you tell?" whispered Vlados.

"I speak it," Crallick grinned. "I learned while adventuring. I think they're talking about eating frog's legs."

"Oh," said Vlados. "Well, I hope they enjoy their dinner, now let's go."

"Garrum! Garrum! Help! Help!" came a deep voice over the chatter. This brought about a round of guttural laughter and jeering.

"Aww, shite," Vlados groaned. "We can't go and let them eat a froggle. That's just not right."

Crallick looked at Vlados. "You realize we'll probably lose half a day because of this?"

"I couldn't face my daughter if I let some innocent thing get eaten and I could have done something about it." Vlados pulled out his hammer.

"Just making sure you know the score," Crallick warned. "I'll make the call if we can do something or not. You will follow my lead on this, understand?"

"Sure," Vlados began.

"Wait for my signal."

Vlados was about to ask what it was going to be when the damned crossbreed flew into the woods, and out of sight. He figured he'd find out soon enough.

Crallick worked his way around the clearing that held the smell of burning pine and maple. He counted five voices other than the froggle. Crallick climbed a towering maple and crawled along a thick branch that was overhanging the clearing by around ten feet. He sat up, unslung his sword sheath, and hung it over a branch in easy reach. He drew his bow and nocked an arrow. By this time, two of the five-foot tall figures had grabbed the froggle's bound form and were fastening him to a pole. Quickly making an assessment, figuring the most physically powerful goblin was the one in charge, he let loose his arrow.

Vlados heard a chorus of goblin yells. Were they of anger or fear? He didn't know. He didn't care. He just figured that it must have been the signal that Crallick was talking about. Raising his hammer, he charged towards the clearing and the screaming.

The screaming goblin hushed when Crallick's blade separated his head from his neck as he dove, spinning, from the tree. Another goblin tried to push his stinking, steaming intestines back into his gut in vain. He sagged to his knees before losing consciousness for the last time.

The two remaining goblins were more alert and swiftly flanked Crallick, coming from either side of the fire. Crallick faced the one away from the road, trusting Vlados to do his part.

The dwarven cry erupted into the clearing as his hammer smashed through the skull of the startled, then dead, goblin.

Crallick's eyes flickered over his shoulder, then glared intimidatingly back at the sole surviving goblin. Its grip loosened on its sword. The goblin raised its hands to surrender. Crallick flicked the tip of his sword across the throat of his victim. A crimson mist spayed the now nighttime clearing.

"Thanks for the campsite," Crallick grimly offered.

"You're kidding, right?" asked Vlados.

"No, I'm not." Crallick started back to the trunk of the maple to reclaim his sheath, bow, and quiver.

"But it's disgusting," protested Vlados.

"Toss the bodies over there." Crallick pointed to a ditch in the gloom.

"What about the smell of blood?"

"Scavengers are looking for an easy meal. They won't come near the fire," Crallick lectured.

"Ooooh, he is smart one!" a new voice piped in. "He knows! He speaks true."

"And then there is him?" Vlados mentioned. "What about him?"

Crallick dropped back down to the ground without so much as a crunch of leaves. "What about him? He saw what I can do. You won't trouble us, will you?"

"Garrumm! No! You saved me! My service is yours!" The froggle wiggled free of his bindings when Crallick cut them off the pole.

With a rapid bounce that easily carried the froggle twelve feet over to Vlados, he grabbed the bottom half of a goblin and flung it deep into the bushes. "I will help! Garrum!"

Vlados, startled, dropped the top half of the goblin. The froggle promptly treated it the same way as the other half. After the clearing was cleaned, they gathered by the fire.

"I'm Crallick, and this is Vlados. Who are you?"

"Hullaboo! Garrum," he replied, licking his eyes with a prehensile tongue.

"I'm a hunter of sorts, Vlados is a brewer, and you?" Crallick asked.

"I am a warrior!" Hullaboo boasted, then became sullen. "My tribe scattered in front of a goblin horde. Garrumm." He licked his head again. "My pondmate, gone. Tadpoles, gone.

Fellow warriors, gone." He licked his back. "Garruum. Some live, more dead. All lost. You?"

Vlados answered for them, "Our home was destroyed and our young were taken. We're going to get them back."

The froggle excitably rose up on his haunches, "Avenge upon them! Avenge upon them! This I can help with! Yes! Yes!" Slurping his wet tongue over his bulbous eyes, Hullaboo continued, "You saved me from death, so I can help you with this! Yes?"

"So you're a warrior?" Crallick put to him.

"Yes, yes!"

"You don't have a weapon," Vlados bluntly pointed out.

Hullaboo quickly glanced about, bulbous eyes leading his square head to and fro. "Snap, squelch, phlllpt!" his tongue lashed out to secure one of the short swords of the goblins and reeled it back in to his waiting grasp. His wide mouth widened even further into a satisfied grin. "I have one now."

Crallick's dour demeanor cracked. "Fine, Hullaboo, let me sleep on it."

Hustling over in a near panic, Vlados whispered, "You can't be seriously considering this?"

"Why not? You insisted we rescue him." Crallick looked over, "I can't help but think he might be more useful in a fight than what meets the eye."

"Huh," Vlados grumbled.

With a wicked gleam in his eye, Crallick softly said, "He has to be more useful than you, in any event." As Vlados huffed indignation, Crallick called over to Hullaboo, "You take first watch, then wake me when the moon is at its highest."

"Yes! Yes! You make sleep time. I'll protect."

"Just one thing before I rest," Crallick said from his bedroll. "How were you taken prisoner?"

"There was a hunting party of many goblins! They found me! Took my spear! My shield! The survivors wanted to eat me! Not even to save me for their tribe. Very selfish!"

Laughing in spite of himself, Crallick asked, "How many more than the number we took you from?"

Hullaboo looked at his webbed hands, then his feet. "More than both hands, but less than adding a foot," he concluded.

"Not bad," Crallick nodded. "Good night."

Vlados asked, "Twelve gobs then?"

Crallick opened an eye. "No, ten. Froggles have only three fingers, with an opposable thumb. More area for webbing. He can probably swim faster than I can run. We'll keep him. He may be useful."

As the spring moon rose into the sky, Hullaboo watched his sleeping comrades. They were noble folk, risking their lives for one they didn't know. Trusting, gullible, or foolish, maybe stupid, he wasn't sure, but they were noble. He would stick around to keep them safe. He would also continue to allow them to think he was simple until he figured them out. Better safe than sorry.

Chapter Four

- *"By gloaming's bloodthirsty grin, the day's march did end.*
  - *By a little hamlet, quaint in the coastal hills,*
  - *Seaview huddled, awaiting doom to descend.*
- *By north and south, two armies did begin to mill."*
  -Verse 5: Ballad of Ser Crallick Carnage-born.

Marahaven was the crown jewel of cities in the Bannathyr Kingdom. It was nestled into the rocky shores on the eastern shore of the ocean. The ocean's name was in contention, depending on which of the three major kingdoms you asked. There were only two details that seemed to be agreed upon. The first was that it was vast. The second was that nobody had managed to transnavigate it to the other side... presuming there *was* another side. The three major powers all held coastal navies, along with dozens of other lesser powers and independent groups.

Those particulars plagued Crallick's mind. He was terrified that if he couldn't catch his quarry before Marahaven, then they would be lost in the chaos of the drama of the high seas. He kept these concerns and doubts to himself, for Vlados's sake, and plastered grim confidence upon his face. Crossroads was less than a tenday away. This was the first place they could split from their path, heading south to Jharrim, the jewel of the south.

He could easily track and cope with that. He was used to following prey through the land, even through cities. Jharrim was a loose alliance of independent city-states that rallied around Jharrim's Sultan. The loose political structure allowed for ease of travel and a ripe environment for bounty hunting and assassination. The slave trade was also alive and well. Vlados had said they had been looking for virgin girls. With a shudder in his saddle, Crallick decided it was best not to think along those lines.

Six more days travel along the Royal Road found the three companions looking down along a descending run of verdant clover fields towards tracks of farmed corn that lead up to the walled city of Crossroads. The city had grown up around a southbound trade route to the Nekomin lands of the south that ran all the way to the Amarallan Kingdom. Crossroads was populated mainly by southern men, Nekomin, and Vitani. The travellers could barely make out an inn just before the fields of corn began.

"Two days until Crossroads," observed Crallick.

"Great, we lose them then," grumbled Vlados.

"Why would you say that?" asked Crallick.

"Well, once they get in there, how would you divine just which way they went?" Vlados spluttered.

"Good point. How, how?" Hullaboo asked.

"How do you spice your ale?" Crallick sneered. "Just don't worry, they won't evade me," he inhaled, unnoticed by the others. "Here," he finished.

Sundown that day marked the end of their fortunate weather. A cool northwesterly wind blew in, bringing with it cool spring drizzles and uncomfortable gusts that found chinks in armor and up sleeves. It chilled sweat from the skin, leaving them shivering. Well, except for Hullaboo. While he reveled in the moisture, his olive green skin beading with vitality, the coolness brought a lethargy to the amphibian.

Concerned, Crallick put to him, "Hullaboo, are you going to be okay?"

A quiet, "Garrum, yes, yes. Just sleepy when cool."

Vlados cantered up to the inn, "Are we staying, or riding on?"

"Staying," Crallick slowed up beside his friend. "Nothing will be gained other than a chill, fatigue, and poor humour by pressing on tonight." He led his horse into the stable. "Here we will revitalize ourselves, feed ourselves, and maybe find information." He took out several of the Amorallan dragons and held one out to the stable boy. "Seen one of these lately?"

"Aye ser, just last night in fact," the boy quailed a bit. "Are they your friends?"

Crallick took the measure of the boy, "No they are not." He took a knee. "What would you say if

I told you I'm a Bannathyr Knight-Ranger, and I'm hunting some very vile villains? Could you help me?"

The boy nervously chewed his lower lip. "I'd believe you. I think they are very bad people. They took Mindy-kitty and they threatened to kill everyone if they were interfered with. They had coins like that one."

"Mindy-kitty?" Vlados asked carefully.

"She's the milkmaid for the mistress of the house's cows out the back. Her mom is a server for the tavern," the lad said soberly.

"Thanks lad," Crallick said. "Keep the coin."

The party left the wooden and straw-thatched stable and walked around the three-story stone building that looked more like a keep than an inn. There were arrow slits instead of windows for the ground floor. A heavy wooden door swung open with some effort. Stone stairs ascended the far wall to the second floor. The tavern had a stone ceiling with iron grates pressed into it. This inn could obviously protect itself very well.

A slender, yet whisker-drooped Nekomin walked up to them. "Please sit where you'd like. I'll take your order soon."

They walked over to a table by the fireplace to take the chill off their bones.

"You're despicable," Vlados lightly declared to Crallick.

"Why would you say that?" Crallick looked sideways at Vlados.

"Who lies to a young boy for information?"

"Who says I lied?" Crallick put to him.

Vlados fell silent as the Nekomin waitress came over. "May I recommend the steamed grog? We also have a lovely corn liquor that we serve warm or cold with cinnamon."

Crallick looked up, "We'll have a round of grog. And by chance, are you the mother of Mindy-kitty?"

The waitress blanched. She sat suddenly, weakened with grief. "Oh my, I'm sorry," she meekly stammered out. "I guess you've been talking to Toby. That was his pet name for my Mindy." She sobbed into her paws.

"Meree, Is everything all right over here?" came a base voice.

The table looked up to see a hulking brute of a man. Bald headed, and grim-faced, he held a freshly bandaged stump close to his left side.

"Yes, Derion," she sniffled. "I'm all right. These men just asked about Mindy."

"Go get the drinks, I'll talk to them," said Derion. He then traded seats with the woman and waited for her to leave the public room before speaking again. "Now I'm not sure whether or not you realize this, but Mindy is a rather sore subject around here right now. I want to know two things. Firstly, how do you know about Mindy, and secondly, why is it your business to ask?"

"Nice compassion, pal." Vlados hissed to Crallick.

Crallick shot Vlados a sidelong glance, "It had to be done. May as well be quick about it."

"Excuse me, sers. Just what had to be done?" Derion put much emphasis on the 'sers' and the 'what', to convey a distinct lack of patience.

Hullaboo spoke up, "Do not worry, these are goodly men. They mean to take revenge on the thieves of tadpoles!"

Vlados groaned.

Crallick chuckled dryly. "What he means to say is that we may have encountered the same villains who took her daughter," he nodded towards the kitchen. "Our daughters were likewise abducted. I'm hunting them down. I plan on exacting revenge upon them, and if I cannot liberate the young women," Crallick gave a wry smile, "Chessintra, I may exact revenge anyways depending on my mood."

Derion nodded, "Okay, let's say I believe you. Are you just in it to rescue your own daughters? Or are you going to help Meree as well?"

"If we are able, we will help every last girl we liberate, regardless of where she rightfully belongs," Crallick assured Derion.

"In that case, they came through just last night. Never even stayed. They just supped and then pressed on, taking Mindy with them. Meree had said that…" Derion paused as Meree brought a round of lightly steaming mugs and placed them around the table with a sullen grace.

"Can I help with anything?" she asked.

"No, that's fine," said Derion.

"Actually, a haunch of mutton for each of us with some bread, onions, and corn would be nice to sup on," put in Vlados.

"Of course ser, I'll be back directly." She scooted back off to the kitchens.

"Where was I?" Derion asked.

"Meree had said something to you," Crallick jogged.

"Oh, right. Yeah, Meree had mentioned that while she had been serving them she overheard them arguing about being on time to get a ship."

Crallick's eyes went huge. That was a vital detail. It immediately told him two things: first, he had two tendays to try to catch up with them, and second, their destination had to be Marahaven.

"There was some talk about sacrificial rites. Virgin counts. Twisted Chessintran type shite," Derion concluded. "You may want to check in with the Flowwvite, or the Jyslinnic church in Crossroads. They would know more Trixiaxi-be-damned shite that would require sacrificial virgins and such."

"Why not just go to a Chessintran temple?" asked Vlados, quite naively.

Both the other men at the table turned in their seats to look at the dwarf. Hullaboo licked his head and eyes with his tongue. Crallick deliberately answered, "Well, Vlados, it's like this. The goddess of death, magic, and time ain't exactly a sweet lady. Her church mirrors her sensibilities. If we went prowling around there, we'd either end up as sacrifices ourselves, or our quarry would soon learn of our pursuit. Get it?"

"Oh," Vlados felt chastened.

Derion stood. "Well, it was good to meet you folk. You get Mindy back, alive if you can… the closure would do Meree good." A few paces away, he turned and added, "And don't sweat the tab. It's on me."

"A moment before you go, friend," Crallick interjected. He nodded at Derion's stump, "Pretty generous for a bouncer. I also want to know how you got that. It may help. In as much detail as you can." Crallick rose to meet Derion, "C'mon, over here, by the fire."

Derion accompanied Crallick over to the fire and took a stool beside him. "First, I'm the owner, not the bouncer."

"I figured," Crallick's battle-worn face gazed intently at Derion. "Most owners wouldn't cough up a limb for a scullery, or a milkmaid."

"Mindy is a sweet girl. Meree's pride and joy. It's the only thing she took with her from Jherrim. I'm … I'm…"

Crallick put Derion out of his misery. "You're sweet on the girl, so you figured that if you could save the day, you could win her heart. That about it?"

"Yeah," Derion looked hard at Crallick. "You know, you don't have much of a sensitive side."

"It only gets in the way." Wryly, Crallick added, "Consider me focused. Now about the arm."

Derion sighed. "I came out to investigate a commotion at the stables. They were packing Mindy into one of the two carts. I reached out and grabbed Mindy's arm. She was crying, yowling at the top of her lungs. I demanded that they release her and go about their way. As cool as you please, someone clad all in furs sauntered up and politely, softly even, said, 'Ser, please remove your hand from my property. You will be compensated.' I told him, her, or it to get buggered. Then, as quick as lightning, there was a flash of metal. I felt a burning sensation in my forearm. I looked. Mindy had fallen the rest of the way into the wagon, my hand still holding her arm. She was screaming now. Meree came running out. The person tossed me a bag of coins. Meree fell to her knees beside me and wrapped her apron around my stump. I'm afraid I was in shock. I certainly wasn't in any condition to take on twenty odd men at arms." Derion cast his eyes downward.

"Don't make excuses. You weren't exactly trained for that kind of situation, were you?" At Derion's shake of his head, Crallick added, "Then you did way more than anyone could have asked of you. Now, let me take it from here. Also, for the record, I'm sure your kitty knows just what you risked for her. Have Meree bring some more corn whiskey. The whole jug. I need to think tonight."

They each got to sleep in separate rooms that night.

In the morning, they convened over breakfast, then stepped out into the overcast morning. Crallick was grateful for the muted light, as his hangover was pounding into his head. The apple cider, bacon, and eggs hadn't done much to alleviate his discomfort. Still, he figured he should be recovered by the time they reached Crossroads by mid-afternoon.

Three hours after midday, they rode up to the towering fortress-like city walls of Crossroads. There were four soldiers outside the gate, all clad in emerald and silver adorned tabards with the livery of Crossroads emblazoned proudly on their chests. Twin towers flanked the gateway, with spires that rose twenty feet higher than the thirty-foot walls. This imposing visage gave the sense of formidable confidence. There weren't any jagged lines or skull-like reliefs to strike fear in approaching travellers. This was a no-nonsense sense of security that it afforded its residents and visitors.

Crallick slowed his horse to a trot as his company approached the gate.

"State your business," the guard dutifully, yet congenially, greeted.

With almost a sheepish glance to his companions, Crallick fished into his tabard that rested over his ring mail to pull free an oiled leather pouch. "I'm Bannathyrran Knight-ranger Crallick Oakentree, of the order of her majesty's royal protectors. My business is on behalf of her sovereign majesty, Queen Kieryanna Bannathyr."

Vlados glanced at Hullaboo, then leaned over to whisper to Crallick, "What buggery is that? You don't honestly expect to get away with a load of bull shite like that, do you?" Then he straightened as the guard returned.

"Everything seems in order, Ser Oakentree. Good luck on your hunt, ser." The guards parted, then moments later, so did the gate doors.

Crallick put the returned pouch back into his tabard, then tucked his chin towards Vlados, "Honesty is the only way to get away with that."

As the trio rode through the gate and into the city, Vlados couldn't help himself. He blurted, "Anything else you aren't telling me? You, a drunk-assed farmer without any friends, killing himself day in and day out, turns out to be a Jyslin-be-damned knight of the realm?"

The clouds began to drizzle again, slicking the mud in the streets. "Actually, that's not entirely true," Crallick corrected. "I'm a Royal Knight-ranger, and I always considered you my friend."

Vlados opened his mouth to throw back something about friends not hiding shite like that from each other, but then shut his mouth, considering that there must be some serious damage for Crallick to keep something like this under wraps. He gave a heavy sigh. "Yeah, well, when yer right, yer right," he conceded. Then he nodded off to his right, "There's the Flowwvite temple, want to try in there?"

"Sure, may as well." Crallick turned his horse towards the street that led to the temple.

The Flowwvite temple rose a towering three stories among the buildings of the neighbourhood. It was crafted from quarried grey-white marble with chrysoberyl veins running cobalt blue through it. A fountain of water cascaded a waterfall perpetually down the crowning parapet, before splitting off to a trough that ran the roof of the third story, then continuing its downward course from multitudinal spouts that gave the illusion of walls of pure water holding the roof aloft. The whole effect would have been far more striking in the sunshine, although the dwarf in Vlados couldn't help but admire the craftsmanship nonetheless.

Leaving their mounts with Hullaboo, they walked up the marble path and stairs that ran between the terraced pools that surrounded the flowing temple. They walked into a cool, refreshing, moist-aired room that was appointed in blue-green satins.

An elven initiate hurried over to them. "May Flowwe's love wash over you. Welcome to the Crossroad's Church of Flowwe. Is there anything I can do to help you?" A warm smile played on his face.

"I need to talk to a priest," Crallick snarled.

"I can send your requests for forgiveness flowing along the river to our goddess," began the initiate, eager to share in his faith's sacraments.

Crallick amputated his enthusiasm, "I don't follow your pacifist goddess, I have no use for her pissy forgiveness, and you can take your righteous indignation and shove it directly up your arse! I need goddess-damned information. Nothing more!"

Vlados gazed at Crallick with shocked concern. "Crallick! Easy, friend." Then, putting a hand gently on his friend's arm, he addressed the now cowering initiate, "Easy chum, we just need to speak to a high cleric about a matter of some import. It involves rites of some sort that we need clarity on. Go get someone schooled well in other faiths, thank you."

"I-I-I forgive you, ser," stammered out the cowed cleric, who then took off swiftly; more so to be away from Crallick than to fetch someone.

Turning on Crallick, Vlados cried, "Just what was that all about, you gobtwat?"

"Relax, I've never met a Flowwevite who wasn't a mewling pacifist. They're a waste of flesh for the most part," Crallick grinned.

Vlados's jaw hung agape, "I swear I don't know who you are sometimes. You were never like this piss drunk in my bar... ever!"

"You are quite a colorful character, Ser Oakentree. I hope I will extinguish your illusion of our worthlessness," A feminine, melodic voice intoned over Vlados's comment.

"Oh just lovely, the High Sister heard you, you lummox." Vlados tried to run interference, "He's sorry."

"He's not," she corrected.

"I'm not," Crallick confirmed.

"You are," Vlados affirmed

"...not," Crallick finished for the appalled dwarf. "You have me at a disadvantage, Sister..."

Apparently unflappable, the turquoise robed woman said, "Sister Wanda Swells. If you wish to consult with me, then I should request a tithe for the Church, then you may follow me to my office."

"Wanda Swells, huh?" Crallick sneered, "I knew an exotic dancer with a name like that once."

"Crallick!" Vlados practically shouted, forgetting himself, and startling several clergy and parishioners. "What has gotten into you?" he added in a more befitting whisper.

"Long story," Crallick simply told him.

"I'm sure she must have been a lovely woman. You may leave your tithe in the alms box." She gestured to a well-crafted box that held reliefs of waves, benign sea creatures, seals, dolphins, and merfolk.

"This should be more than ample," Crallick said, holding aloft a sapphire the size of a sling stone between his forefinger and thumb.

Wanda's breath caught in her throat. For the first time, an emotion other than blissful serenity passed her face. "My good ser, that is too much for a simple consulting fee. I mean, tithe."

"Why? It is just a gift for the poor," Crallick said coldly.

"Well, bring it and yourselves to my office. We will discuss matters there." Wanda turned and practically flew up the stairs in her haste to reach the security of her office. Once there, she ushered the pair inside, then followed, turning and locking the ornate door. "All right now, gentlemen. Why are you waving around enough wealth to feed an urchin for his lifetime? Why are you really here, Crallick? Just cut the shite, and get to the chase."

"My daughter was taken, Wanda." His voice was still gravelly, but the softest since he had walked into the temple. "I need to get her back."

"Oh my Goddess, Cral, not Amalae," Wanda clutched at some turquoise prayer beads. "You know I'll help you. You don't even have to ask. But why the …"

"They took Vlados's daughter as well; also a few other virgin girls. There was some overheard talk of sacrificial rites. Who, or what does that sound like to you?"

Wanda paced a moment. Then she shucked her vestments, revealing a pair of aqua dyed leather pants and a light pastel blue tunic that flowed about her torso. Her hair was tied back into a long ponytail. She went over to her wall of shelves and grabbed four volumes from them. She dropped the pile of tomes on her desk. There was a black one with silver chased pages; one that had a red scaled cover, one with gold filigree edged pages and a ruby adorning the spine; one which was two plates of thin slate bound together over reams of vellum, and a fourth which was a white leather-bound book with bone decorations.

"All these evil faiths run with sacrifices. Particularly of living souls. The desirable option of virginal sacrifices comes from the purity of the spirit. Lack of sin. They're more for use of particularly vile results." Wanda was beginning to run through pages while she talked, "Asha Trixiaxie, Goddess of Elemental Fire and Consumption. She likes her sacrifices burned. I don't find many rites that require more than one virgin, but, who knows?" She gave a nervous laugh, "Maybe they're stocking up for the winter?"

"Not funny," growled Crallick.

"No, no, of course not." She cleared her throat, "Kragg, the Elemental God of Earth has little use for sacrifice. Even though he is the god of murder, he is a greedy god and not one to promote sacrifice. Still, if someone was to misinterpret why they were gathering victims, and think that it's for a sacrifice rather than a religious hunt, then it could be…"

"No, he wasn't mistaken. The word sacrifice was assuredly used," Crallick interrupted.

"Well then, we can rule out Kragg." Wanda gave a shudder, "That leaves the Chessintran church. Chessintra is the evil twin of Jyslin. She is the Goddess of Darkness, Death, Magic, and Time. Her sister is of Nature, Light, and Life. They say the Vitani and the Moritani elves are the children of Jyslin and Chessintra respectively."

"That's if you believe in that shite," Crallick drawled.

"Of all the times you've been healed by divine magic, Crallick, how can you say that with a straight face?" Wanda countered.

"Easy. Magic is magic," Crallick grunted.

Vlados watched the continuing exchanges and interactions with growing interest. He was going to have to talk to Crallick or Wanda about this later.

"In any event, there are several rites of a forbidden nature in the Chessintran texts. None that directly involve virgins, but as I said, there are rites that work better with virginal sacrifices."

Scanning the black book, she said, 'The Soliloque of Shadows' is Chessintra's Holy text. The Bone Diaries is the high book of forbidden rites." Wanda was starting to murmur almost to herself. She switched books, suddenly pulling open the Bone Diaries, and scanned the table of contents. "Saint Angellicana preserve us! I found it!"

"Found what?" Vlados leaned forward in his seat. Crallick straightened.

"The answer must be in the Malefecorum." Wanda stabbed a finger at the text in front of her, then resumed reading, "The Malefecorum is a sacred tome that was scrivened by the archdemon of death. Imari, the handmaiden of Chessintra, instructed that with the slaying of thirteen pure souls and the incantation therein, one could wrest control of the greatest of servants to be bent to your will for a time."

"For a time?" scoffed Crallick. "How long does the life of thirteen virgins buy you?"

"I don't know," Wanda said.

"Who would do this?"

"I don't know," she repeated.

"Then what DO you know?" Crallick growled, pacing in front of her desk.

Wanda rose, placed the two Chessintran volumes in her rucksack, then grabbed a turquoise lacquered volume and put it in as well. She opened a cabinet and withdrew a rapier on a belt from a peg. "I know that whoever has your daughters, has the Malefecorum. I know you are dealing with a devout Chessintran. Only the most schooled in the theologies would have even heard of the book. I know you are in over your head here. And, in conclusion, I know I am coming with you."

Crallick opened his mouth to protest.

"Don't waste your breath, Cral. You need me, your daughter needs me, and you're smart enough to figure this out."

Crallick's shoulders sagged visibly, "How long do you need to get ready… and thanks."

"We'll meet outside shortly." Wanda left them sitting in her office as she ran down the hall searching for the mother superior.

The pair found Hullaboo lounging in the Flowwe temple's pool. The two mounts were drinking, and Hullaboo was swimming. After collecting the frolicking Froggle and waiting on their mounts for a short while, Wanda joined them.

"Oh, my goddess," her hands flew to her mouth. "You never told me you were travelling with a froggle. I'll get a second mount from the stables then." Her mirth was barely contained.

"Something wrong?" Hullaboo asked.

"A lot," Crallick simply replied.

Wanda returned with a pair of horses and she led one over to Hullaboo. "Here, you may ride this one."

Thanking her profusely, the froggle leapt into the saddle. Thus ready, the group headed towards the western gate of the city.

Chapter Five

*"Bannathyrran troops began their mighty advance
Amarallan lines sounded with draconic screams.
Arrows, bolts, shot, and spells flew across the expanse,
Perforating both armies. The blood ran in streams."
Verse 6: Ballad of Ser Crallick Carnage-born.*

At the market square that made up the west gate of Crossroads, Wanda pulled up short. "We should rest up first. It's almost eventide, and we have a two tenday ride to Marahaven."

"No, I don't think that is wise," said Vlados. "We already wasted too much time figuring out what we were up against at the temple."

"No, Vlados," Crallick countered to Vlados's surprise. "She's right. Also, any time we have lost today, we can make up on the road over the next two tendays. We need to rest while we can. The road can be hard on folks."

They detoured to a small cottage style inn to the south side of the Western Gate. The next morning, they rose with the dawn and got underway with a Spartan breakfast. The road held drizzle and a coat of clouds for most of the day. That evening, after setting a twelve-hour ride behind them, they got as comfortable as they could under an increasingly heavy spring rain. Hullaboo seemed to be happier the wetter the weather became. For the rest, they camped in sullen silence.

The next morning had them wolfing down a cold breakfast, then setting out under a grouse grey sky. The following three days likewise held varying shades of grey and degrees of dampness for the travellers.

The piercing rays of sunshine greeted them as they rose for their fourth day of riding. As the blue chased scudding clouds across the sky, Crallick grumbled, "Well, there goes our advantage."

"Huh," snorted Vlados, "leave it to ye to find a rusted lining after a cloudy day."

"Think about it, my friend," Crallick mounted up. "They are fleeing us, not realizing that they are. They are dragging wagons. Wagons go slower through bogging tracks along the road. Mud is our friend in this matter. Now it will dry up."

"Yeah, well so will my undershorts," grumbled Vlados.

"Don't feel so bad," smiled Wanda. "Crallick was just as dour a long time ago. I also prefer riding in the sun."

"I like the rain," Hullaboo said.

The troop rode with Crallick pretty much keeping to himself at the head of the column by about twenty to thirty horse lengths. Then Wanda and Vlados rode side by side, and Hullaboo pulled up the rear. There was little of interest along the Royal Road as it ran through the civilized lands of the Kingdom of Bannathyr.

There was plenty of time to get to know each other a little better. They spent the rest of the tenday sharing stories. Vlados was an innkeeper and a really good barkeep. Wanda hadn't always been a sister in the church. She knew Crallick from back in the day. No, nothing romantic. She had been an exotic dancer to supplement her income while she attended the bardic college of history in Marahaven. She became a treasure hunter and that was how she knew Crallick. Yes, he was an honest to goodness knight. He had always felt she abandoned their group's calling when she took her vows and left for the church. Vlados's wife was back in his home town. Their daughter and Crallick's were fast friends. He missed the mining community of Vein-Crag.

These tidbits and more were shared as they rode hard after their prey. The nineteenth day had the Spires of Marahaven come into view. They were riding into the shadows of the capital with still an hour of mounted travel while the sun began to set behind the city. This lent a slightly more foreboding image to the city than necessary. There was nothing sinister about the city itself, just that the jagged dark spires seemed to splay groping dark fingers across the land with the dying sun.

They could taste the tang of salt in the air as they rode closer. There was a sweet undercurrent of decaying fish meat to go with the slightly more pungent waft of rotting seaweed.

Crallick sighed, "I'd hoped I'd never have to see this place again." Half turning in his saddle, he caught Vlados's attention. "Once inside, you go get yourself a good crossbow and whatever other supplies you think you may need. Get Hullaboo a weapon of his choice, and armor as well. Wanda will come with me dockside to secure our prey. Understand?"

"Sure Crallick," Vlados furrowed his brow. "Why are you taking Wanda to such an unsavoury part of town? Won't that be risky? Would she not be better off coming with Hullaboo and meself?"

Crallick barked out a short laugh. "What do you think Wanda? Got your purse? Want to go shopping?"

Shaking her head she replied, "Crallick, you really are an asshole."

"Language," Crallick mocked.

To Vlados, Wanda said, "I'll be fine, remember that I knew Cral way back. Also, I wasn't always a good girl. I know my way around the docks of a city. I'm good at finding things out and taking care of myself. Don't you worry your mohawked head about me."

They rode up to the liveried and armored men guarding the gates. One grey-haired human glanced up from a table to the side and exclaimed, "Crallick! Crallick Oakentree?" Rising up from his seat, he added, "Well as I live and breathe, it is you! How are you?"

Crallick squinted, "Horace? By the six creators, how did you even recognize me?"

Horace snorted, "You may be greyer and more wrinkled than when I last laid these peepers on you, but that sword, mail, and attitude are all you!" Horace laughed, "Man, it's good to see you. What brings you?"

"Some Chessintrans stole our kids for some shite-smelling ritual," came the short answer.

"Shite," breathed out Horace. "Sorry to hear." Then to the approaching seargant at arms, he added, "They're fine. I'm admitting them on my authority."

The city guards fell back, then turned their focus on some more travellers approaching the gate.

Crallick and his companions followed Horace off to the side. "Have you admitted a group of armed men, around twenty to thirty in number?" Crallick asked once they were out of earshot of the others at the gate.

"Not today," said Horace.

"Yesterday?" prompted Hullaboo.

"I was on the south gate yesterday," Horace said. "But let me check the records." Horace took several moments of poring over numerous sheets of vellum that made up the lined ledgers from the prior day. The volume itself represented the current week. Horace stabbed a finger triumphantly at a page. "Here! I'm sure this is it!" Then he read, "On the 27th of Hannois, during the eighth hour of the day, there came to the eastern gate a company, numbering eighteen in all. In possession of Amarallan trade documents, legally in possession of four slaves, all young females. Two possible humans, one dwarf, and one nekomin. In their party were fifteen men at arms, two reptilemen drivers, and one Chessintran Mage. Upon declaration of their business, they did so declare they were late from Jherrin to catch their ship home."

"Well, that tells us three things," Crallick grinned viciously. "First, they lied about both their origin and their destination. Second, they'll be only a few hours out of port due to the tides. And third, Horace the guard still doesn't know shite about Amarallan trade counterfeits."

"Well, other than your criticism, pal," Horace grinned, "I'm glad I could help. Good luck and goddess speed."

"Thanks," Crallick led the rest of his troop into the bustling, colourful gate market. Turning, he addressed Vlados, "This is where we part ways. Watch your purse."

"All right," Vlados creased his brow in a bemused chastisement. "I'm sure I can handle a cut-purse or two."

"Crallick grinned, then mounted up, saying, "Who's worried about them? I'm talking about the children." With a clicking, he rode off towards the sea.

"He's right," Wanda told the shocked Vlados. Then she too rode off, heading after Crallick.

Crallick dismounted and hitched his horse to the tethering post by the side of Warehouse Road. Wanda replicated the action a few moments later, and joined Crallick. "Ready for this?" she asked.

"I was born…" Crallick glared. "Shite Wanda, why do you even ask?"

Smiling good-naturedly, Wanda patted his ass, "'Cause I almost had you. And one day, you'll slip." She began to wind her way through a throng of cavorting street urchins.

"Women," Crallick cursed to himself. Then he began to follow Wanda towards the seedy line of taverns and inns that lined the dock front.

Wanda had selected a blue-walled wooden building that rose over the docks and the water. It was actually three stories, although only two were visible over the level of the docks. The third story actually just skimmed the surface of the water. The Porpoise's Pleasure was the only building built on the docks proper, and not on land. Its other distinction was that of a bawdy house. Wanda entered the eastern facing main doors, stepping onto green carpet. This entry was strategically poised to provide a grand view of the entire bottom floor at a glance. This presented a very stunning view, as not only the pretty and lithe dancers grabbed the attention of those coming in, but the lead glass floor upon which they danced gave the illusion of dancing on the waves themselves. Arranged in tiers climbing away from the sunken stage were carpeted drinking and dining levels, where patrons could slake their thirst with any number of potent potables and could satisfy their hunger with either the catch of the day or seasonal dishes. Female companionship would wander these tables seeking to take lonely sailors to private booths, or to an upstairs boudoir. A fairly comely bard used illusory spells to augment the lighting for her musical performance that had the nude dancers writhing suggestively to set the mood for the establishment.

A hulking bouncer of some human-goblin bloodline rubbed his eyes in disbelief. "Wanda? Wanda Swells?" Then laughing, "As I floggin' breathe, it is you! What brings you here? Jerreth will be happy to hear of your return."

"Whoa there Thogg, I'm just a patron tonight. I'm looking for a fast ship and some information, that's all." Wanda put her hands up admonishingly.

Thogg nodded thoughtfully. "I know of four Captains in here tonight. You cozy up to the bar..." he gestured to the bar that ran off to her left, "and I'll set up a booth for you. I'll bring any interested parties to you to negotiate." Thogg glanced around, "You bring any muscle, or you want me to guard for you too?"

Wanda cracked a sweet smile. "Oh Thogg, sweetie, you don't need to worry about me. I have protection. And more than just what is on my hip." She patted her rapier.

Thogg scoffed, "That toothpick? Nothing more than a utensil to clean the shite from me boots. Who is your help? So as I don't accidentally bar his or her entry."

"Oh, you would remember him as soon as you saw him," Wanda coyly demurred. Then, as instructed, she headed over to the bar.

Thogg went and cleared out a booth usually reserved for private dances that offered both privacy and a clear view of the stage and exit. After hanging his 'reserved' rope across it, he made a few rounds of the privateer, pirate, and smuggler captains he knew were there. The merchantmen captains he ignored, because if ol' Wanda was looking for a fast ship, then clearly she was up to no good. After she was set up and her security was in place, he would go up to Jerreth's office to let him know what was going on.

Crallick strode into the Porpoise's Pleasure and his nose was immediately assailed by the stink of human sweat, female sex, soured whiskey, and shitty beer. He, even as a drunkard, had been spoiled by Vlados's fine ales and meads. Damn, that dwarf could brew. His memories of the place flew back into his mind. The intoxication of the night his crew had celebrated their triumph. Their elation of the plans to adventure after the war. The guilt of his cheating dalliance with the young human dancer. All these memories flooded back as a ghostly voice haunted his eardrums. "Crallick! Crallick Oakentree! What the demon brings you here?" Thogg's voice grated Crallick out of his reverie.

"I see you have yet to build that manor house and retire," Crallick observed coolly.

"I see time hasn't made you prettier," Thogg retorted. "Why are you here?"

"I'm with Wanda." Crallick's eyes challenged Thogg.

"No shite," Thogg mused. "Well, let me set you up here. You can see her clearly there. How is that?"

"Fine," Crallick agreed. "This will do nicely." Crallick set an arrow on the bar and handed his bow to Thogg. "Keep her strung when you put her away," Crallick warned, rather than requested.

"Of course, Crallick, no problem." Thogg placated. "I remember your trick. It'll be ready for you."

Wanda looked at the first captain to show his face at her booth. A grunt, a spit, and a "No way. Women be a worthless curse on the sea," ended the interview before she could even say 'Hello'.

The second, rather bloated man to grace her booth pinched his gut over the table, pushed up dirty bronze spectacles over his bulbous nose, and with a sniff announced, "I am Captain Steffan Jackman, the Stormy!" Then with a trickle of drool that slathered down the left side of his limp lip, he added, "You may find that some seafarers have no interest in taking women as either crew or passenger. I just want you to know…" his bald head inclined slightly as his eyes greedily drank in her curves, "I share no such qualms."

"Heh, heh." Wanda chuckled nervously. "Well, that is very nice to know. I'm looking for a very fast ship." She thought his ship would surely travel faster if he were overboard. Then in a chastising voice inside her head, she reprimanded herself with a 'Floowwe would not approve of such attitudes'. Instead, she smiled and asked. "How many masts?"

"Two my dear, unless you count my personal mast." The belly rumbled the table. "Ho, ho, ho. We run a light and shallow draught."

"How soon can you make ready?" She bore through a salty stench that she was certain was not the sea.

"Day after tomorrow, my dear. We are berthed three docks down, slip nine, the Stormrunner."

"Thank you, I'll consider it." The stench was becoming nauseating.

"Wish to discuss terms?" Steffan pushed.

"I'll consider it, then get back to you." Wanda huffed, trying to breathe through her mouth, which only caused her to taste the stale, sweat-laden air.

"If you're concerned about price, we can negotiate on services," he leered.

"I'll consider it, and I assure you, I am not pressed to exchange services." Wanda's hand tightened on her rapier as she denoted the tone of finality in her voice.

"All right then," Steffan sweated profusely as he hauled his mass out of the booth. "I'll discuss fares with you dockside then." Turning to face her before he left, "Adios my lady fair." Then he lumbered into the crowd.

Wanda flashed her hand out of the booth. A waitress glided over. She crinkled her nose, then spritzed some perfume to guise the lingering scent of the Captain. "May I get you something?"

Wanda, wishing she hadn't taken her vows for just moments, asked for water with a lime wedge. "No, no gin or vodka, thank you."

Whisking her wish away through the crowd, the waitress was eclipsed by a Reptileman of no small stature. His scales were a series of blue hues with yellow striping over the side of his head. Loose, yellow cloth hung from his corded torso and arms. Cowhide breeches that were customized to accomodate his tail completed his outfit. There was a rich blue sash that tied a cutlass to his hip. Wanda liked the reptileman immediately.

"You ssseek a fassst ssship, yesss?" He drawled.

"I do." Wanda simply replied.

"Ssserpent'sss Tongue isss fassstessst sssloop on the ssseasss," he sibilantly boasted.

"Sure." She wasn't sure if she unconsciously elongated her own 's' with the sibilance of the reptileman's own accent. She hoped not. "How soon and how much?"

"My name is Captain Ssstrathosss Wavebreaker. I can make ready as soon as required. The cost dependsss on three thingsss. One isss cargo, or passsengersss, or both. Two isss the danger involved – do my crew merely have to hide you, or are they expected to be marinesss? Three is the time of voyage. I value my twenty-eight hand crew. What sssay you?" Sarthos concluded by crossing his arms over his chest in an all-business gesture.

'Wow, he is professional,' Wanda thought. "What about women as passengers?"

The reptileman spat on the floor in front of the returning waitress who held Wanda's water and lime. "That isss a mammillian sssuperssssticion."

"Thank you," Wanda told the server and tipped them, taking her drink in turn. Then to Sarthos, she added. "Only passengers, unknown time of travel, and maybe, though I'd have to confer with my backers."

Blue nostrils flared. "Thisss isss a hunt then. I would need an official letter of marque! I refussse to engage in piracy!" He rose abruptly, spun on his heel, then as his tail lashed, he looked back and added, "If you posess those documentsss, then you may bring them for inssspection at dock four, ssslip ten." Then he strode off.

A letter of marque? Fat chance of that. She would have to talk to Crallick about that one. Too bad too, he seemed a good fit.

"Is this seat taken?" Sultry notes intoned over the singing and the crowd.

With a small shudder of revulsion about the inference, Wanda said, "No thanks, I'm not looking for a companion."

"But I hear you're looking for a fast ship," the dulcet voice amended.

Wanda looked up from her drink to gaze into emerald eyes. Those were framed by copper skin, in turn framed by strikingly scarlet hair.

"That I am," Wanda acquiesced. She gestured to the seat opposite her.

The woman languidly sat where indicated. She smiled, then roughly grabbed a passing server. "Rum, bring the bottle."

Wanda looked at the fit, lean human. "I presume you are a captain...?" she let the thought linger in the air.

"Aye, I am. Captain Raquel Firebrand at your service." She tipped her head in lieu of a bow or curtsy.

The rum arrived. Raquel tore the cork open with her teeth and swilled back a full swig before wiping her mouth with her sleeve then proffering the bottle to Wanda, "So who'm I drinking with?"

"I'm Wanda Swells." Wanda began.

"Dancer?" Raquel interrupted.

"Sister of Flowwe." Wanda patiently corrected.

"Good, 'cause dancers don't usually have the type of money for the type of voyage you seem to be trying to charter."

"What makes you say that?" Wanda put out.

"Try this on for size. You need a fast ship, so you're either running after or away from something. You have no cargo and probably number under half a dozen passengers. You don't know how long the voyage would likely be so you either have no seaworthy experience, or you don't know the location of your arrival, which means you are likely chasing something, not running." Raquel took another draught of rum. "You're probably evenly matched, or slightly under strength, so you may need my crew as marine protection. But you're not sure. My brigantine is the fastest on the seas. No boast, no shite. Not the strongest, but damn fast. My crew is seasoned, as am I. But you'll be paying for the quality. Gems, no minted coins. Also, no letters of marque required. We can leave on the moonlit tide if necessary. Whatever you need, I can provide," she paused, half-lidded her eyes and breathed, "for a price."

"I see," Wanda shuffled in her seat. "You don't have an issue with women aboard I see. So no premium for female passengers?"

Raquel barked a short laugh. "No, I won't ding you for having a vagina." She laughed again, "Some idiots, huh?"

Wanda laughed along with the crass woman, "Yeah, some idiots." She took another pull of her lime and water and again spoke, "Let me tell you how you did. You have moxy and streetwise skills to case the prospective interview in order to get the rough details of the job. You are smart enough to use maybe some eavesdropping enchantments. You are smart enough to fill in the blanks. You aren't as charming as you think, though. You confused lack of interest in male wiles as deviance, not devotion. You are crafty enough to present the opportunity for brazen greed to dictate your pitch, ensuring a top price. How is that?"

"Wow, you are cynical, sister," Raquel mused. "What did you say you did before becoming a cleric?"

"I didn't," Wanda tritely stated.

"Well, anyways, after that fat lummox finished breathing over you, I figured that'd be enough to turn any woman gay." Raquel smiled into her upturning bottle. *Gulp. Gulp.* "Ahhh. But yeah, you pretty much have the rest. So Are you chartering the Flamerunner, or not?"

"Depends on your price."

"Two thousand crowns in gems, half up front, plus danger pay and incidentals," Raquel said.

"That's twice as much as anyone else would charge!" snarled Crallick, coming up on the booth.

"They're not as good," Raquel stated flatly. She squinted at the new arrival. "Have we met?"

"Doubt it," Crallick growled, taking a seat beside Wanda. He smelt of whiskey.

Wanda rose her hand, palm up towards Crallick's chin. "This is my backer, Ser Crallick Oakentree."

"No shit, the butcher of Xod? The High Protector of the realm? I thought you were dead?" Raquel laughed. "Well, shit, if this is the royal coffers, let's just triple the price right now." She was positively beaming.

"I was drunk, not dead," Crallick glared sullenly at Raquel. "I haven't held or used titles for ten years now."

"Oh." Some of the opportunistic mirth left Raquel's eyes. "Still, once you earn the titles, only the Queen can take them from you."

"Yeah. I suppose that is true." Crallick reached over, uninvited, and pulled a slug from the bottle of rum. It hit the tabletop a little harder than it should have. A spiderweb began to dampen the side of the bottle. "I'm trying to rescue my daughter and several other virginal girls who are to be sacrificed to some dark goddess or another. Cut us a fucking break, you greedy… huh?" His mounting tirade had been cut short by a gently placed hand on his arm.

"Hush, Cral. Let her think."

Raquel glanced at the diminished hero and the caring priestess, and cursed her damnable luck for having a heart at all. She knew she was going to give them a deal. Damn. Damn. Damn. "Damn. Sister, you really know how to kill a girl's mood. I'll charge you a thousand up front, and a full fifty percent of the spoils. Not negotiable."

Wanda grinned and extended her hand, "Great. Done. What time do we meet you at the docks?"

"Four hours from now, if you want to make the moon tide," Raquel said. She rose, and scribbled a note. "That's where I'm berthed. See you there." Then she was gone.

Crallick gave a halfway grin. "Great job recruiting…. Now we just have to figure out how to track them."

Wanda grimaced. "No Crallick, you need to figure out how to bathe before we set sail on a ship. She checked the note, "I have things to do. Tell Vlados and Hullaboo where we're to meet." She handed Crallick the note, patted his hand, shook her head, and then was gone.

Crallick figured he'd just have one more drink.

***

Wanda ran up to the central city fountain a full two hours after they were supposed to meet. Vlados was furious. He was a nice and even-tempered guy, but when you finally got to him, he became a force of rage. His complexion was almost scarlet. Hullaboo, far more patient, was happily licking the salt out of the moist air and playing with his new spear. The head was steel and it was shod like that halfway down the haft.

"Where have you been!?" she breathily rasped. Sweat beaded her brow, and gave a sheen to her forearms as well. "You were supposed to be dockside an hour ago!"

"Well, so nice to tell us this!" Vlados roared. "Just where the hell have the two of you been!? I'm not some errand boy to be left hanging around!"

Wanda's perplexed and hurt look took Vlados aback. "Wait, where is Crallick?" she asked.

"With you," offered Hullaboo, not liking the yelling.

"No, I sent him to get you, then to get to the docks; dock three, slip seven." Wanda's eyes widened. "Where is he?"

"Where did you leave him?" Vlados asked. He was trying to reign in his anger by taking deep breaths.

"At The Porpoise's Pleasure," Wanda offered. "My goddess, you don't think he got hurt, do you?"

"Crallick?" scoffed Vlados. "No, but he's probably shit-faced by now. You left him in a bar. This man has been drinking himself under the table for ten years now." Vlados sighed heavily, "Nothing to be done about it now but to go and collect his sorry arse."

"My goddess, I'm so sorry," Wanda looked distraught, worry sagging the corners of her eyes and mouth. "We found a ship. We were going to set sail on the moon tide. I was so excited to find out the possible destination for the ritual sites of Chessintra, I never stopped to think or even ask how Crallick had been these last years. I just assumed…."

Vlados shut her up. "Quit that. Act like a good priestess and focus on what you do right, and forgive what ends up as shite. Deal?"

Tears had begun to flow from Wanda's eyes, "Deal."

Raquel was waiting for them at her berth. A crew of about a score of hands bustled about, rigging and hauling supplies into the hold, and making things fast on the deck. She watched with grim curiosity as her passengers made their way up the dock towards her. A dwarf and a froggle suspended the 'backer', Crallick, between them. He was obviously in a drunken stupor. Before the shepherding Wanda could speak, Raquel had turned to her Nekomin first mate and in a hushed tone whispered, "Mr. Tritts, our guests are here.

Make ready. Don't let the crew note the state of that one."

Mr. Tritts roared his reply, "Ma'am." Then turned to bellow at any crew that were starting to lollygag at their duties to watch the approaching arrivals. These crewmen quickly bustled off to return their attention elsewhere.

Raquel approached and said, "Quickly, follow me. You can stow him in my cabin 'til he rouses. Introductions and payment will have to wait until we are underway. We have no time to spare."

Everyone, sensing her urgency, hustled up the gangway. Crallick was tossed on her cot.

"Release the mainstays!" Raquel hollered.

It was done.

"Gaff sticks and poles. Clear the slip!"

It was done.

"Run out the sweeps!"

The two banks of eight oars bristled out the sides of the ship.

"Clear the harbor, then raise the mains," Raquel concluded. Then directly to Mr. Tritts, she added, "Come find me when we're clear of the harbor, I'll set you your bearing."

"Aye ma'am," came his crisp reply.

With that, Raquel turned from the receding lights of Marahaven to enter her cabin, to settle her business with her new passengers.

Chapter Six

"Vita I, Mortani, dwarf, and man all fought hard
Amarallan and goblin kind were just as fierce
Heroes and clashes provide matter for the bard
Then three dragons, the Bannathyr lives, did pierce."
Verse 7: Ballad of Ser Crallick Carnage-born.

Raquel surveyed the misfit group collected in her cabin. One drunk and passed out Vitani blood hero. One human, one dwarf, and one hulking froggle sitting around her cabin, looking nervous and concerned. Well, it was time to make their voyage feel as pleasant as possible, after business.

"Which of you has my fare?" she asked bluntly.

Wanda nodded towards the cot.

Of course it was. Raquel walked over to the man and, rather unceremoniously, began pawing through his clothes. Coin purse... felt a trifle light; probably travelling coins. Oilskin pouch for papers; upon inspection, she grunted, "So this drunken lummox really IS a knight-ranger of the realm. He even is a Ser, and all that." Tossing the skin back in the tabard pouch, she continued her search and yielded a bodkin on his ankle. There was a leathery pouch of two... no, wrong type of stones. She grinned sadistically. Finally, hanging from the small of his back, at the crown of his arse, was a pouch of gems!

Pulling the pouch free, she upended it on her desk. She counted out three: a pair of emeralds, and a smaller ruby. She put the rest back in the pouch. Tossing the pouch to Wanda, she explained, "This will do for my fare. When he awakes, tell him we are underway and that his current debt is settled. Expenses accrued during the voyage shall be levied against him at the time of his debarkment." Raquel nodded, "Agreed?"

"Agreed," confirmed Wanda. "Our current destination is Fairaway Cove."

"The southern Pirate Isles?" Raquel looked to confirm.

"Yes," Wanda smirked. "As opposed to the northern ones?"

Raquel smiled wryly. "Yes, ma'am. There are two independent archipelagoes that are havens for Pirates. They are affectionately known as the northern and southern pirate islands."

"Oh."

"That notwithstanding, the southern islands shouldn't be a problem. If you'll accompany me," she gestured at them all, "I'll get you stowed at your berths." She led her guests from her cabin and immediately to her left, she opened a plain wooden door. "This is yours," she addressed Wanda. The door opened into a barely closet-sized room that held only a six-foot cot on one wall, and a fold-down table that allowed the bunk to cleverly be used as a bench as well. There was one shelf that could be used to store effects. A porthole and a hanging lantern provided two options for light.

"This'll do well enough." Wanda glanced over at Raquel, "As long as I don't have to share it."

Raquel laughed. "No, not at all."

The cabin beside Wanda's was twice the size but held four bunks, not one. "This is for the rest of your companions. The Dwarf…"

"Vlados," he extended his hand by means of introduction. It was accompanied by a cheerful smile.

"And the froggle…" she shook the dwarf's hand.

"Hullaboo!" he grinned widely, tongue lolling loosely to the top of his britches.

"Right," Raquel headed up the steep stairs to the deck of the ship. When the others came topside she looked at Wanda while she addressed Mr. Tritts. "Mr. Tritts, please make for Port Fairaway under full sail."

"Aye, Aye, ma'am." Then bellowing at the top of his lungs, "Making bearing south, by south-west! Making all sails!"

Turning from her jumping crew, and feeling the sweet salty air moistly kissing her face, Raquel smiled, then walked over to join Wanda at the rails of the aftcastle of the Flamerunner.

"So what makes you figure these people you're hunting are sailing to Fairaway? There are closer and safer ports of call to be found. How do you figure they'll run so far south?"

Wanda looked up from the roiling waves. Her eyes twinkled in the silver light. "Well, I'm not all the way certain but I can't afford to be wrong with this. I did a lot of communion with Flowwe. Also, there is mention in the Bone Diary of a port on a southern island chain that marked the direction to the sacred ziggurat, where the darkest rites could be performed with the most potent results. When you couple that with my suspicion that they're in possession of the Malefecorum, then Port Fairaway seems to be the most likely destination."

"But why?" Raquel put to her. "Assuming they have the sacrifices that they need, why not just make a straight run to the ziggur-thingie? Unless the port is directly on the way?"

"I don't know. And I figure they don't either. It hasn't been viewed by mortal eyes as far as I'm aware."

Raquel laughed, "You mean to tell me that they're chasing a faerie tale? Seas below, we're chasing idiots chasing faerie tales. That's rich."

"Well, Raquel, whether you believe in the divine or not, faerie tales or not, there are those who do, and they have abducted thirteen maidens to sacrifice to Chessintra's amusement. Rich or not, that is why we are hunting them. To save those lives if we can. That rich enough for you?" Wanda held onto the gunwale rail tightly.

"Hey, I meant no insult to the virtue of our mission. I just don't understand how religious zealots can go off half-cocked without thinking things through. It makes no sense," Raquel parried.

"What? Sailors don't set sail for parts unknown for the sake of exploration?" Wanda countered.

"Not without a pretty good idea of a destination; even if you've never been before. You at least have a bearing that you keep to, and can return by. Jyslin made sure we can find our way, day or night," Raquel said.

Wanda smiled in spite of her rising temper. "So you do believe in the divine?"

"Aye. As I said, I'm not pissing on our mission. Why else would I have taken such a lousy fare for such a risky mission?" Raquel feigned being put out.

Now Wanda had to try not to laugh. "I'm sorry, of course, you're right. I suppose the trip seems quite mad, and very ill-conceived."

"But noble enough to undertake." Raquel then lowered her voice. It lost all the levity that it had once held. "But speaking of noble; what of the drunken ser in my cabin? What manner of aid, or hindrance, is he to be?" she somberly concluded.

"Crallick?" Wanda asked first, then heaved a great sigh, punctuated by a rolling wave that lifted the ship along with her unspoken prayer. What would he turn out to be? She would have been swift to answer once, but that was long ago. Now she was gravely uncertain. She looked into the emerald fire of Raquel's earnest gaze and barely whispered, "I don't know."

"You don't…" the voice trailed off as the ship dashed down the swell.

"You have to understand, I travelled and fought alongside him through many tribulations. I would have sworn him indomitable. That was ten years gone now. When he appeared to beseech my aid in my office, I recognized the old flame of his wrath at injustice and was immediately moved by Flowwe's spirit to aid him again. Now, I fear, I may know why." Wanda turned her back to the rail, to face Raquel directly. "Vlados told me that Crallick has been farming and failing at it for the last ten years. He has taken to the bottle as a companion after the loss of his wife. It is only the fruits of his rather illustrious career that have kept him and his daughter fed."

"How old is his daughter?" Raquel inquired.

"Fifteen," Wanda smiled. "I remember her playing with my braids when she was five. She declared I should be a princess."

"You knew them back then?" Raquel paused a moment. "Is she your daughter?"

"Heaven's no!" Wanda laughed, then blushed lightly. "No, she was Triella's daughter."

"Oh, right," Raquel nodded, understanding. "You did say he was widowed. How?"

"Pox took his wife, and apparently his spirit went with her."

"I see," Raquel said. Then looking up at the moon, she added, "The hour is turning late upon us. You should retire for the night. Sleep well."

"Thank you. I shall." Wanda turned and headed below.

The lidded eye of the moon looked down on Raquel. The cool evening air filled her sails and toyed with her hair. Her sweet home, her ship, creaked and groaned comfortingly in ways familiar and soothing to her and her crew. It was a great night for sailing. The padded footfalls of Mr. Tritts came up beside her.

"Yes?" She tilted her chin to her shoulder to take in his gold-green eyes as they gazed at her, they were almost luminescent in the night.

"Get your rest my lady, Captain. The night is pleasant enough, but tomorrow will be long and hard. You need to be more rested than I, and my sight is keener than ye." This was accompanied by a feline fang-lined grin.

Patting his furred shoulder, Raquel looked at the calico complexion of Mr. Tritts' face. "Thanks. I'll see you in the morning," she called out before she went below decks.

Opening the door to her cabin presented her with a view that she hadn't needed, yet one that filled her with more pity than wrath. Crallick had rolled off her cot and was curled up on her red plush carpet with his hand shoved down his breeches. Drool trickled down the side of his slack lower lip. His snores were muffled by the carpet.

Raquel decided, not for the first time, to sleep with her clothes on. She untied her seal-hide sword belt and looped it over her chair. Then locking her door, she stepped over the slumbering man. She wrinkled her nose as a trumpeting bout of flatus erupted from his upturned bottom. She shook her head. Disgusting. She crawled in her cot and soon drifted into the easy sway of the sea.

Morning poured molten sunlight through the stern windows. Raquel's eyes snapped open. Crallick was gone from her room. She collected her weapon belt, put her hat on in a jaunty left-slanted tilt, and headed up to the deck.

There she let the sun kiss her eyes and the breeze stroke her face. The ocean rocked her in its arms, and she basked in the glory of the cobalt sky that was wisped by platinum gossamer in the morning air. Raquel breathed deeply. This was going to be a glorious run. She saw the four companions huddled amidships. Rather, three were huddled, unsure of where to be so as not to interfere with the bustling crew. The fourth, Crallick, was over at the quartermaster's rum barrel looking a little sallow. *'Well, that will soon be dealt with,'* she grimly thought.

"Captain on deck!" alerted Mr. Shneed, a wildly tattooed, pierced, bronzed, and bald muscular human.

Mr. Tritts looked up from the aftcastle, yawned, stretched, and padded over to her. "Ma'am. I turn the watch over to you. We're on bearing, and making good time. We have favourable winds and are only needing to tack about twelve degrees per run."

Raquel smiled. "Excellent. I relieve you Mr. Tritts. The watch is mine. If you could send the passengers to see me, I'll acclimate the poor dirt dwellers. Your guess to Carib? I'm guessing eighteen days."

Mr. Tritts waved his whiskers about pensively, then said, "I stand relieved. By my calculation, if the weather holds, we should make Carib Island in about sixteen days." He smiled, "I'll send the litter to you."

Raquel ran up to her station, behind the main wheel of the ship. Her helmsman was grinning broadly through chestnut lips. "Morning' ma'am."

"'Morning Mr. Martine," she replied to her dark-skinned Vitani pilot. She sat in her chair, which was bolted to the deck, behind a table that was likewise bolted in place. There was a frame that pinned a pane of lead glass in place that could anchor a chart to the table under almost any conditions. She had paid a pretty crown for it, but had never regretted any of them. She began to pour over her charts. Mr. Tritts had laid a favorable course. She concurred with his work. She looked up as she heard the deck boards creak the arrival of the passengers.

"Please gather round," she invited with a smile.

Crallick had a surly glower on his face and was licking chapped lips. Vlados had a wide grin under a short strawberry blond beard. Wanda smiled politely. Hullaboo had his tongue furiously licking over the exposed skin on his arms, lower legs, and his own head.

"Now," Raquel began, "I'll start by bringing you up to speed on our voyage. If we maintain favourable weather, we should see Carib in about nineteen days. So you have plenty of time to relax and enjoy yourselves, or make whatever preparations you feel you need for when you catch up with your marks. You won't be bothering my crew, they're experienced. If you ask them questions and they're not busy, they'll answer you. If they're busy, they'll ignore you. Don't take it personally. You'll eat with the officers. Your dining mates will be myself, 1st mate Mr. Tritts, 2nd mate Mr. Shneed, Quartermaster Mr. Drake, and Surgeon Syllethra. You will each be entitled to one ration of rum per day, this may be taken as a single measure or a half measure. This is not negotiable. The crew usually has a spell of leisure time around evening, and you are welcome to join us. If, in the unlikely event we are boarded, you will leave all negotiations to me. All combat and spellcasting will be handled by my crew. You will not participate unless directly asked. Now, all of you savvy my rules?"

Vlados nodded.

Hullaboo and Wanda said "Yes" in unison.

Crallick grunted.

Raquel smiled, "Great. Now, do you have any questions?"

"Nope, crystal clear!" Said Vlados.

Hullaboo asked, "Any water that isn't so dry?" This was punctuated by his tongue running over his yellow eyes.

"Ahh," said Raquel, reason seeping into her green eyes. "I see, you need something to help keep your skin moist. That it?"

"Yes," he said, smacking his lips together. "I feel the water in the air, just can't understand why it's so dry!"

Stifling a smile at the froggle's obvious discomfort, Raquel explained, "It's the sea air, m'dear. The salt in the ocean and the water coming off it will dry yer poor skin as badly as any desert. I'll instruct the quartermaster to talk to the cooper. He can get you a large cask with wash water to let you freshen up with that. Will that do? That would be in addition to your drinking allowance, you understand?"

"Yes, yes, thank you, thank you. You are very kind!" Hullaboo wandered off then with a happy expression on his face.

"Can we take your leave?" Wanda asked.

"Of course," Raquel shooed them away. "At your leisure."

"Where can I exercise?" Crallick asked.

"Anywhere you like," Raquel said. "May I ask you something, with you ensuring you shan't take offence?"

Crallick gave her a suspicious look. "All right."

"How are you going to handle your drinking problem?" Raquel figured the best route was to simply get to the point.

"That's not your problem."

She saw that one coming. "Well, Crallick," she deliberately tried to sweeten her tone. "As this is my ship, and I am her Captain, and all are my subjects, then my subjects' problems are my problems. Savvy?"

Crallick looked hard at her, "Sure. I'm savvy."

Raquel pressed, "So how do you plan to take care of your drunkenness?"

"You're not very polite are you?" Crallick growled.

"Neither are you," she shot back. "Now quit changing the fucking subject."

"I'll deal," Crallick said.

"How?" she pressed.

"Exercising," Crallick said. "I'll stay focused on my mission."

"Like you were focused in Marahaven?" Raquel softened her voice. "Look, I'm not trying to be a hard ass here. I'm here to help you. When you hired me on, you hired a professional. This includes all the benefits that come with that while shipboard. If you ever have any issues while on board my ship, you do not take matters into your own hands knight-ranger, you take them to me. I'll take care of you. Savvy?" She forced a smile.

"You really like that word, huh?" Crallick muttered.

"Yeah, it means, 'Do you understand what I'm saying, you salt-headed scallywag?' in Nekomin," Raquel smiled. "I learned it from Mr. Tritts."

"Well, yeah, I savvy," Crallick growled. "And thanks."

The following tenday fell into a pleasant routine on the ship. The early summer weather was conducive to great sailing. The crew handled the ship like symbiotic lice crawling over a fen fox. The Flamerunner cut smoothly through the waves with a gently unending rolling motion that never felt like it was cruising at a swift nine knots. The four companions fell into routines of their own around the pulse of the ship and her crew.

Wanda woke, broke her fast, said her morning prayers, and then turned to researching in her Chessintran tomes. The afternoon had her practicing her rapier in the heat of the noon sun. After an hour of that, she would seek out the company of the ship's surgeon, Syllethra, who turned out to be a female mortani who held some rather interesting ideas about Chessintran religion. After some time with her, they would usually head to the officer's meal together. After dinner, Wanda would take in the entertainment of the crew's social hour. Then she would observe her evening sacraments before retiring to bed.

Vlados fell head over heels in love with the ship. He had never been to sea before so the new experience was exhilarating for him. He enjoyed the ribbing of the other sailors who razzed him about the dwarven racial fear of wide open places and there being no caves around. He laughed it off. They joked about dwarves not being able to float because they were made of too much rock. Yet, they accepted him wholeheartedly as one of their own as he showed genuine interest in knots, sailing, and ship construction. He climbed the rigging with them. He helped them trim the sails. He helped keep lookout, he helped in the holds. He took his meals with the crew and became quite good friends with most of them. Vlados even took some night shifts. Vlados had taken to running around without his shirt and his formerly pasty white flesh was beginning to redden, and slightly darken. Two of the crew even shared their rum rations with him; this helped convince Vlados to get a tattoo of a flame-wreathed anchor. This was an ink brand shared by the crew of the Flamerunner. Vlados was having the time of his life.

Hullaboo seemed to have the most difficult time of them all. He woke, then ran to the cask of water and dove in. He then grabbed morning breakfast as swiftly as he could before running back to the cask. All afternoon he slept immersed in the cask, breathing through his skin. When Raquel was told by the quartermaster how much time the froggle was spending in the cask, she doubled the fresh water allocated to keeping Hullaboo healthy. He would come out and sup with the others, and hop around in the evening social. He tried to be active in the cooler evening air, the nasty salts weren't so present on his skin then, though he could still taste it. He slept in his bunk until morning. Often he gave his rum share to nice Crallick who saved him from the nasty goblins. Hullaboo didn't like the sea at all.

Crallick's routine ran along the lines of: see the dawn, get a half measure of rum, and then eat breakfast. After that, track down Hullaboo for his day's rum chit. Exercise. Eat lunch and get another half measure of rum to wash it down. Exercise. Find sailors to gamble with for more rum rations. He would only allow himself to lose a half ration. Often he would have 2-5 full rations in a day. There was the odd day where he only had one and a half. He thought he was being clever, but Raquel and her quartermaster had their eyes on him and were keeping very close watch on his actions. He usually skipped the socials, electing to brood in his bunk over his missing daughter, and Vlados's missing daughter, and all the other daughters that it was on him to rescue and reunite with their families. Jyslin above knew why he got saddled with this shite. But that was that.

The first hiccup on their run to Carib came on the eleventh day. About an hour after their breakfast, the ship suddenly seemed to slow in speed. It was a smooth deceleration, almost a glide. Raquel looked up at her sails with a furrow to her brow. "Wake Mr. Tritts, now! Quartermaster, open the arms locker!"

"Shall we run out the sweeps, ma'am?" Mr. Shneed asked.

"No, Mr. Shneed, that would just mire us more." Raquel was striding over to the gunwales. She looked over the side. "Shite," she concluded.

"What is it, ma'am?" asked Vlados, coming up behind her.

Raquel turned to him and was about to dismiss him, reminding him to stay out of the way of her crew, when she remembered that it was the dwarf who seemed smitten with maritime life. So, instead, she said, "Aquans. They're an aquatic people of the seas. They often will solicit the aid of enormous jellyfish to snare passing ships. That's what has us."

"If we're in snares, then why didn't we all just stop, and wind up upon our collective arses?" Vlados put to her.

"Guile, my friend," Crallick snarled, joining them at the rail. "Guile."

"Now what 'n blazes do ye mean by that, ye scallywag?" Vlados poked his friend.

Raquel laughed at the unlikely friends, but added, "He's right. The jellyfish has caught us in its tentacles, then has ballooned up like a sea anchor, gradually bleeding off our speed until we barely crawl along. If there is more than one, it can stop a galleon cold. While the ship is slowing, it allows time for the Aquans to catch up to the vessel and begin to board, hopefully catching the crew still unawares, or at the least, barely ready. That won't happen with us, though."

"May I assist?" Crallick asked.

She gauged him for a moment or two before deciding. "As long as you stay out of my sailors' way." Looking away from Crallick, she continued. "Mr. Ironforge," she addressed Vlados, "While you are under no obligation to do so, you may report to the weapons locker and prepare to stand with your mates."

Beaming like a child who had just been given a whole mountain of rock candy, Vlados giddily cried out, "Aye, aye Captain!" then scampered off.

Shaking his head, Crallick asked, "What did you do to him?"

Raquel's smile was infectious. "Nothing, but the sea, she can bewitch with the best of them." Her smile vanished, "When you help, no flame-based incantations. Or the use of oils, or flame-based magic of any kind. Clear?"

"I savvy." Crallick wandered off to find some liquid fortitude before the fighting would commence.

Crallick walked over to the keg that held the day's rum. Knowing that the quartermaster was busy with the serious issue of dispensing arms to the ship's company, Crallick lifted the iron ladle, pried the oaken top off the keg, took a full ladle's worth of the dark amber liquid and poured it directly into his open mouth. He relished the burn that slaked down the back of his throat. He relished the warmth that radiated comforting fingers outwards through his legs and arms, all the way to his fingers and toes. Oh yeah, he was ready for a fight. He grinned.

Wanda rushed to gather her prayer beads and get her rapier from her bunk.

Hullaboo was nowhere to be found.

Vlados's curiosity got the better of him on his way to see the quartermaster. He took a moment to glance over the side. Transparent, almost invisible tendrils were adhered to the side of the ship's hull. Each was as thick around as his rather stocky calf. They undulated and pulsed with the strain of their hold on the ship. They glistened in the bright sunlight. In fact, they seemed to glow with an inner light of their own, though this might have been a trick of the light. He'd have to ask Raquel about that later. Suddenly a thought struck him. Freshwater marsh leeches, even the giant ones, would drop off you when exposed to salt. Now this bugger who held fast to the ship would probably not be bothered by that form of alkali. But pour enough alcohol on it.... that might be toxic enough for its system to make it recoil from the ship. He changed his course and headed to find the rum.

Running up to the rum barrel, Vlados noticed Crallick lifting a ladle to his lips. "Hey, brother, give me a hand here."

Finishing his third draught of rum, Crallick said, "Sure, what do you need?"

"We need to grab a bunch of glass flasks. Got to fill 'em all with rum. Earthenware would do as well. Quick man, meet me at the starboard gunwale with the vessels. I'll have the rum there." Vlados wrapped his arms around the massive cask.

"Who, wha', wait a minute. What're you thinking, friend?" Crallick's eyes narrowed with suspicion.

"No time to explain, just get the damn jars before it's too late!" Vlados grunted as he worked the cask over to the side of the ship.

A sailor paused to curiously watch him. "Where you going with our rum, mate?"

"Ah, relax Toby, I have a plan to free us up from those tendrils. Now, what say you give us a hand?" Vlados replied with a grin.

"Sure, mate." Tobias Fent decided the best way to figure out what was going on with the rum was to help his newest shipmate. Planting his feet, he shouldered up half the weight of the cask onto his hips. The two made the gunwale much quicker, then set the cask down.

While waiting for Crallick, Vlados took the time to glance over the side. The roiling waves had an eerie calming near the hull of the ship; Vlados was beginning to understand that the calmed water was where the bells of the jellyfish were acting as breakwaters, mollifying the rolling force of the ocean. Then he started. There, at the base of the tendrils, the water rippled away, then broke revealing his first view of what he assumed was one of the aquans. These... fish? *'Well,'* Vlados thought to himself, *'for the sake of argument, let's just call them beings.'* These creatures, beings, had massive eyes, adapted to the gloom of the depths. Their sallow eyes had to be twice the size of his palm. Those eyes were offset to either side of the fishlike skull. Gills flanked either side of their necks. A lean, tapering trunk was clad with heavy but streamlined scales. Long and flexible legs seemed to act as a bifurcated tail; each foot providing half of the fin of that appendage. There was a dorsal fin that crested the spine of the beings. The aquans sported harnesses that held several spears, not tridents as the land-dwelling myths often said of sea-folk. Vlados thought he'd have preferred tridents. These spears seemed to have been fashioned from coral. They were savagely barbed and irregularly pointed in such a way to be sure to leave gaping, rending wounds in their victims. Their forearms ended in fin assemblies that held a membrane for swimming between very flexible fingers.

Damn it, where was Crallick? Vlados began a quick count of the aquans trying to ascend the side of the ship.

"So what's the deal with the rum?" Toby's question jarred Vlados from his reverie.

"Ahh, me boy. It's like this," Vlados began. "Ye alcohol should be nice 'n nasty and toxic to our gelatinous friend there. Like leeches don't fancy salt… you see?"

"Yeah, but why does it have to be the rum?" Toby pressed, feeling rather concerned about the fate of the crew's rum.

"Well, I suppose we could break out the stores of the captain's wine?" Vlados sarcastically mused.

"Never mind," came the glum response.

Peering over the side again, Vlados exclaimed at the top of his lungs. "Borders! Five here!"

Crallick ran up with an armful of crockery vessels. "The ship's chef is going to have it out with me after the fight, I suspect," Crallick growled. "Here you go."

"Thanks, no, just keep those fishy things off me back!" Vlados said, and got to work filling his soon-to-be arsenal of grenades.

"With pleasure," Crallick smiled. With barely a thought, Crallick reached through the ethereal plane of luminescence to touch the spirit of his blade. He beckoned it to his hand, and with a sparkling of light, it materialized there.

Vlados hadn't the time to remark on the phenomena. *'Later,'* he thought to himself.

Cries of 'boarders' and numbers rang up from around the ship after Vlados's alert. The fore-port called out six, while the fore-starboard called out five. The Stern-port cried out seven, and the stern-starboard another two. For the twenty soul crew, they would be hard pressed indeed.

As the first wave of boarders scaled the slimy tethers that held the ship fast, the ship's company made ready to repel them. Those not already armed were running to the arms locker to retrieve crossbows and swords. The surgeon prepared her room for the casualties that would be certain to visit her.

There were only four sailors in the bow of the ship. One in the forecastle took sight with a short bow, and loosed an arrow over the side. It impaled itself to the fletching in the gill of an aquan who, with a gurgling noise, fell free, back into the ocean. First blood went to the crew of the Flamerunner.

The stern of the ship, meanwhile, had Mr. Tritts holding a rather small four-man skirmish line in an attempt to protect the sailor manning the helm. The other side of the ship had Raquel and Wanda, side by side, set to receive their fishy guests.

First blood may have been the Flamerunner's, but the drop belonged securely to the aquans. Within the span of a heartbeat, fins were touching down on wood decks. With jagged coral-grown spears leading the way, seven aquans charged the three defending sailors. The archer in the forecastle cabin, who was trying his best to cover the sole sailor on the starboard defense, didn't notice the two aquans who hadn't stopped their ascent at the deck, but kept climbing to the roof of the cabin. Two spear thrusts were swiftly batted aside with lively parries of men, fresh and amped up to fight. The port defenders felt confident that they could hold their own. The poor mook on the starboard side likewise batted away two initial thrusts, though his movements were more harried, and fraught with worry.

The two sailors on the port bow delivered light cuts with their sabers to the aquans, who were wholly committed to winning the deckhead.

The archer took sight of an aquan flanking the solitary defender on the starboard bow and fired, mumbling "I got you mate" as he did so. The arrow sliced harmlessly off of the dense and very curved angle of the aquan's skull. The defender fared no better; as it was all he could do to stave off the rain of thrusts that tracked in towards his body.

Along the port gunwale, one flopped over the rail, surprising Crallick, causing him to veer away from Vlados and Toby. Vlados, by sheer accident of fortune, was on the far side of the cask of rum that he was working feverishly to fill flasks with. Toby shrieked a shrill cry of surprise-laced terror when four aquans leapt over the rail, not feet from where he stood. His cry was horrific enough to shock the closest aquan into dropping its spear. The aquan just down from the startled invader was not so easily spooked and promptly ran his spear along Toby's left side. The hooked and barbed coral nature of the savage weapons became readily apparent as a spray of blood spurted out from the force of the strike. Toby had the flesh flayed clean away from his left hip. He howled in pain.

His cries caught the attention of both Crallick and the other aquans in his immediate vicinity. Crallick cursed under his breath. He couldn't be everywhere at once. But he had to back up Vlados. So, giving the solitary aquan a baleful glance goodbye, he turned and charged to try to save Toby. Toby tried to stab the aquan who had dropped his spear, hoping for some quick, gratifying revenge, but in his haste he slipped on the deck, now slick with his own blood. This caused him to wind up on his own arse, looking up at the impending doom of the aquan spears.

With an unintelligible war cry, Crallick leapt onto the stairs beside Toby that lead to the aftcastle. This did two things: one, it interposed himself between the aquans and their prey; two, it allowed him the advantage of elevation. Taking his greatsword, he launched a devastating blow at the aquan closest to Toby. There was a crunching sound as though a salt pillar had just been split in two. The greatsword sundered the aquan's spear, along with the aquan's forearm, cleaving them free from their former owner.

Higher up on the aft deck, two rapiers flashed in the daylight, foiling two attacks. Raquel turned her attacker aside with a flourish, embedding her rapier to the hilt in the liver of the boarder. He wouldn't be long for this world, even if he somehow survived the battle, which Raquel was going to ensure he didn't. With her free hand, she pulled free a pistol to level it at the one bearing down on Wanda.

Wanda, parrying a savage thrust, quickly prayed to her benevolent goddess, Flowwe, mistress of the waters of life, to take back that which was hers to give. Divine energy pulsed through the cleric's spirit, channeling out through her fingers to envelop the charging aquan with a desiccating miasma that instantly leeched all of the water from the attacker's body. The dried husk fell to the deck in a pile of shimmering scales and lumpy bones.

Seeing that Wanda had things well in hand, Raquel pivoted the pistol back to the dying aquan, and then decided not to waste the shot.

On the aft port, Mr. Tritts had a spear sheer into the flesh on his right shoulder. His clavicle broke on a barb and sent him yowling with pain. Beside him, Mr. Shneed fared little better, catching a spearhead literally in his hand. While this saved it running him through the bowel, it ruined his right hand. A sailor in the aftcastle shot the head of the aquan threatening Mr. Tritts. Then he began to reload his pistol. Mr. Shneed yanked the spear free of the grip of the boarder, and spun it around with a growl. "Ye like to play in the coral, mate? Well, have at it then!" He thrust the newly acquired weapon back at the aquan with such ferocity that when the jagged head lodged in the aquan, and the body sagged back overboard, it caught Mr. Shneed so unawares that he was pulled along with the dead body over the side. They collided with the bell of the jellyfish, where tendrils of a poisonous nature quickly scavenged the free lunch from its surface.

Mr. Tritts barked a command through gritted teeth at the only other sailor by him. "Fall back and hold the line! We have to keep the helm."

"Aye sir," was the grim reply.

Back at the port bow, unbeknownst to the defenders, an aquan slipped down the cargo hatch to the next deck down. There he found a cask filled with fresh water. He knew that mammals couldn't live with only salt water, so he decided to vandalise the cask. He burst the seams to reveal a very shocked and angry froggle.

Topside, the confidence in the fore-defending sailor rose as he expertly swatted away another spear thrust, not giving any ground. But then it came crashing down as his mate's spine, along with the barbed spearhead that carried it, ruptured through the back of his mate. The nearly instant iron stench of arterial blood, along with the acrid urine and pungent fecal stench, exploded in the briny air around him. His morale was instantly soured. Craving vengeance, his cutlass found a chunk of flesh to take from the left thigh of his now wailing and limping opponent.

Back below deck, Hullaboo grabbed up his fancy steel spear and promptly jabbed it at the aquan who had destroyed his sanctuary. The aquan contemptuously caught the thrust and pinned the spear against the deck with its own, then he glared at the froggle. *'Fine then,'* Hullaboo thought. *'I'll use your spear.'* With a cat-blink fast reflex, his tongue lashed out to seize in its adhesive grasp, the aquan's spear. Thinking it didn't taste right was an afterthought, as he launched it into the astonished aquan. Then, with his foe dispatched and his shiny spear free, Hullaboo uttered a mighty "Croak!!" and leapt up through the cargo hatch to land on the aft deck.

The starboard side of the foredeck saw the sole defender surrounded by four aquans, his back pressed against the rail towards the main deck. Four spears frenetically thrusted at him. His hands were a blur; desperation drove him. Parry one, Parry two, and fumble with other hand for pistol. Parry three, and draw pistol. Too slow! Burning pain. Blurring sight. A cough. Taste of blood. Hard to breathe. Whistling around the frothing wound on the left side of his chest, where a good four inches of spear spitted him like a roast.

It was hard to draw a bead when firing into melee. That's why he never heard the aquan behind him on the deck. It was the rending of his right arm as he was drawing the bowstring taut that loosened the arrow, through no will of his own. Pain flooded over him. He saw with feeble relief that his arrow had found its mark in an aquan's kidney. In defiance more than anything, he spun around with his bow still in his left hand to drive it into the gill of the yammering aquan. The aquan flexed the gill covering closed, but still lost a chunk of flesh and heard a crunch of cartilage.

The sole defender managed to fire a shot into the belly of the aquan wearing his mate's fletching. His sword too busy to do anything but parry, he wanly smiled relief as blood loss gave him a comforting feeling of woozy bliss at seeing one less enemy at his last stand.

At the starboard main deck, the aquan that Crallick had ignored noticed the dwarf working furiously on something involving a keg. He figured it had to be stopped. With a silent charge, his long loping strides carried him on well-flippered feet to the quarry with great speed. There came his thrust. Right on the mark! But, with the pitch and roll of the ship, even dulled as it was on its jellyfish bed, the dwarf rolled forward through blind luck and grunted as the spear only seriously bruised his back as it caught on his leather jack. Dropping his work, Vlados whipped out his hammer and turned to meet the offender, knots beginning to form in his shoulder where the armor had saved him. "What buggery is this?" he roared.

Before Toby could make his feet, the unarmed aquan leapt upon him, leathery-slick fingers grabbing for his neck. Little hook-like nails embedded in his neck and a viselike pressure mounted in his windpipe, causing him to gasp then wheeze. His sight began to swim. Snot drooled from his nose.

A vicious thrust of a spear lanced into Crallick's side. Too bad for the attacker that Crallick never paid attention to the warnings against wearing metal armor on ships. The coral head shattered against his ringmail. Shards were still driven into his side, and he grunted as two of his lower left ribs cracked their displeasure.

Toby flailed about, desperately trying to hang onto consciousness. His battering hands uselessly fluttered against his murderer's scaled hide.

Crallick caught his breath, then uttered a brief incantation. The planks of the deck and the rails suddenly erupted in life, growing woody vines that snaked and coiled around the four aquans in front of him. He then cleaved his sword towards the one directly in his path. As it tried in vain to pull free of the vines, it never noticed the serrated sword split the air before splitting its gills, trachea, jugulars, carotids, and finally, it's spinal column. The vines held the macabre piece upright, and the head balanced on the body, venal blood pouring down the sides of the cadaver while arterial blood spurted crimson out of its mouth in a sick parody of a garden fountain.

Raquel deftly riposted a clumsy thrust of a spear before, to her horror, she felt her grip on her rapier pull free, caught in the barbs of the spear. The aquan flicked his spearhead sideways, launching the blade off the end of the ship.

"You bloody cuss!" she exclaimed. Then she fired. The shot punctured a third eye into the aquan's face. Its skull never ruptured. However, its eyes did a rather erratic dance before the whole body sagged limply to the deck. "That was my favorite blade, you sodding panty waste!" She began to kick the inanimate corpse with a fury.

Wanda jumped with a fright. She wasn't used to hearing such loud noises in such proximity. That momentary lapse in concentration cost her. She felt the tip of a spear drag along her lower thigh. It opened up both her breeches and her flesh with a searing hot pain. She clutched the weeping wound with a yelp. Then she besought Flowwe to salve her pain. With a wash of relief running over her as a waterfall, she then flashed her blade towards her assailant. It struck home, but not severely. She barely pinked the scaly hide.

The sailor on the aftcastle heard the creak of the longboat and knew he was in trouble. It took every bit of discipline he could muster to continue loading his pistol. Fortune smiled upon him, and he rolled away in time to see a spear lance the cabin roof where he had been mere moments before. He fired in retaliation. The force of the shot caught the aquan full on in the chest, shattering its sternal plate into flechettes that made short work of the organs behind it, and blew the thing clean off the roof to further feed the jellyfish.

Mr. Tritts took another savage blow that tore a chunk of flesh out of his calf. His mate let out a shortened scream. A spear had plowed through both lungs, and when it passed the aorta, it ruptured it, causing an eruption of blood to vomit forth. The lad had only been seventeen. Mr. Tritts abandoned his reason, dropping his weapon in favour of his claws and teeth. He leapt upon his foe. Clutching its shoulders with hooked claws, he then began furiously kicking, his lower claws rending flesh and slewing out loops of intestines. With a feral growl, he looked up from his victim to its adjacent ally. He leapt again.

Below decks, the quartermaster finished doling out the weapons and made ready to lead the last four sailors out with him. Three more had gone before, to render aid as quickly as they could. The surgeon glanced about nervously. "Chessintra, help me. I may need more beds," she said as she listened to the screams of terror and pain from topside.

Back topside, the port bow of the ship continued a stalwart, pitched battle, with one sailor desperately holding off a brace of aquans. One sliced a ribbon of molten pain on his right thigh, while he used his cutlass to direct the point of the other spear into the shoulder of the one who had just injured him. He then finished the job by lopping off the rapidly weakening aquan's right arm. Rapid blood loss did the rest. As the body toppled unconscious over the rail to feed the jellyfish, the sailor backed up to give himself a little breathing room. He almost backed into the looming Hullaboo.

Hullaboo croaked out a loud "C'mere!" then flayed his tongue out and yanked the aquan off his feet with such force that he was able to drag him a good ten feet to rest at his feet. He jabbed his spear down at the struggling aquan. The frustrating thing had no interest in dying that day and managed to yank to the side, causing the froggle to narrowly miss his own tongue. He missed the aquan altogether. He narrowed his eyes in threatening concern.

Behind them, on the forecastle roof, things went from bad to worse for the gallant archer. One rammed his spear at him, but only managed to lock him up with his bow, keeping the tip at bay. The archer growled his defiance. The aquan stared back silently with gaping eyes. They were so alien, it was impossible to tell if there was malice or any emotion at all in them. The archer felt himself being turned in a vital dance for leverage. Then after turning almost a full half circle, an electrical jolt of pain blossomed in his lower back, then a massive pressure in his stomach. Moisture inside his pants. Then nothing below his waist. The archer's eyes became confused. He watched the fish-face in front of him change colour, from blue and orange to scarlet. He was vomiting. He was no more.

The aquan who had skewered the evil mammal who travelled on their ocean from behind, carefully turned his weighted spear to the edge of the ship and dropped the body for the jellyfish to clean up. His mate popped his bony palates together three quick times, letting all who spoke aquanni know that they held the forecastle.

Underneath their drama, the lone sailor on the starboard bow deck frantically batted away blow after blow. He ducked low under one spear thrust, rolled backwards under the rail to the main deck, then grabbed the spear that followed him, twisted it violently, and stabbed at the aquan head that followed the point through the rail. Thus trapped, the aquan was helpless as the blade carved up under his jaw to seek out its hindbrain. The aquan convulsed spasmodically as his grey matter became acquainted with the curved cutlass. Then the aquan stilled. The sailor, holding his own wounds, cried, "Help me mates! I'm almost done!"

His voice carried over the starboard main deck. There, Vlados was scratched on his right thigh whilst kicking away a thrust of a coral spear. "Back off me, ya fishy lummox!" he bellowed in rage.

Help arrived from an unexpected quarter. The lookout charged from the mainmast, where he had finally completed his swift descent. Barreling into the aquan's right side, he crushed it against the rail. All could hear the splintering bones. They noticed the panicked flapping of the aquan's lower jaw. Blood seeped out of the gill slits around its neck.

The aquan trying to crush the life from Toby, instead, found a vine had trailed around his own gill-covered neck. It crushed the gills closed, causing him to lose his strength. He released Toby, instead grasping at the bindings choking the life from his own body. Crallick kindly solved the suffocating aquan's problem by decapitating him. The body slumped to the deck. Crallick sardonically noted to himself that it was beginning to smell like a fishmonger's cart. He could really go for a fish and crisps. A coral spear tip lancing towards his right flank jolted him out of his reverie, as he was barely able to deflect the point away from his head. All the same, it carved a series of nasty furrows that wept furiously up the length of his left arm. At the top of the stairs, in the melee, was Wanda. With water-like grace, she swished past a spear thrust, taking her a stride closer to the top of the stairs. The overbalanced attacker fell victim to her merciful counterattack. She plunged her rapier into its eye. There was only a little resistance as the tip skidded along the back of the orbital bone before popping with a sudden release through the hole for the optic nerve. The brain behind provided no resistance at all. The only trouble was, the aquan was dead on its feet, but didn't quite realize it yet.

Raquel, disarmed of her blade, was frantically reloading her pistol. She looked up just in time to see an aquan lunge forward, spear zeroed in on her throat. "Fuck," was the last word to pass her lips as her trachea and jugulars were sheared from her throat with a bubbling scarlet deluge that caught even Wanda in its spray. As blackness overtook her vision, she forced her quivering hand up for one last shot. Raquel couldn't tell if the roaring in her ears was the blood draining from her head, or the roar of her pistol.

On the aftcastle roof, the sailor heard the fate of his captain. Damning it all in a heroic effort to save the day, he ran across the roof to leap into the air and, sword outstretched, plummeted towards the murderer of the captain. Sadly, though, he misjudged the distance and ended up falling tragically short, burying his sword into the kidney of his swooning captain. Looking up he saw the blank face of the aquan menacing him. Shite, his day couldn't get any worse.

Mr. Tritts continued his carnage, leaping onto the next aquan before he could even turn his spear towards him. Fore-claws latched his shoulders, rear claws disemboweled, and his teeth tore into its gills. A heartbeat later, he was looking at the last aquan, who tried to run for the helmsman. Mr. Tritts' powerful pounce brought the aquan up short. Both collapsed to the deck at the feet of the helmsman, the coral spear skittering away over the lip, to the main deck below.

By the port cargo hatch, three sailors poured onto the main-deck. Hearing their ally's plea for help, they charged, bellowing all the way up to the foredeck.

An aquan, unseen in the commotion, slipped below deck. He hid in the gloom of the porthole lit deck, waiting for an opportunity to inflict a great blow. Ideally, he wanted to get below the waterline and release a vial of kraken stomach acid. But he had to be smart. He would wait and see what happened.

The tide and the momentum of battle began to shift in favour of the defenders. Even though the cost was dear, the sailor by Hullaboo finished off the aquan for him. This freed up Hullaboo to leap away with a barely comprehensible, "Thank you," from his slobbering, overextended tongue. Hullaboo leapt clear to the roof of the forecastle. The foremast provided a nice anchor to loop his tongue around to fling his jump in a sweeping arc. This allowed him to massively kick off an aquan who had his back turned to him. It sent the aquan reeling, off-kilter, and it careened over the side of the ship, ricocheting off the anchor on the way down. The jellyfish were getting well fed. This kickoff allowed the froggle to launch the opposite direction back around the mast, like a two hundred pound blue and yellow tetherball. He then struck the surprised aquan, who had just turned towards the commotion of his friend being kicked overboard. Instead of facing an opponent, the aquan felt the breeze of the same fate plow into his own back. He, too, fed the jellyfish.

Holding the starboard bow of the ship, the two aquans suddenly found the tide reversed upon them as their initial quarry continued to stab at their ankles, and three new sailors charged into the fray. The mammals were so noisy. They seemed to bellow nonsensically. "We got you mate!" and "You can fall back now, mate!" and other alien curses flowed freely from their fleshy red gobs. The two aquans combined their efforts against one sailor who foolishly got trapped between them. Spears hungrily feasted on flesh from his gut and his arm, and he painted the deck red and brown. He made more animal noises. His sword arm still found a thing to take revenge on. Unfortunately, all it found was the deck as he fell to one knee.

A biting slash from the original defender brought the aquan to its knees right in line with a lateral swing of a meat cleaver. The ship's chef opened the aquan up from gill to gill. The head flopped back from the clean laceration, and the eyes went milky.

"Who's up for one hell of a good old-fashioned fish fry tonight?" roared the ship's chef.

"Where'n creation did all these vines come from mate?" asked the lookout.

"Buggered if I know," said Vlados, as his hammer rose and smashed the skull of an aquan who could barely breathe as it was.

The lookout stabbed the dead thing just to be sure. The vines held it aloft in a rather suspicious way.

On the stairs, Crallick spat a glob of poisonous spittle at the aquan. It caught the creature in the face, blinding it and causing great pain. His sword finished the creature off with a jagged slash across its bowels. He left the carrion on the stairs and stepped over it to see what was going on behind Wanda.

Wanda stepped back from the dead aquan, who stabbed the air a few times in vain. Then she saw the ruin of a body that was the dying Captain. Well, her goddess was just going to have to interfere with this one. With all the focus of peace and harmony that she could muster, she knelt beside the failing captain. Laying her hands on the woman's throat, she began praying.

After seeing the human priestess kneel by the captain, a move he was certain was suicidal, the sailor's alarm rose when he realized an aquan suddenly ignored the captain and the priestess. It came right for him. He just managed to roll right, out of the way of the blow, before it sundered him. He urgently lashed back, with his cutlass doing nothing more than bruise the aquan.

Mr. Tritts finished goring out the aquan at the feet of the helmsman and then he remembered just how injured he was. He sagged back against the wall of the aftcastle cabin, and murmured, "Just need a quick cat nap…" He closed his eyes.

Now, the reason that most seafarers preferred the cutlass to other weapons is that, in addition to use as a sword, its haft was heavy and sturdy enough to double as a hatchet. After staving off the onslaught at the port-bow of the ship, the deckhand sought out ropes to cleave free from the ship.

Hullaboo leapt fifteen feet over the remaining aquan to catch him within a triangle of angry sailors. The aquan quickly dropped his spear and rose his hands. Asking for mercy, Hullaboo suspected. It just made his execution easier. Two cutlasses from the front and a spear from the back ruined the internal organs of the overwhelmed being. The grievously wounded sailor who had held the position, after seeing the final foe drop, allowed himself to succumb to his wounds. Sliding to the main deck in a puddle of his own blood, stool and urine, he closed his eyes.

Vlados tossed two flasks to the lookout. "Run these forwards, and smash them on the tentacle thingies holding the ship. Then come back and let me know how they work."

"Aye, mate." He grabbed the flasks of amber liquid and obeyed.

Vlados chucked one of his own down the side where he stood, and observed. Three of the scintillating tendrils writhed as though hit by a torch, and flayed themselves free of the ship before swiftly withdrawing into the water. "Yeah!" Vlados exclaimed.

"What the bloody mess is it?" Crallick yelled back.

"The flasks! They work! Just chuck them down on the jellyfish! It'll let go as sure as froggles hop!" he called back.

Slicing an aquan in half as it barred his way up the stairs, Crallick retorted, "Great! When I'm finished mopping up, I'll feed your pet!"

Another aquan started down the stairs toward Crallick, missed its footing on the first step and fell face first at Crallick's feet. Puzzling over the odd behavior, Crallick finished his deliberation by simply driving his greatsword into the base of its skull. Mystery solved. Now maybe he could finally get up the damned stairs.

Wanda's prayers of peace allowed her to work beneath anyone's notice who held a violent motive in their heart. Her subsequent prayers of healing waters and restructuring mantras flowed out of her and rushed cool energies into the body of Raquel. Throat tissues began to knit back together, beginning with the two severed jugulars, who danced around like miniature snakes before striking at each other and binding true to one another. The process was taking way too much time for Wanda's liking. She switched the focus of her healing prayers to reflooding the woman's barren circulatory system with new blood. Wanda watched with relief as the colour began to seep back into the pallid form on the deck. *'Thank you Flowwe, there is hope yet for this woman'*, she thought.

Scant feet away, the prone would-be rescuer wished he had timed his leap to save his captain better. A heartbeat past his wish, he felt a spear rupture his stomach, causing searing pain and burning as his gastric acid began to digest his own bowels. Pulling the aquan closer by the jagged spear, he wedged his cutlass into the gill, and skewered it upwards, driving it towards the thing's brain. Both of their breathing labored. Both of their struggles ebbed. The light of life flowed from both sets of glaring eyes that softened as death took them.

The quartermaster, leading another three sailors, came topside. Upon seeing the chaos of combat had died away, he called out, "Captain?"

No answer.

"Mr. Tritts?"

No answer.

"Mr. Shneed?"

No answer.

Calling over to the Vitani lookout, the quartermaster said, "Mr. Reillane, you're in command here, I'm going below to search for stray boarders. Try to get us free if you can!"

"Aye, sir! Save Mr. Ironforge has the issue well in hand," the lookout called back.

"Well, defer to him then!" With that, the quartermaster led his men back below.

The lookout returned to Vlados about the same time as Crallick. "Well, you heard the man, Mr. Ironforge. What's the call?" the lookout asked while Crallick smirked.

"Uhhh," Vlados stalled. Then, shaking his head, he recovered. "Well, how did the vessels work?"

"Very well, mate," the lookout beamed. "Very well indeed."

"Well then, you take these," he handed him a sack of six, "and keep going. Come back if and when you need more." Looking at Crallick, he added, "Cral, can you find out how many hale bodies we have left on this tub, on deck?"

"Sure, Mr. Ironforge. And what should I do about them?" Crallick dripped sarcasm.

"Get two men up to man the sails, and get the others to take the bodies below to the surgeon. Get two more to come help with freeing the ship." Vlados paused to breathe. "Savvy?"

Crallick couldn't help stifle a laugh. "Sure, Captain." Then, shaking his head as he walked away, he murmured, "A dwarven sea captain. What next? Just when you think you've seen it all…"

Chapter Seven

"The Knights of the pyre used weapons wreathed in flame
To focus their efforts on the east Wood Wyrm's wrath.
Two grand knights made fire to put mount Dratho to shame
Oil fed fire charred all, Wyrm included, in its path."
Verse 8: Ballad of Ser Crallick Carnage-born.

Vlados leapt up to the aft deck. "You know what yer doing with keeping us on our... uh, bearing?"

The helmsman smiled, "Aye, ser. That I do."

"'Kay then, keep us heading to Carib while I figger out how we be sitting," Vlados's dwarven accent was becoming more stressed with his increased anxiety.

"All the tentacles are free of the ship, ser!" called a deckhand from the main deck. "We're free and easy now!"

"Excellent!" Vlados called back. "Now be a good lad and run and fetch the quartermaster!"

"Aye, aye, ser." The hand trotted off to the hatch below.

Several moments passed as the unscathed crewmen gathered up their wounded counterparts and got them stowed below deck. The ones who seemed beyond help were left for the moment, along with the stinking offal and the blood that stained the deck boards. Vlados waited patiently and soon enough, the quartermaster presented himself to the dwarf.

"Aye, ser?" came the questioning acknowledgement.

"Mr. Drake, may I ask you something?" Vlados put to the man.

"Aye."

"Why the infernal blazes are you not taking command of the blasted ship?"

A sardonic grin split the bronze cheeks of the massive quartermaster. "Truth be told ser, I know more about the operations of this vessel than any alive. I just don't have the heart to carry the load of being responsible for my shipmates' lives. I just can't do that, ser. Any advisements or information you need, I'll gladly supply, but I won't order my mates in life and death situations." He shook his ragged blond hair.

"All right then, when the surgeon has a few moments, have her come up and let me know how we stand with the health of the crew. Then I can worry about the watches," Vlados put to Mr. Drake.

"That sounds fine," Mr. Drake said. "I'll see if either she or the ship's chef can expedite that for you."

"Thank you." Vlados turned to the desk, trying to puzzle out the maps. All the while, fervent, earnest praying chanted from Wanda on the starboard side of the ship.

A while later... about the time Vlados had figured out where north was on the map, and actually in relation to the ship, Mr. Drake returned. "Syllethra apologises, but she's far too busy, as is the chef. They gave me the rundown."

Grimly, Vlados mused that this couldn't bode well. "Please do, Mr. Drake. Let me have it."

"If I may respectfully suggest we do this in the Captain's quarters, and make sure you enter it in her log?" He smiled sympathetically at the dwarf.

"Of course, what'd I do without you?" Vlados rose and headed below.

"You probably wouldn't be in the insufferable position you find yourself in now ser," Mr. Drake confessed. "On behalf of the ship's company, thank you for stepping up."

"Yeah, well," Vlados's shoulders heaved, "it needed to be done."

"Aye, it did." Mr. Drake waited for the dwarf to rummage through the Captain's desk to find her log book. He then waited patiently for the acting Captain to find the inkwell and quill. Then he began. "The Flamerunner, a brigantine running with twenty-one souls crewing her, with four passengers aboard, ran afoul of an aquan ravager school. There were two Mallay jellyfish, and about two score aquans. In the defence of the ship, the following were the results of the fracas. Deckhand Fieri Tijahni of Jherrim; 2nd mate, Mr. Archibald Shneed of Bannathyr; deckhand Braken Wade of Bannathyr; rigging rat, Dale Goreman of Amoral; and rigging rat, Ichobod Arlois, of Bannathyr, all lost their lives defending the ship. These tragic passings bring the shipboard compliment down to the minimum recommended crew for the brigantine. Of the remaining sixteen crew and four passengers, the following are no longer whole and hale, and are currently under the care of the ship's surgeon, Syllethra. Deckhand Tobias Fent, of Bannathyr, is requiring stitches for a deep gash over his left hip, and he is being cared for due to having his throat brutally crushed in an attempt to squeeze the life from him. His recovery is estimated at 2-3 tenday, barring sepsis. Rigging rat, Dester Wyrmbane, of Amoral, is requiring stitches for his right leg, recovery estimates one tenday, barring sepsis. Rigging rat, Vessae Sarath, of the Jharrim Jungles, has a punctured left lung, and her recovery is thought to be 4-6 tendays. 1st Mate Jarlois Tritts, of Jharrim, needs the setting of a broken right clavicle, stitches on the right shoulder, and stitches on the left calf. His recovery, barring sepsis, should be 3-4 tenday. And finally, Captain Raquel Tallanthyre, of Bannathyr, whose condition is critical due to severe damage to the throat and the left kidney. She is not expected to recover. The remaining eleven crewmen are unscathed. Two of the four passengers are unscathed. Ser Crallick Oakentree of Bannathyr has two broken ribs and has refused treatment. Wanda Swells of Bannathyr requires stitches on her left thigh. 1-2 tendays should set her right, barring sepsis. Vlados Ironforge of the Ironforge

Clan is acting Captain until further notice. We are continuing at best possible speed for Port Fairaway." The quartermaster looked up, "That should about do it, ser. If you have any personal thoughts, you may add them on your own volition."

"Thank you, Mr. Drake," was all the heavy-shouldered dwarf could muster at the retreating back of his quartermaster.

Vlados went to the aftcastle and bellowed fore, "All hale crew, to me!"

After they assembled, Vlados took count, then continued, "As we are woefully undermanned, some changes to duties will have to take place. Until we hit Carib, we'll have to run on twelve-hour watches. We have no fit rigging rats, so the look-outs will have to double as such. Also, they will each have an apprentice rat from the deckhands. Lawrence Marley, you'll take first watch, and have Eli Puraji with you. Show him the ropes."

"Aye, aye." The two men dashed off.

"Robert Marquis, you have the second watch, and Izzy Nunez will assist you. Go get some shut-eye."

"Aye, aye," came the parting reply.

"Jacob Mortine, since you have been piloting us for some time, you'll finish out the first watch, then turn the helm over to Mr. Drake, who'll pilot the second watch."

Mr. Drake nodded approvingly, then called to Jacob, as he turned to head to his bunk. "I'll relieve you in a few hours, mate."

"As we only have four available deckhands left, there will be no use of the sweeps. The sculls will be made fast in the hold. The first watch will belong to Jaroll Hawthorne and Fransisco Nunez. Second watch will be yours," Vlados nodded at Brom Corr and Lovarth Nordhome.

"Aye ser!" yelled the four men before splitting company.

Hullaboo hopped from twenty feet away to mere inches from Vlados's nose. "What you want from me?"

Vlados sized up the massive bipedal frog. His leaping ability would be able to move him quickly about the ship, but would his size overbalance him aloft in the rigging. "Would ye feel uncomfortable up there?" Vlados pointed to the sails.

Hullaboo grinned and licked his salt parched skin, "Like tree frog?"

Vlados laughed, "Sure, sure. Like a tree frog."

"Okay!" Hullaboo leapt up to the first brace without touching a rope, then just about scared the shit out of the lookout as he landed above him and asked what he could do.

Wanda was still chanting over the body of the Captain.

Crallick walked up, "Well Captain Ironforge, what can I do to chip in?"

Grinning from under his slowly re-growing beard, Vlados said, "Nothing. Just protect the ship."

Crallick scoffed. "Just me? I think you may be giving me too much credit."

"No, my friend," Vlados stared daggers at Crallick, "I believe it is you who haven't given yourself enough credit. Just who are you really, Cral? Who?" He shrugged. "Making vines grow from a ship but can't get a farm to run, so you cannae be a druid. You are a noble living like a pauper. Chessintra's blessing, Crallick who the fuck are you, really?"

Crallick scratched his head, looking balefully at Vlados. Then he growled, "I'm your friend. That should be enough. Don't let your new post get you too full of yourself. I am who I am. Don't think you can demand shite from me... little dwarf." Crallick let the contempt for the perceived invasion of his privacy drip heavily from the last two words.

Not allowing the dwarf to get another word out, Crallick spun on his heels and headed to the bow of the ship.

After no less than ten hours of chanting, Wanda collapsed into a fitful sleep, her body having been ravaged by divine energy flowing through it. The next morning she awoke in a smelly medical bunk, Syllethra tending to her wounded charges. Wanda felt a painful tug when she went to slide her legs off the bed. Looking down, she noticed her thigh had sixteen tight stitches holding the cut in her leg together. There was no bandage. Syllethra noticed her up, and came over to her. "Good morning, Wanda. How are you feeling?"

"Like I've suffered a severe case of divine diarrhea," she laughed weakly. "Thank you for my leg. Why didn't you bind it?"

"I'm finding that the coral tipped spears left wounds that are falling to sepsis quickly if bandaged. Leaving them open is having a better effect. That and a lot of alcohol," Syllethra smiled wanly. "The Captain lives, thanks to your ministrations. However, she still slumbers deeply. I don't know how well, if ever, she'll recover. Regardless, thanks for all your efforts."

"Hey, I'm not done yet," Wanda smiled. "You have a lot of work here. I can help."

A weak smile punctuated Syllethra's response. "I will gladly accept all the help I can get."

The next tenday and a half proved uneventful. There was mounting fatigue from the overworked men. They were doing the tasks of two men each and working half again as long as they were used to. Nevertheless, the trim of the ship was kept well, and they still managed close to nine knots an hour.

Clouds scudded swiftly along the trade winds as the Flamerunner flew towards Port Fairaway. The lookout, Mr. Marley, squinted to the south. Then there, just on the lip of his vision, was the crowning of a new tooth in the ocean. The triangular cusp of a sloop's sail rose out of the waves.

"Sail ahead! Sail ahead! Sail ahead!" he cried out.

"What is she, Mr. Marley?" called up Vlados.

"Dunno yet, ser! She's about a league out, but closing," Marley returned. About an hour and a half later he called again. "She's a sloop, ser!"

Crallick walked up to Vlados. "Trouble?"

"Buggered if I know, mate," Vlados confessed. "This is my first time doing this shite."

"So then, tell me, what does your gut tell you?" Crallick prompted.

"Well, we're heading to the pirate islands, so my bet is that if we don't play our cards right, yeah, there's a might chance of trouble," Vlados confessed.

Crallick grinned. "All right then. This could be a break in the monotony at last."

Crallick had been either working out, or brooding sourly at the bow of the ship. He had spurned all attempts to see if he was all right, even from Wanda. Soon enough everyone, Vlados included, had decided to leave him to his own melancholy. That is not to say that Crallick's friends weren't concerned, but more a measure of the impasse that they found themselves in front of.

Later that afternoon, the sloop began to drop her sails to slow her tacks towards the Flamerunner, who still had the season's prevailing wind mostly behind her. As the sloop closed, the lookout called down, "Ser! She's running off! There are at least twenty souls crouched down on deck. I figger she's pirate or slavers. She's got ballistae!"

Too late, Vlados gave the order to make full sail away from the sloop; shuddering thunks shivered the hull, just under the main deck. Following that was the groan of thick hempen ropes, pulling taut between the two ships. There was a black banner that ran up the mainmast of the sloop, unfurling in the warm breeze. It revealed an octopus wrapping its tentacles around a ship.

"Ahoy mate!" called a voice across the water aboard the sloop. "Don't ye be running off now just as we made yer' acquaintance!"

"Wouldn't dream of it," growled Vlados under his breath. Then aloud. "Why'n did you have to go shoving pointy things into me hull?"

"Just a minor bit o' patching is all! She'll be fine!" called the voice.

"Who's going to be doin' the patching? You?" Vlados countered.

"Well, mate, depending on how we get along, maybe!" laughed the voice, along with an accompanying chorus of others joining in the mirth.

Crallick then added his two pennies to the discussion. "You got any rum over there? We're running a touch dry! It might be cordial of you to invite us to a sociable event!"

Vlados strode across the deck while the sloop continued to draw closer. "Just what do you think you're doing?" he hissed.

"Being polite and conversational," Crallick grinned malignly.

"Well mate, that's an awfully imposing thing to put to a mate at sea. While of course we got stores of rum, as should you, one doesn't usually make sociable demands on a first encounter. It's not polite. One should wait to be offered, not ask." The voice tisked its disapproval.

"Well, as I am not accustomed to sea travel, and the idea of someone shooting at me sours my etiquette, and I'm not sure how polite piracy is in any event, and it is my intent to make landfall at Port Fairaway, a known pirate port, I figure slaking my thirst is the least of my concerns," Crallick said.

The far voice began to bluster, "Now wait just one Flowwe-be-damned minute here! Who be in charge there? Your rudeness is surely putting a sour note on the day, mate! Firstly demanding drink from fellow seafarers, then accusing them of piracy, then taking offence to grappling on to safely make parlay! Those are fighting words indeed!"

"I'm sorry, my good man," Crallick's predatory grin broadened. "You mistake my meaning. I was not accusing you of piracy, I was simply telling you of my intention to partake of it myself."

The roar of laughter erupted from the sloop. Twenty to thirty souls rose up, no longer interested in surprise at this outlandish fool.

Crallick joined in their merriment.

Vlados, pale now, rushed about getting those below decks up and armed.

"You!" called the voice. "You seem to have a light crew for engaging in piracy, mate. And how, pray tell, do you plan on carrying out this ploy of yours?"

Again Crallick laughed, "You again mistake my meaning. I do not mean to implicate my crew, as they aren't mine to command. I simply mean me. Just my need. My intent. My act. Alone. Give me half your stores of rum and I'll let you all live. Fail to comply and I'll kill you all."

The mirth left the voice that answered Crallick. "There are thirty of us, mate. You sure ye be liking them odds?"

"Yeah, I am," growled Crallick. "There's only one ship, all sealed up with pitch and tar. Wood and men burn pretty well together. Ignia lanca."

Extending his hand, Crallick launched a bolt of magical fire just yards from the bow of the sloop.

"Shite!" came the now panicked voice. "Are you bloody insane!?"

"No." Crallick grinned. "But, my friend didn't believe me when I said I'd kill for a drink. He really should have listened."

"Yer bat shite crazy! Yer daft! You know how much pitch and tar make up the waterproofing of that there tub of yours? One errant spark and ye go up just as swiftly as we!" Fear tinged the words with an uncertain weight.

Crallick practically beamed in twisted delight. "Well now, we wouldn't want that now, would we? By now, you've figured out you can't cut free, turn around and get out of range before I've had time to light you up like an Asha day bonfire. So I strongly urge you to get two casks of rum and throw them into a cargo net that you'll sling between the two lines with a draw rope tied to it. Then you'll throw the draw rope to my colleague here." Crallick gestured to an incredulous Mr. Drake. "Who'll proceed to pull my rum over here to me. Only then will I allow you to safely cut free. Any questions?"

"Aye, one. And what if we test yer resolve and decide to come to blows here and now?"

"Then, I fire the ships and we find out how long you can tread water?" Crallick smiled. He cracked his knuckles and wiggled his fingers, "So tell me, you feeling lucky?"

A pause was only punctuated by leather on wood, rope on rope, and grumbles from the would-be pirate vessel. With a begrudging thud, the draw rope was thrown to Mr. Drake. He then began to pull the two casks over to the Flamerunner.

"Thank you, my good gentlemen." Crallick waved, and smiled at the opposite crew. "I'll toast your health!" He then swung his greatsword, cleaving the ropes free of the ship. "Happy sailing, I hope your future ventures are more profitable, and safer than this one!"

Amidst the grumbling of discontent, and the creaking of ropes and timbers as the sloop began it's frantic turn away, Crallick's fine Vitani hearing picked up the cries of 'Can we sail with you?' Bolstered by this, he called out one last time, "Any who can make it to this ship may sail with me!"

As soon as the words cleared his throat, a full eight crewmen dove from the sloop and began swimming furiously for the brigantine. Crallick never bothered to watch their progress. However, as he helped himself to the rum, he heard the gathered crew watching and laying bets on the projected outcomes of what was to happen with the desperate swimmers.

Vlados walked over to his friend, "Crallick, I'm worried about you."

"Why?" Crallick sipped from a cup of rum.

"Well, for starters, ye drink like a dwarf,"

Vlados began.

"Why, thank you," Crallick interrupted and toasted his friend.

Shaking his mohawked head, Vlados corrected, "Not meant as a compliment, mate. Secondly, you risked everyone's life for what, a couple of shitty barrels of rum?"

Realization dawned in Crallick's rum-softened mind. "Ah, I see. You actually think this display was about the rum." At Vlados's nod, Crallick continued, "No, my friend. It just happened to be a seemingly insignificant thing that I was sure no one would willingly want to die over. But something I'm sure they would be in possession of. It was a bluff, a ruse, a hoax, tomfoolery at its finest." Crallick drank again from his cup before refilling it. "The loot was a perk."

"What about the unnecessary hardships you're putting those other sailors through?" Vlados gestured to the seven men in the water. Wait, hadn't there been eight?

"Again, spoils of war. Anyone who on a whim can turncoat will never be trustworthy. Anyone who'll risk their life has invested in you completely and therefore will be more trustworthy. You see?" Crallick took another pull on his mug.

"You are a cold man, Mr. Oakentree." Vlados watched as the first of the water bedraggled sailors pulled themselves aboard the main deck to both cheers and curses.

All in all, five men bolstered the crew of the Flamerunner by the end of the morning. Initially there was some confusion over exactly who was in charge. No, it wasn't the psychotic elf mage-who wasn't a mage. No, it wasn't the former captain, who was in her sickbed. Yes, it was the dwarf. Really, truly, it was the dwarf.

There was a slender human rigging rat who went by the name of Marc. Another rigging rat, Nespyran, was vitani. They allowed Vlados to place them on alternate watches. This doubled the number of actual rigging rats up in the sails for each watch. There were two more deckhands, a lizardman, and humans Menshirre Orram and Ronald Noble, who looked anything but, respectively. They were also separated to alternate watches.

The fifth crewman was Wallace Pallan. He had been an officer. The first mate of the other ship, in fact. This rankled Vlados. He was very unsure of what to do with this one.

"How can I trust him?" he asked Crallick and Drake.

Wallace took it upon himself to answer, "For starters, I could have just not told you my position on the ship. I was honest with you."

"Says you," Vlados quipped.

"Aye, says me," Wallace replied.

"How do I know you aren't lying about that too? Maybe yer just a glorified cabin boy? Maybe you're just looking for more pay?" Vlados mused aloud.

"No, that doesn't make sense," mused Crallick.

"He wouldn't lie about that," confirmed Drake.

Laughing, "Damn straight, I wouldn't. First, if ye half a brain in yer head, I'd just imagine, you'd confirm it with the others. Second, it'd be a lot easier for me to not be an officer in this position. Savvy?" Wallace scoffed.

"All right, so why did you jump ship... Mr. Pallam, is it?" Vlados asked.

"Pallan ser. And easy ser. Captain Ernstman has not been faring well and to get taken as he was just drove in the final nail for me. I'd had it. Getting taken by a mark? That was the last straw. Even two full shares aren't worth a damn when there's nothing to share. So when your lad here held out the auditions, I figured I'd try my hand. And here I am." Wallace paused. "I'm good at navigation, and I'll take a second mate's or third mate's role. I'll be trustworthy."

"We'll see about that. Mr. Pallan." Vlados made sure he got the name right that time.

Fair weather followed them for the rest of the day. In the evening, they could make out the lights of Port Fairaway before they could make the distinction between land and sky. Underneath the deep blue mantle of night, the ship slipped into the sheltered harbor with only the slightest moans and creaks.

Chapter Eight

"The seaside Knights of the plume were found not to fly
The water drake plied the coast with peals of thunder
Bannathyr soldiers fell to the surf to die.
The savage cliffs the drake completely did sunder."
Verse 9: Ballad of Ser Crallick Carnage-born

The lapping waves sloshed more noisily as the brigantine, Flamerunner, slid up to the outermost berth. She was small enough to barely make use of the berth, unlike some of the other frigates and galleons anchored out in the harbor. Evening cast a dark pall over the sea. Port Fairaway turned into a violent stab against that pall. Lights from candles, lanterns, and bonfires mixed with laughter, mirth, clinks of crockery, moans and shrieks of pleasure, and some of pain. All leant to the symphony of delights that was Carib Island.

"Welcome! And what's your business?" called a portly fellow from the dock with a friendly wave.

If it had not been for the man's beaming grin acting as his own personal lantern, Vlados doubted he'd have even seen the man, so dark was his complexion. "We're in hard from Port Marahaven! We're looking to take on supplies and crew!"

"In hard you say?" the man mused. "There be a story there, I say!"

"True enough," Vlados agreed, "But not one I'll be yelling across the harbor."

"To be sure of that! Well then, come ashore and we'll discuss your needs," concluded the harbormaster.

Turning to Crallick and Mr. Drake, Vlados asked, "Will you accompany me?"

"Sure" and "Aye" marked the two men's assent.

Wallace came up to them. "With your permission, ser," and he waited.

"With my permission, what?" Vlados vainly hid his confusion.

Chuckling to himself, Mr. Drake said, "He's asking permission to talk to you, ser!"

"Oh." Vlados looked a little sheepish at that. "Sure then. Fine. Go ahead. Talk."

To his credit, Wallace didn't do a thing that could have embarrassed Vlados any further, even keeping a straight face when he spoke. "Permission to come ashore with the landing party, ser. I can be valuable in assisting with the acquisition of the new crew. Also, might I suggest running up the absentee pennant. You might also want to check with the ship's surgeon to find out what her immediate needs are, and what accommodations need to be made for the injured. Several of these duties are out of the purview of the quartermaster, though I'm sure he'd do an admirable job in his efforts. As for me, I'm an old hand at these tasks. Having had to do it for several voyages as a first mate, and several as a second mate. What say you, Captain?"

Vlados couldn't help but fluster and puff up a bit with pride at the title being addressed directly to him. "Soundly put, Mr. Pallan. Go find the surgeon's needs, and have the pennant run up, then come along and join us on the wharf."

"Aye ser," came the smart reply.

Crallick felt an unexpected joy at having his feet on solid ground… or at least on solid jetty… again. He tried not to chuckle as his stalwart friend took a few wobbly steps before finding his feet solidly again. The three men were deep in their tale to the harbormaster, for as assumed, that was what he was; when Mr. Pallan joined them. After the conclusion of their tale, the harbormaster asked what did the Flamerunner need and what was her length of stay.

Crallick was the first to respond. "I need a money house to make change for payments. We plan to have a short stay to get our chores done, no longer. We are chasing an unknown vessel which carries nefarious villains with intents on sacrificing virginal maids…"

"I could use some virginal maids," the harbormaster good-naturedly joked before he swiftly became puzzled at the lack of laughter that usually accompanied a bawdy joke like that.

"His and my daughter are among them," said Vlados quietly.

"Oh," humbled the harbormaster. "I'm sorry."

"Also," Crallick growled, "they don't intend to sacrifice their virginity that you inferred, ser, but their lives. Thirteen girls, I believe."

"Well that's a terrible waste of virtue," the harbormaster said before he could clamp his hand over his mouth. "My God, I'm sorry. I talk when I'm nervous. I just don't think sometimes. I'm so sorry."

"Well to make up for it, you can save your skin, and our time," Crallick's grin was more intimidating than friendly. "Any of the ships pass through here with a female Nekomin wearing Chessintran robes, and accompanied by some scary-assed lizardmen, and other men at arms? We need their ship's name and bearing if possible."

"Heading," Vlados corrected for the benefit of the harbormaster.

"Aye, good sers," the harbormaster said. "I can take care of that for you. Moneyhouse is..." he gently took Crallick by the elbow and pointed to a stone building to the immediate left of the main street that ran inland from the dock street. "Just there." Then, he turned to Mr. Drake who, through the tales, he garnered to be the quartermaster of the ship. "Stock stores and ordering is in my office, there." He pointed to a light timbered, open fronted shack in front of a massive wood warehouse. To Mr. Pallan and Vlados he concluded, "The apothecary is just up the road on the main street there. It will be on the left-hand side. The hospice is the next building beside that. Hotels and bars are closer to the docks."

Confused, Vlados asked, "Well, you handled everyone's needs well enough, even where to get meals, but I need replacement crew. Where is your guild hall?"

Laughing, Wallace grabbed Vlados by the arm, not unkindly, "Ah my Captain, you jest so well!" Then to the now chuckling harbormaster, he said, "Thanks mate, we'll be back for the information in a bit. Please look into it swiftly."

"Of course." The harbormaster ran a chain to the anchor-chain and padlocked it. "I'll have it for when you pay for your berth and supplies."

***

Crallick entered the low, stone brick structure. There was a dim glow provided by a single candle on a candelabra that rested upon a clerk's podium that faced the door. There was a stool upon which rested a gnarled little lizardman, of a variety Crallick hadn't encountered before. The little fellow looked up as Crallick entered, the scratching from his plume ceasing.

"Evening, ser," the squeaky voice said. "How may I be of service to you tonight?"

"I need some local currency," Crallick said.

"Well, all three main currencies are handled on the Carib Archipelago. Any in particular?

What merchant said you couldn't purvey your coin?" a confused clerk asked.

Laughing, Crallick clarified, "You misunderstand me. No one has denied my coin, as I have none to give." Crallick held up a few glinting gems between his thumb and forefinger.

Drawing in a breath that came as a squeak of surprise, joy, lust, or greed – maybe a little of each – the clerk jumped from his seat, ran over, slammed and locked the door behind Crallick, pulled him urgently by the arm to a seat, and then rushed into the back room squeaking furiously all the while.

Crallick tried not to smile as he thought of a reptilian mouse.

Heavier footfalls sounded from the back room. The door swung open to reveal a half-ogre that loomed over the little three and a half foot clerk by the span of a tall dwarf.

"Critchure here tells me you have some gems that need my attention. I am Horace Dandywine." He extended a head-sized slab of a hand towards Crallick in greeting.

Unflinching, Crallick shook the hand, "Ser Crallick Oakentree, of Brannathyr."

A deep guffaw shook up from his lard ringed torso. "My old home country. You, like me, seem not to be of pure Vitani stock. Human for your other half then?"

"That'd be about right," Crallick conceded. "Look, I am in a bit of a hurry, not to be rude, but

I need an appraisal and currency exchange for these gems; some, or all, depending on their worth in this part of the world." Crallick gave a predatory smile, "I trust you are as good at your job as I am at mine. Consider what you see as a small amount of my earned savings."

Bellowing a great guffaw, Horace turned the three gems in his hands and said, "While ser, I grant you these are fine specimens, they are by no means anything to brag so about."

Crallick grinned, "I just gave the trinkets to the clerk." He opened the strings of his pouch, "These are the goods."

It was the half ogre's turn to draw in a breath, "Aarison, man! Do you intend to buy the whole island?"

"Impressed?" Crallick put.

"I'll say. That is more than enough to buy the entire archipelago." Putting a more serious expression on his countenance, Horace continued, "Ser, if you are travelling at sea, let me advise you on several things. First, the average able-bodied seaman gets one crown per tenday, and are thrilled with it."

Crallick was happy that Horace was using currencies familiar to him.

"This stone," Horace pulled a small one from the pile, "Will keep a company of forty souls paid for a year. This one," he pulled a smaller one from the pile, "will keep the ship supplied for that same time. All these, you should leave with me for safe keeping. Take this for incidental expenditures," he added a few gem chips to the now five stone pile that represented Crallick's expenses. A full thirty-five gems laid on the side.

"All right, Horace, if I take your advice, what is to stop you from running off with my wealth?" Crallick not too delicately put to the large man.

"Fair question," Horace smiled, choosing not to be offended by the blunt challenge of his honour. "Firstly, I don't want to spend the rest of my life looking over my shoulder. You strike me as someone who is not easily quailed and holds a grudge. Second, I'd rather earn ten percent of this magnificent trove legitimately, and have you on my side if I'm ever robbed." He laughed, "Not that that ever happens anymore."

"Oh?" Crallick asked.

"Not since I impaled the last three who tried on pikes up their arses as a punishment. One screamed for a day and a half before he finally died." Horace grinned, "Never had a problem like that again."

Crallick felt his anus pucker sympathetically from the idea of such a cruel crucifixion. "All right then. At five percent we have an accord."

"Aww, come now, seven percent?" Horace patted his opulent tummy, "I'm Part Ogre, and Critchen has twelve mouths to feed."

"Seventeen, master Horace," the diminutive lizardman corrected. "Etchen had another clutch of five eggs that survived."

"Really? Congratulations." Horace turned to Crallick, "Sorry, seventeen mouths to feed."

Laughing and shaking his head, Crallick said, "Fine, seven percent it is then, and you make my payments for what I need. My ship is the Flamerunner, in the third mooring."

"I shall, ser Oakentree. You take this, and have a splendid night." Horace took a pair of large pouches and gave them to Crallick, "This one is crowns for larger purchases." The other he hefted, "this one is scepters for smaller purchases."

"Thank you, I'll see you when I return," Crallick concluded.

"Safe faring!" said Horace. Then to Critchin, whom he told, "Take the list of supplies and the roles for Mr. Oakentree to his quartermaster."

***

Mr. Drake had walked purposely over to the massive wood structure and began wandering the rows of stacked crates, making mental notes as he went of what they would likely need. Damn, their ship's captain was greener than any officer he had ever sailed with. Hell, he wasn't even an officer. Second, the backer was some psychotic knight, looking for a bunch of virgin girls. Other than the fact that one was his daughter, there was something creepy about that. He sighed. He should never have agreed to quartermaster for a woman. He supposed he got what he deserved.

After a few hours itemizing a list of things, he took it to the warehouse manager. The manager gave him the change from what had been preauthorized by his charter. Then Eric told him the berth to have the supplies delivered to.

Vlados and Wallace headed up the street towards the apothecary. The street was rich with smells, noise and colour. Smoking dens, brothels and taverns ran up the righthand side of the southbound street, while markets and more reputable shops lined the left side. At this time of night, however, there was very little in the way of reputable trade going on in the street. Courtesans plied their wares, wearing next to nothing in the balmy tropical evening. Pushers of opiates and other mind-altering substances brazenly strolled the main fare, often offering free samples of quality. Callers of both genders advertised gambling houses, brothels, and taverns, both on and off the main street.

Wallace advised Vlados, "Don't let them take you anywhere off the main drag unless you're tougher than the toughest cats in port. Also, tonight we're in a bit of a rush, so I suggest we leave the sightseeing for the return trip perhaps?"

"Agreed," Vlados concurred. Then, upon finding the apothecary and hospice, they went into the yard of the ajoined buildings.

"Here we are then," Vlados said, then proceeded to knock loudly on the door.

"Just a minute!" Hollered a sleep dulled voice, laden with the gravel of age. "If you all would stop yer shenanigans and keep regular hours like, you'd not be wakin' poor old Betsy up and ye'd might be livin' as old as she too!" The voice was accompanied by thudding footfalls down wooden stairs. The door then opened to a bleary-eyed woman in her late sixties, silver-white hair akimbo from the pillow, and care-worn face trying to take in the people at her door. In a softer voice, she said, "Now, ye look worried. What can I do for you?"

Vlados bowed deeply. "I'm afraid I have two errands that I'm here about. The first is that I need accommodations for four crew who range from moderately to gravely injured. Second, I need this list of reagents," he proffered the scrawled list of ingredients from Syllethra.

Taking the paper, the woman squinted down at it, then exclaimed, "My, are you a chichurgeon? These are a rather comprehensive stock. With the number of coagulants, I expect you suspect to see battle?"

Shrugging, Vlados replied, "I'm no chichugeon, but yes, we expect to see battle at least once more only, the gods willing."

Nodding slowly, Betsy shrugged off the last fetters of sleep and said, "Well, let me get dressed. It'll take me about an hour to get these together for you. Have some of your shipmates bring me your casualties next door there. I'll get them set up right proper."

Vlados said "Thank you" to the closing door. Then to Wallace, "Is she always that... ummm.... rude?"

"She says she's efficient," Wallace grinned. "Not rude. C'mon, there are men to gather in the meantime. Let's go to the 'Carib Pride'!"

"All right, lead on," Vlados grumbled.

The Carib Pride was a two-story building that was back towards the docks. Light poured out of two open windows to pool on the inky street. There was a symphony of sound cascading out of the windows and the double doorway. There were the sounds of clinking glassware, belching and other gaseous exchanges, laughter, and voices. All backlit by a steel drum band.

The wooden planks on the exterior were worn by weather, but still retained a bluish-grey tinge barely discernable in the ambient light. No door, just a curtain of beads impeded entry to the place. With a rustle of those beads, the pair of men strode into the place.

There was a long bar along the left side of the room, being the north wall, with several tables and booths arranged opposite. On the other side of the door rose a small stage, upon which four chocolate coloured vitani – or were they mortani? Vlados wasn't sure – played a stringed instrument, a couple of sets of steel drums that had been cut and hammered into pleasing sounding plates, and a wood pipe of sorts.

The tables had been fashioned out of cogs that had held spools of anchor chains. The stools that surrounded them and lined the bar were all old kegs of black powder or other dry goods. Vlados nodded appreciatively at the sensibility of the tavern's décor. He suddenly missed his own wayside tavern very much.

"Wait over there," Wallace said, indicating a corner table. "You need to be both visible, and defensible. I'll be back shortly."

"All right." Vlados took the seat closest to the joint of the walls. From there he watched Wallace walk over to the bar, indicate towards him, smack a serving girl's ass, then wander over to the stage. There, Wallace got the attention of the singing elf, who was also playing the stringed instrument. When the group finished their song, Wallace had the elf bend low, and he whispered something into his ear. The elf nodded, then got back to his spot and started into a lively song. Wallace made his way back to Vlados, arriving at the same time the serving girl brought up a pitcher and three mugs.

"All right. That's taken care of," said Wallace, pouring a drink for Vlados, then himself. "The band will announce..." He was cut off by a raucous clamor on the stage.

"Yo, yo, yo! Me mates and hearties! Any of ye lookin' to catch yerself a billet of a ship huntin' some dogs, then getcher self o'er to the dorf inna' corner 'der. Vlados be 'is name an' he bein' a pers'nal friend o' mine. So you make shoor ye' chat nice. Or'n I'll shove me banjo up yer rassclott batty hole! Ye savvy, elfe?"

There was much laughter, some applause, and several heads turned to look at Vlados's table.

"Showtime," Wallace said, as the next song was struck up and the first sailors began to make their way over to line up by Vlados's table.

It took the better part of three hours, from the first 'hello' to the last 'better luck next time, mate', to hire the thirteen souls that would round out his crew. Vlados was very tired at the end of it and wanted nothing more than to find his way back to his bed. With a start, he suddenly realized that he had considered the Flamerunner's captain's bed as his. Poor Raquel. Being left behind on her own. Granted, he was sure that Crallick would see that she was set up nicely, but there seemed little comfort in that. His daughter needed him. With that simple thought at the fore of his mind, Vlados steeled his courage to do the unthinkable. He would leave the wounded here and leave with Raquel's ship. His daughter needed him.

Morning broke with the injured having been relocated to the Port's hospice. The existing crew were gathered on deck, and the newly pressed crew were aligned on the dock. The minor repairs had been serviced, the supplies had been stowed in the holds, and extra rum had been stored, although Vlados swore he had nothing to do with that order.

Standing on the aftcastle cabin's roof, Vlados called in a resonating voice so all could clearly hear him. "Ahoy, all! To the old crew and the new blood alike, we come together under one purpose! We seek to bring justice and right a tragic wrong! This is a hunting expedition, make no mistake, there will be harrowing danger! We will make your service worthwhile! Your souls will know they are on the side of right this time, regardless of what happens! You will each get more of a share than what you would otherwise earn, as we have little guarantee of lavish wealth! But as a thank you for your dedication, an extra ration of rum to set sail on!"

Cheers erupted from the men.

"For those new to the Flamerunner, I am Captain Vlados Ironforge. This is my first mate, Erik Drake…"

Erik opened his mouth, about to protest, then thought the better of it. Instead, as he towered beside the dwarf, the words that came out were, "Aye! Hello all. Now even though I may not always see eye to eye with our fearless captain, I'll always stand beside him!"

There was scattered laughter, applause, and a few 'huzzahs!'

Smiling, Vlados continued, "Since Mr. Drake is being promoted, one of the lucky new deckhands, Mr. Burrowwell…" He paused, looked at his notes, and then asked, "Is this true, Mr. Pallan? Is Mr. Burrowwell a dwarf?"

"Naw, she ain't," bellowed a voice from the throng of sailors on the dock. "But aye, SHE be a dearf! Tandi Burrowwell at 'cher service!"

"Bugger! Did we find the only dwarf on this rock other than me?" Vlados said, half to himself.

"Aye, might be that ye did! Imagine my surprise to find a dwarven sea captain! At that I say to meself, now there is someone I have to serve with!" Ms. Burrowwell called.

"Aye, then. Back to this. Ms. Burrowwell will take over the duties of quartermaster, in addition to her lighter deckhand duties. Shifts will be a touch on the long side, twelve hours each. There'll be one lookout, three rigging rats, and eight deckhands per watch. There will be at least a brace of officers on watch at all times. Now, welcome aboard and find Mr. Pallan to get your berth and watch."

Seeing the harbormaster walking up to the crew swarming ship, Crallick and Vlados both took routes that independently converged on him as he approached.

"Evening," said Vlados, at about the same time that Crallick, less politely demanded, "So what did you find out?"

"Well sers, it only took light digging. My notes are very good," the harbormaster boasted.

"Cut to the chase," growled Crallick. "We have to do the same."

"Uhh, ahem, of course." The harbormaster jittered his hands about before continuing. "On the 21st of Dracois, just after dawn, a white-sailed, three-masted ship anchored in the harbor. She sent three longships ashore to secure supplies. She had black paint or enamel applied to her hull. Very expensive. She had silver letters astern, and upon her flanks at the bow. The name read Chess's Blight. Her captain signed as Temelia Grimm. She asked about Jamtown. They left around dusk, headed towards the island of Bian. I know that they took supplies to last many tenday. Definitely more than just a cruise to the islands, and more than what raiders take to pillage the main coast for a while. I hope that helps my good sers." At the end of his speech, he bowed deeply.

"What do they want in Jamtown?" wondered Crallick.

"Best slave market on the ocean, ser," the harbormaster glanced up. "To be sure, they were looking for seven slaves."

Crallick found a predatory grin claw his cheeks tight. "Perfect!" Glancing at Vlados, he said, "C'mon, our quarry is at hand! Let's not tarry here!"

Vlados followed his suddenly enthusiastic friend. "Thanks," he said as he parted with the harbormaster. He followed the practically exuberant Crallick onto the Flamerunner. "Step lively lads! We got a three-masted ship to catch;

make as much sail as fast as possible and make our course for Jamtown, Mr. Drake!"

"Aye ser!" came the rousing replies. Then with the chattering of sailors and the creaking of timbers, the Flamerunner made into the night. It was the 24th of Dracois, they were only a few days behind an apparently slower ship. He began to see why Crallick was enthusiastic. For the first time in almost two months, he didn't feel like this entire venture was in vain. He had been secretly going along so that his friend wouldn't kill himself, and for something to salve the loss of his own daughter and bar.

By midday the next day, Vlados heard Mr. Marquis call down from the lookout, "Jamtown ahead!"

Rushing to the bow of the ship, Vlados found Crallick already there. They were swiftly joined by Wanda.

"Hey all," she said as she came up. "Don't mind saying that it's a nice change of pace to be not slaving over wounded men all day."

"Aye, to be sure." Vlados watched the growing details of the approaching island harbor. He was a little awestruck.

Nestled in the verdant brush of a jungle paradise, with snow-white sands running to either side of the crowded bay, lay the natural harbor of Jamtown. That, however, was where the natural beauty of Jamtown ended. The thirty odd masts that crowded the bay made it difficult to count the masts, let alone the ships. It was also difficult to tell what the true size of the town was, as its details were buried behind the ships at the end of the bay. The only sure thing that could be told was that there was a lot of browns of untreated timbers forming the structures.

"We got to make this quick," stated Crallick to his viewing companions.

"Aye, that we do," Vlados agreed.

"I really don't like the feel of this place," Wanda commented.

"Not many do m'lady," said Erik Drake, coming up behind the onlookers. "This is a warehouse of sentient trade."

"Sorry?" asked Wanda, not comprehending.

"A massive flesh market ma'am," Erik gravely intoned.

"My goddess," Wanda breathed. Horror laced the fringes of her tone.

"No ma'am, I'm sure your goddess wouldn't approve such a thing," Drake went on.

"No, he wouldn't, and that's why ye be staying here with me an' the ship. Okay?" Vlados soothed Wanda's obvious discomfort. "Crallick— you, Pallan, and two others take a longboat o'er there and learn what you can. I'll have us quietly come about and be ready to run to open water should things go amiss. Savvy?"

"I savvy." There was a twinkle in Crallick's eye. "Just what makes you think something will go amiss?"

"Because it's you, son," Vlados smiled under his ruddy blond beard. "Because it's you. By design, or fluke, someone will have a bad day, and in some way things will go amiss."

Nodding, Crallick conceded the point, "Fair enough."

Half an hour later, Crallick, Wallace, Mahar, and the monitor lizardman, Jetten, were lost from sight as they sculled the ship's launch through the maze of masted islands. A full hour later had them clamouring out of the launch, onto a decrepit jetty.

"You two stay with the launch," Crallick commanded Wallace and Mahar.

"Just a minute," Wallace Pallan began to protest. "I'm supposed to be in comm…"

His voice trailed off at Crallick's glare. "Firstly, a lizardman and a half-blood that's vicious looking and wears a string of trophies around his neck…." Crallick pulled a not-quite-properly preserved thong of goblin ears, aquan fingers, and a length of unidentified matter that was not handling Crallick's attempts to preserve it very well. "Will be taken as flesh traders more readily than a couple of human pure-bloods." He finished among the two men's "eww's" and the chuckling of the salivating lizardman. Crallick, noticing this, snapped, "No! You cannot eat my trophies. They're mementos, not hors d'oeuvres. Savvy?"

The sullen monitor nodded. "'Kay," it hissed.

"Good, now let's go." With that, Crallick left the two men at the launch and strode into the town, leading his lizard companion.

"The slave pens are this way," Jetten hissed, wrinkling his nostrils at the side of his elongated head up toward the air. "I can barely smell them over your tasty necklace though," he finished, conical teeth showing by means of a grin.

"Keep dreaming of my trophies like that, and soon I'll be wearing a tooth and a new belt," Crallick advised.

Sniffing indignantly, Jetten added, "You know, for a Vitani, you're quite violent."

"Only half. Not all the way Vitani." Crallick smirked, "Enough to get the ears, though."

Thus bantering, the two headed down narrow streets choked with refuse and the sentient population who lived in the ramshackle shanties that lined the streets. Then, as though bursting into a clearing, the pair erupted into a large square, roasting under the hot tropical sun. No breezes made it into the stale market. Vast pens, half dug into the ground, half lined with filth and sugar cane cages, lined the perimeter of the square. Light tents and stalls clustered around the sides, creating a pair of avenues between the pens and the central stage.

Almost immediately, the pair were accosted by purveyors of human flesh, offering all kinds of uses for unuk guards, castratae boys, fertile breeding stock, and hard labourers. Deals were made available for singles, pairs, and grosses. Crallick set his face in a hard, determined mask. He figured he had to set his mind to his quarry. Whatever it took, he would not, nay could not, fail Amalae and Bekka. Or Mindy, or any of those other condemned girls. With that in the back of his mind, he pounced on a spry looking chocolate Vitani merchant. "You!"

"You batty boy? Ser, me no batty. You want batty, me can get you though!" The suddenly wide almond eyes turned to fix themselves on Crallick's severe countenance.

"Do I look batty to you?" Crallick growled, not even sure what that meant. Then taking a deep breath of resolve that he hoped would be interpreted as frustration, he continued, "No more bullshit! I want the choicest pieces of virginal meat you have to offer in this market! Now, who do I talk to for that?"

"Let Soulo go, my friend. He can't help you there," said a voice from the gathering crowd. "His trade is younger... options. You have a discerning quality to you, ser. If you seek the best, you seek me."

Crallick's ears tracked the owner of the smooth voice to a cleanly dressed, chocolate skinned Vitani blooded man. Startling white teeth that matched his tunic broke his face apart in a dazzling display. He extended his hand, "Come now, I am Levvan Dazzathry. Mr. Dazzle, if you will."

Crallick shook his hand with mock enthusiasm, "Well, it's about time, someone who looks like they understand culture and finesse. Where can I get the ripest maids to pluck?"

"Why, as I said, with me, good ser." He gestured to the side, through the bickering, dickering, jostling throng of market-goers. "Come this way."

He led them through the crowd to an opulent looking tent that proclaimed *"Mr. Dazzle's Domain of Dazzling Delights."* Stepping into the white linen tent felt fresher than the outside clamour and miasma. Out there, the stink of unwashed people, effluvia, and rank pens multiplied in the stale, unrelenting heat to make it almost nauseating to those not acclimated to it. In this purveyor's stall, however, there was a fresh collowood incense burning in a censure. There were potted flowers that gave off a pleasant perfume. Hand-picked, no doubt, to also put one in the mood to make a purchase. Crallick knew such a plant could sway one's mood and one's ability to think rationally with just a hint of its aroma. Crallick decided he immediately sensed another predator just like him, though governed by his own set of rules. He would have to be very cautious to get what he needed.

"Very nice," Crallick said.

"Hmmm," Jetten grunted agreement.

"Thank you," Mr. Dazzle said. "But, first, you didn't come to gander at my stall, you came to gander at my flesh! Also you have me at a disadvantage, I dislike doing business with those I do not know the names of. Also, I refuse the sale of any of my wares to those who seek to abuse them." He finished by winking.

Crallick scoffed. Then he caught himself. "How could you enforce such a claim?"

"I can't, directly," Mr. Dazzle smiled. "But I can refuse to sell to one who I find has slain or seriously harmed any of my merchandise in the past."

Scrunching up his face, Jetten said, "How is that possible?"

Laughing, Mr. Dazzle leapt up and grabbed a small chest. With a flourish, he produced two gems. They were tiny enough, but they scintillated brilliantly. "With these. Each flesh comes with one. My master crystal can tell which gem goes dark and which flesh it was. I cross reference the name, then bam! Onto my blacklist they go! Clever, no?"

Crallick smiled, "That, my friend, is the best news I've heard all day." Grimly he added, "So where is your stock hiding?"

This is where Mr. Dazzle's countenance flickered for just a heartbeat, before he offered an excuse, "Well, usually I have on hand twelve to thirteen heads, but at the moment, I've just had a run on virgins." He laughed, "I wonder if there is some new lewd holiday I really need to learn about. This guy came in with two Komodomen and bought up eight. That's right! Eight! All different breeds too! Now that's kinky!" He laughed again, then he saw Crallick's expression.

"When was your stock depleted?" Crallick asked.

"Why, just yesterday. They took some time to browse, then chose their wares." Mr. Dazzle's smile tightened to a grin, "Now, look, I make it a strict policy not to discuss others' transactions. I'm starting to get the feeling you're not going to be a paying customer, so our business is done."

Crallick, barely controlling his temper, growled softly, "Show me the flesh."

Sizing up the fellow, if not much paler Vitani blood, Mr. Dazzle pulled on a rope that drew a panel open. As the fabric panel slid open, it revealed seven young girls, all dazzlingly beautiful, all barely clothed in sheer wraps of complimentary colours. They all straightened, posed, or swayed suggestively as the curtain revealed them to Crallick and Jetten.

"Well ser, there they are. I'm afraid I'm out of martini, jaragua, and hobgoblin. I have four humans, a vitani, a tree froggle, and a demonic ephemorae." He crossed his arms, "Now ser, which suits your fancy? Be warned, the more exotic the flavor, the higher the fee." He then emphatically nodded at Jetten, "And they are not to be eaten. They are playthings, or pets to be cared for, not consumed. Clear?"

Jetten grinned widely, "Got it."

Crallick glanced over the lot of them. He justified what he was about to do by reasoning it was best for his daughter. As his eyes wandered over the girls, the ephemorae caught his gaze with her own. She gave him a radiant smile, nodding slightly as to encourage him to choose her. Well, since she seemed the most eager to go with him, he made his choice. "I'll take the Chess-blessed," he said, using the racial slur for the demonic ephemorae.

Laughing in delight, Mr. Dazzle beckoned the girl forward. She obediently crawled forward on her hands and knees, scarlet skin highlighted by the gold gossamer wrap that left little to the imagination. Her cocoa-red hair fell about her heart-shaped face. She lifted her delicate chin to Mr. Dazzle and received the gem between her lips like a Flowwvite receiving communion. She swallowed delicately, her yellow eyes locking onto Crallick's grey ones.

With much less pomp and ceremony, Mr. Dazzle turned to Crallick and said, "Now, Crallick. This gem will cost you 5,000 crowns." Smiling widely again, he added, "or equivalent."

"Why so high?" Crallick grunted.

"Premium product. Premium beauty. Premium purity. Premium health. All comes with a premium price. You treat me well, and I'll serve you better." Mr. Dazzle's pitch fell like quicksilver on an alchemist's table.

Suddenly grinning, Crallick said, "Of course! Why not? You only live once, unless you believe the Jyslinites. I'll take of her," he good-naturedly jabbed Jetten, who accepted his role as friend who was pushing his mate into a big luxury purchase.

"Good deal, mate," Jetten said. "She smells sweet."

Trying not to cringe, Crallick fished out five thousand in gold coins. He then pulled another one hundred platinum coins and set them aside. Locking eyes with Mr. Dazzle, Crallick said, "Let me have it." He took the offered gem and swallowed it.

His newly bought slave sighed.

"What is that for?" Mr. Dazzle gestured at the pile of platinum on the edge of his desk.

"Consider it a rebate; an insurance policy. I'm going to treat you better, so you can help save those eight virgins you sold to that guy with the two komodomen. I know for certain that they plan to sacrifice those eight girls, along with five others, in some messed up rite to Chessintra. I've hunted them for five tenday now. I'm almost on them." Crallick was almost snarling now with anticipation, "I know you have their names! Also, if there is another way I can track them…?"

"Hold friend!" Levvan's hand came up, all signs of his song and dance gone, "You're telling me you've hunted them across land and sea, and bought a slave, just to get to these men?"

"Yeah," Crallick growled.

"They have something of yours." Levvan put together. At Crallick's darkening features, he corrected, "No, they have someone of yours."

"Yeah," Crallick said, this time very softly. He felt the magic itching his hand to call his blade to it.

"Well, shite. I have no interest in pissing the likes of you off," Levvan smiled weakly. "The man's name is Eli Bligh. He is from Amaral. The two Komodomen are Takk and Serr. They're probably from the northern pirate islands. All the flesh are obedient to the gem that he alone swallowed. If you have a means to track magic, then you could follow the charm dweomer that rests upon the stone. It is identical to the ones within you and her," he gestured to the nubile woman that now wrapped her arms around Crallick's leg. She sat upon his foot, smiling up at him.

"I sincerely thank you," Crallick said, pulling his foot free of the woman's behind. "You may have just helped me save those girls, and my daughter. Well earned." He slid the platinum to the slaver. "Let's hurry," he said to Jetten.

The two men turned and bolted from the tent. The din of the market drowned out the padding of bare feet that followed as swiftly as they were able. It wasn't until the men stopped back at the launch and Mr. Pallan waved at the two of them that they became aware of something amiss.

"Let's get going, Mr. Pallan," Crallick said, hopping down into the boat.

Jetten started untying the aft rope.

Wallace looked at Crallick, "Is it to be the five of us returning to the ship then, ser?"

"Huh?" Crallick asked, dumbfounded. Looking up, he realized with shocked amazement that in his rush of hunter's focus, he had forgotten his purchase. She had dutifully run through the streets, pell-mell following her new master. "Bugger it all," Crallick was not going to enjoy explaining this back at the ship. "C'mon then."

The slave-girl hopped gracefully down into the boat. "I'm sorry I wasn't quicker, master."

"No need for apology," Crallick attempted to soothe in a surly voice.

"Of course, sorry master," came the sweet-sounding reply.

Amongst the snickers of the three other men, they swiftly sculled out to the Flamerunner. Oh yeah, when he got back to the ship it was going to be a long bit of explaining indeed.

Chapter Nine

"Knights of the Cairn avenged their fallen brethren
Slaying thousands of foes and the water drake too.
With heroics, they'd be proud to tell their children,
With their dwindling forces, many a foe they slew."
Verse 10: Ballad of Ser Crallick Carnage-born

Pulling alongside the Flamerunner at the edge of the thicket of ships in Jamtown's harbor was a tricky prospect. Even though it was a naturally sheltered bay, there was much in the way of navigation that needed to be done. Also, the tide was wrong for the current to be cooperative. Eventually, the task was completed without mishap. The landing party and launch were brought aboard and the stunned crew were confronted by a stunningly beautiful, barely attired ephemeron woman.

"Ahem," Vlados cleared his throat. "Crallick, is there something we need to discuss?"

"Oh, I'm sure there is," Crallick pined. "In your quarters."

"I'd say…" Vlados began, but then was swiftly interrupted by the righteous ranting of Wanda.

"By the goddess's benevolence! Why in the serene grotto is there a naked woman on the ship?" Her piercing eyes swiftly found Crallick. "You know about this?! What were you thinking?

You were supposed to go there for information, nothing more!"

She would have continued, except Vlados stepped in front of her and said quietly, "Hush. Not here. My quarters. Now."

Heeding his advice, she turned and stormed off to Vlados's cabin. Before following, Vlados turned to Crallick and sighed. "Good luck mate," was all he could muster.

"You're telling me," Crallick muttered. As he led his slave to follow Vlados, he overheard the gossip swiftly running the ranks of the crew. He knew by the time he was done with Vlados and Wanda, even those off watch would know of the sultry slave girl.

Upon entering Vlados's cabin, Crallick was again set upon by Wanda. Vlados had to sit her down in a chair and admonish her that if she never gave Crallick a chance to speak, she would never get to the truth.

With a reluctant "Fine, speak!" she crossed her arms over her breast and sat in judgement over Crallick.

'Of all the sanctimonious shite,' Crallick thought. He shook his head.

Vlados broke the increasingly awkward silence. "Crallick, what is this?" he gestured at the girl hiding behind Crallick's shoulder.

"It's a woman, Vlados. That is plain to see," Crallick sarcastically chided.

"Of course it is. She's not wearing anything to

disguise that, is she?" Wanda scathed.

"Give it a rest!" Crallick snapped.

"Just tell us what happened," Vlados soothed in his best bartending voice. And, not knowing what else to do, he pulled out his personal bottle of rum, three glasses, and began to pour.

"Look," Crallick began. "I just had to go wandering through a disgusting flesh market, pretending that I had an interest in owning a slave. After making a scene with the help of Jetten, I managed to get onto the right track. I was introduced to some Vitani who fancied himself, called Mr. Dazzle."

Wanda scoffed at this. Vlados rolled his eyes.

"Yeah, yeah, I know," Crallick agreed. "Anyways, Mr. Dazzle says that he's the last word in luxury pleasure models, particularly ones who have never been driven…"

"You hear yourself speaking right now?" Wanda shot him, horrified.

Growling, Crallick sniped back, "I do. And I had to do what I had to do to save Vlados's daughter and my own. I make no goddess damned apologies. Now, do you want to hear the rest of this or not?"

"Go ahead," Vlados said.

Wanda chewed her inner lip, or cheek, and nodded once.

"Fine." Crallick's voice was taught, rimmed with anger. "I got in and found out that he had sold eight girls to Eli Bligh, which is the name of the villain responsible for our kidnapped daughters, by the way. The name I got only after I agreed to purchase some flesh from him. This, and the tidbit of information that Mr. Dazzle somehow likes to ensure his wares are only used as intended. Not to be abused…"

Wanda again interrupted, "How the fuck can you say that Cral? It's blasphemy. You can't treat women like property and then claim to care for their well-being. It's not possible in any form of creation."

"Again with the interruptions," Crallick snarled. "Doesn't your goddess teach tranquility and peace? Why don't you exercise it?" Before she could muster a retort, Crallick continued. "After I purchased the 'flesh'," his voice betrayed just how much disdain he had with the admission, "he made her swallow a gem. I then swallowed the other gem. After he saw I was legitimate, he was persuaded to help me. He told me that the gem allowed him to know if his former property was physically harmed, or killed. It also holds some sort of charm dweomer upon it. He said that all eight girls were slaved to Eli. His two Komodomen, Tukk and Serr, ate none of the gems. They left just yesterday. We're only one day behind! We have a chance to catch them! We have a chance to save those thirteen girls. That is why I now have her." Crallick gestured to the cowering ephemorae.

"She has a name, doesn't she?" Wanda shot in.

"If we save the girls at the expense of one, you should at least tell us her name."

"Uhhh..." Crallick stammered, then fell silent. "There was so much I was focused on, I never even thought to ask."

"You're despicable!" Wanda got up and stormed out of the cabin.

"Well," Crallick muttered sheepishly, "that could have gone better."

"Aye, that it could," Vlados agreed. "Look lad, give her some time to process this turn of events. And by gods, I know what that cost you to do that for our daughters. While they might not be here right now to say it, I will. Thank you m'son, you did great."

Unable to contain herself any longer, the slave girl spoke up quietly. "Have I displeased you, my master?"

As Crallick rolled his eyes at the unwelcome title, Vlados said, "And sure as a lad wants no buggery, ye better be doin' something about that."

Crallick turned to the bow-lipped woman. "No, you haven't, except please don't call me master."

"Then what am I to call you, my lord?" she asked.

Vlados choked back a snorted laugh. "Oh, this is rich."

Crallick glared him into silence, "Don't you start too."

"Wouldn't dream of it Crallick," he smiled.

"Crallick will do nicely," Crallick informed the young woman.

"Thank you my lord Crallick," she said. Then at Vlados's muffled laugh into his clasping hand, she corrected, "Crallick."

Crallick smiled as sweetly as he could remember. Could he remember the last time he tried that? Was it at his five-year-old daughter, while he was still sober, or was it at his wife, begging him not to leave, years before. He shook his head free of the memories. Jyslin damn it, he needed a drink. He faked it as best he could. "That sounds beautiful, the way you say it like that. It'll do nicely." He hoped that would come across as praise.

She beamed, "Then, as it pleases your ear, so shall it leave my tongue."

More words dripped off that honeyed tongue. Crallick suddenly felt very uncomfortable. He wryly noticed Vlados fidgeting. "What is your name?"

Sashaying over to him, she leaned up to whisper in his ear, "My name is Kittalae Gathrae, but you can call me whatever you wish, my master."

Ignoring the heat on his cheeks, which was almost as difficult as ignoring the press of her against his side, Crallick observed, "Kittalae Gathrae is a very lovely name. It will do nicely. Is it Vitani?"

"Yes it is. My mother was bred by a demon of seduction..." she smiled coyly. "You might say that I'm the product of perfect breeding, Crallick."

Not wishing to offend, Crallick grunted, "Some might say that." He then tried to disentangle himself. Moving across to Vlados, he asked, "How are we to dress her? Where do we bunk her?"

Vlados, not able to contain himself much more, guffawed, "In whatever pleases you, master."

"Drop it," Crallick said.

Kittalae added, "He's right Crallick, I'll wear whatever you wish, if this doesn't please you." She swished the gold gossamer gown around her body. "And I'll simply sleep with you, and your wife."

"My wife?" Crallick gawked.

"I'm sorry Crallick, was the jealous woman not your wife?" Kittalae bit her lower lip thoughtfully. "She acted so possessively, I was certain she was..."

"Wanda?!" Crallick shook his head emphatically. "She's not my wife! My wife has been dead for ten years now." The admonishment ended more somberly than Crallick had intended. Jyslin, he needed a drink.

"I'm sorry Crallick. It is good she is not your wife. I didn't mean to distress you," Kittalae said soothingly.

"I need a drink. Solve this, Captain," Crallick suddenly commanded, then left the cabin, door barking on the frame with his exit.

Kittalae sighed, and Vlados groaned. His eyes then softened, in spite of his frustration with his friend. "Look, miss," he started, catching the young woman's attention. "It's not your fault. My friend, Crallick, he carries around a lot of pain, guilt and grief with him. He is a good man at heart. But it's a might bit difficult to see. Do ye understand?"

Kittalae nodded.

"Now then, how 'bout ye tell me a few things about yourself? How old are ye, and how did ye come to find yourself in such a place to be sold to my friend? Though knowing his heart, you're probably in better hands than close to anywhere else ye could be."

The woman smiled; it was sincere, not applied for presentation. She looked genuinely pleased. "Yes, I know, the wood told me." She nodded, "I communed with the wood every time a would-be master came into the show-tent. When I got a favorable reading from the element, I …" she looked up, chewing her lower lip lightly in thought, seeking words. "I tried to be more pleasing. When I didn't feel it, I became plainer. When Crallick came in, the wood cried to me that he walked with life, and light. I was pleased when he chose me. I am barely two decades old."

With her natural scarlet complexion, Vlados couldn't tell if she blushed, but her body language suggested a coy humility.

"My mother sold me at the age of fifteen when I still hadn't garnered any suitors. The boys at my home town, Fenhold, in Bannathyr, used to call at me 'Kitty Hellcat, come to kiss your soul away.'" She hung her head at the memory. "I was sold for two hundred crowns."

Vlados spluttered a bit, "But slavery is illegal in Bannathyr! How could you?"

Smiling again, "Just because it's illegal, doesn't mean it doesn't happen. Also, I'm from close to the Tarranthyr marshes. Things are wilder there."

Nodding, Vlados concurred, "I suppose so. Now look lass, I understand that Crallick finds you more than a bit distractin' in that see-through thing yer all wrapped up in. And yeah, in a very pleasing way to be sure. But he needs his wits about him. I need my crew thinking about things other than spending time with you."

"Well, they never could unless my master permitted it, and if I'm not mistaken, I don't think he shares well with others." Kittalae smiled for effect.

"No he doesn't, but that don't change the direction that men's minds take. Savvy?"

"Savvy?" came the confused response.

"Sorry," Vlados clarified, "I think that be a Jherrim word meaning 'understand'. I picked it up while sailing. Sailors use it a lot."

"I see, and yes I savvy," she smiled.

"Now, I just happen to have a trunk full of ladies attire over there that I inherited from the first captain of this ship. You are welcome to any of it that fits you." Vlados dragged out a trunk that he had been using as a table, then opened it for her to rummage through.

"Ohhh, she had good taste!" Kittalae practically squealed with delight. She dove at the trunk. Without modesty, she shucked the sheer that draped her nudity in a golden cloud. She then plopped cross-legged in front of the trunk, pulling out and discarding items of clothing until she found things to her tastes. This took an exceedingly long time for poor Vlados, who tried to focus on charts, on his log, on the sleeping arrangements, on anything other than her.

Finally, after what seemed like a tenday, she rose up clad in tight red breeches that so matched her skin, he thought at first she had forgotten pants. Likewise, her feet were sheathed in red boots, adorned with gold appointments on the tips of the leather at the calf and at the toe. Eyelets and buckles were likewise gold. The shirt she had selected was of white silk, and was a little too short and a little too tight to be modest. However, the fabric did its best to conceal her chest, though it failed to hide the darkness at each breast. She had also selected a pair of elbow length gloves that matched her boots, inasmuch as they were red, leather, and had gold eyelets where red leather thongs tied the gloves in place.

Looking quite pleased with herself, Kittalae asked the gobsmacked dwarf, "Would this suffice?"

"It'll have to, I suppose." Though in his head he was wondering how the presentation improved the situation. Aw, Grotto. It was Crallick's problem, not his. "You and Crallick will sleep in here from now on. I'll move my things to Crallick's cabin. It's big enough for what I need. Also, Crallick may want you sleeping on a different cot from his." Then he winked before any insult could be taken, "For reasons of his own, and having nothing to do with you."

She nodded.

Moving from the lantern-lit cabins, to the maindeck that was less lit by glowing lanterns and more by the silvery shine of the tropical moon, Vlados led Kittalae to the bow of the Flamerunner.

"I'll let you know when I've moved my things out." Vlados wandered off, grabbing a deckhand on his way, "C'mon, I need a hand mate."

"Aye Captain," came the dutiful reply.

Left alone with the sea breezes playing warm tales across her face, Kittalae allowed herself to be lulled into a sense of reverie, losing herself to her own thoughts as she had done many times in the slave pens. She reached out to the wood of the ship. Even though it had been poisoned with pitch, tar, things of fire, and death, there was still power in its structure and vitality in its presence. She was comforted.

"I'm sorry," a soft feminine voice jarred her from her self-induced meditation.

"Huh?" Kittalae turned to see Wanda standing in the moonlight.

"I'm sorry," Wanda repeated. "I must have come across as very harsh and untranquil. I am a Flowwvite sister, so my behavior is unseemly. I apologise. Your lot is not your fault."

"No apologies needed, ma'am. I'm quite suited for my role," Kittalae said.

"No, child, you are not. No one is suited for slavery. Tell me, do you have faith?" Wanda swelled up her sermon voice.

"I'm no child, ma'am. And indeed I have a faith. It is what Crallick choose me," Kittalae said.

"Really? How old are you?" Wanda said. "And pray, do not refer to me as ma'am. Wanda or Sister Swells will suffice."

"Of course sister. I am nearly twenty."

"As old as all that?" Wanda smiled graciously. "Well, one can have a lot of wisdom packed into so short a time. I shall not judge, save by your actions. As to the matter of your faith?"

"Of course, sister," Kittalae smiled. "I commune with the element of wood. The element guides me. It showed me that Crallick, despite his outward appearance and smell, was an ally."

"Smell?" Wanda was perplexed. Had she travelled so long with the knight-ranger to become acclimated to something distasteful?

"Yes, his trophies he hangs around his neck fouls an otherwise pleasant musk." Kittalae dropped her gaze, "Forgive my bold observation. I hope he'll allow me to tan his trophies properly."

Laughing, Wanda said, "Good luck with that my dear. Mind you, he is a dear friend. I was unable to tear him away from his wife while she lived, and I respected him for that. When it became apparent her death spelt the end of the man I knew, I turned to the cloth. He turned to the bottle. Do not hurt him though, for I care deeply for him, and my vengeance shall be most… un-Flowwelike." Wanda's face softened, "That said, I abhor slavery and all it entails, so if you are ever mistreated, I shall end my friend to spare his soul."

Kittalae's face darkened, "I shall have to tell Crallick of such treacherous words."

"No need," Crallick's voice cut out of the moonlight. "I would expect no less from the holy harlot, the spiritual stripper, the penitent prostitute. I hold her to keep those words. I too, abhor slavery. If not in such a dire way to find my daughter, you would have still remained there, with no ties to me whatsoever."

"Then perhaps tied to someone less kind and benevolent…" Kittalae interrupted to try to soothe his spirit. "I am pleased to be bound to you. My place could have been much more grievous."

"It may still be," Crallick growled with a bit of a slur in his voice.

The two women wrinkled their noses at the odor of stale rum on his breath. He staggered a step on the rolling deck. He caught a soft rope, then realized it was Kittalae's arm that had lashed out to steady him.

"Wanda, sorry if I disappointed you, but my daughter…"

"You're forgiven." Wanda helped him down onto a lashed down cask. "Let's put the unpleasantness behind us. How do we move forward?"

"I dunno. You're the expert in divinations, not me. I play with nature and mess people up," Crallick muttered.

"I knew you walked in light," smiled Kittalae.

Wanda laughed. Her laughter was infectious, and soon the others, one quite drunkenly and unaware of what he was laughing at, sent peals rolling across the deck. Getting control of her humour, Wanda said, "Allow me to find the stone inside you. Then, from there, I should be able to track the residue from the passing of others like it."

"Do what you got to do," Crallick said.

It took until the dawn breaking for Wanda to break down the basic elements of the slave jewels.

As dawn bathed the water and the ship in blazing gold, the Flamerunner looked all the part what her name suggested; a magnificent swift ship, leaving a blazing wake in her passing.

Wanda gathered Vlados, Crallick, Drake, and Kittalae together on the roof of the aftcastle cabin. With a wide yawn, she began, "The breakdown of the magic is as follows: there is an abjurative spell that prohibits a desire for violent action towards one another. A clever way to protect both owner and slave from one another. Second is a one-way empathic dweomer that allows the slave to feel the owner's emotions. Only vaguely mind you, there are no details conveyed. The third is a transmitting pulse that chirps, if you will, the life force of the slave. This is received by both the owner and the slaver." She looked pointedly at Crallick, "You'll always know where your little slave girl is, Cral."

He began to protest when she interrupted, "Save it. I'm buggering your mind. This situation won't get old for a long time, I suspect."

Resigned, Crallick grunted and leaned back against the smooth rail of the ship.

Kittalae snuggled herself against his side for warmth in the tepid morning breeze. "That's okay Crallick, I like that you can find me."

Vlados couldn't hide a grin, even under his thickening beard. "That's nice Wanda, how does that help us?"

"Every pulse leaves an imprint on the etherea. If Crallick knew what he was doing with more than just his sword..." She let the double entendre hang in the air for a few moments. "He'd actually have an easier time tracking them than I would, as he draws most of his energies from Jyslin's realm. As it sits right now, this is their direction." She pointed west-northwest.

Vlados and Drake both swallowed; Vlados incredulously chiming in. "Are you sure, girl? There's nothing out that way but open water."

"I am. After I get a few hours sleep, I'll check again, then spend some time casting an incantation to enchant a pendant, or chain, to track them with."

"All right then. Mr. Drake, make for that heading. We have a plan, and a means to execute it. Now let's catch those sons of bitches."

"Aye, Captain." With that, Mr. Drake flung himself over the cabin roof to land beside the helmsman, in order to give him the instructions.

Wanda retired below decks.

Vlados said, "Alright, you two get some sleep. I've slept all night in my new cabin and love it! Nice and cozy, just like the mountain halls back home. You two fen pigeons have been up too long. You're also," he directed at Crallick, "too drunk. Sleep it off. I'll get ye if anything comes to pass."

With a mocking "Aye, aye", Crallick stumbled his way to his new cabin.

Kittalae mouthed a 'thank you' to Vlados before she swiftly followed Crallick, subtly making sure he never overbalanced.

Once alone in the cabin, she asked, "Isn't this lovely?"

Crallick dragged himself over to the lower of the two cots and threw himself onto it, letting the momentum of the sway of the ship counter his dropping form. "Sure," he grumbled, already half asleep.

Kittalae drew the shades over the windows and then, as she undid the lacing on her blouse, she pulled a sheet up over her master's prone form.

Crallick half noted that her tail was quite nimble. Wait. Had she a tail? "Where in Etheria did you hide that?" he slurred the query.

Smiling, Kattalae swished her tail around her waist, forming an almost invisible belt. Topless, she curtsied, "You like?"

A snore greeted her.

"Damn," she pouted. All her showmanship and effort was for naught. Next time she would woo and impress, of that she was certain. Her Chessintran-blooded nature nudged her desire to crawl into the bottom cot with him. No, she chided herself, that would have to wait. Let him wake to the tease of seeing her splendours sleeping above him. Smiling wickedly, she shucked the rest of her attire and swung herself up into the cot above. She allowed herself one personal pleasure of contact with him. She slid her tail between the ropes to find his hand and twined into his fingers. In this way, along with the sway of the ship, the distant cries of the laboring crew, she fell into the sweetest sleep she'd had for as long as she could remember.

Chapter Ten

''Twas the drake of fire who threatened to break the lines.
Cunning was he, staying aloft, out of harm's reach.
With strafing flames, he tried to break Bannathyr's spine.
General Skywyn plotted, then began his dire speech."
Verse 11: Ballad of Ser Crallick Carnage-born

Thirty days into their pursuit of The Chess's Blight found the toll wearing hard on the crew of the Flamerunner. The high summer heat sweated men dry. Day after day, the tedium of not seeing sign of either land or mast wore on everyone's nerves. Things that seemed trivial inconveniences roused fits of anger, flaring tempers to temperatures that rivaled the midday sun.

It was around the 26th of Ariois, high summer, when the taut sing of rigging and the creak of masts loaded with full sails went quiet. The only sound was collapsing canvas impotently losing whatever wind it had once gathered.

"Ah, what fresh buggery is this?" Vlados asked, squinting up through the glare of the mid-afternoon sun. "Why aren't we catching any wind, Mr. Drake?"

"We're foundered in a doldrums, ser," the shirtless Amorallan responded.

"A what, you say? Do we need Crallick to kill it?" Vlados suddenly asked, adrenaline beginning to spike.

Laughter erupted from those close enough to hear the exchange, including Erik Drake, who, not unkindly, answered. "Ah, if only that were so, Captain. You see, doldrums are a mysterious death of the wind. We usually run into them around high summer, and in the tropics. It's where Asha's heat is so strong, she even manages to kill Aarison's winds. So unless Crallick can kill the goddess of fire..." He smiled broadly at the thought of such a lark.

"Aye, I see now," said Vlados glumly. "So how do we catch the wind?"

"I'd have to be pretty damn drunk to take that woman on," said Crallick, topless, lying in the shade of the foredeck, but alert enough to overhear the conversation. One could see the rippling muscles across his frame, crossed by several jagged scars from lucky strikes of long-dead foes.

Ignoring his friend's weak attempt at humour, Vlados prompted Mr. Drake, "Well, mate?"

"Well, the Flamerunner has one advantage that our prey does not. We're small and light enough to carry sweeps. I'd suggest we drop and secure all canvas, to reduce any drag, then scull after the blighters who are stuck with only sail. We may gain on them, though the men will not enjoy their time," Drake warned.

"Like they're enjoying it now?" Vlados scoffed. "Assemble all hands to the main deck."

"Aye ser!" Mr. Drake spun about, and as Vlados mounted the aftcastle cabin roof to address his crew, Drake began crying out, "All hands to main deck! Send it below. All hands to main deck!"

Soon a chorus of the cry was taken up, then the scurrying of sailors, not rats, flooded from every corner of the ship to the main deck, facing aft. The only exceptions were Mr. Drake and Mr. Pallan, who flanked Vlados; Crallick, who never bothered to move; and his slave girl who seemed to only recognize his sole authority. The final exception was the stoic fixture at the helm, the massive Jacob Martine, who continued to hold his post under Vlados's preferred podium.

Once all assembled to his liking, Vlados began. "My friends, firstly, my deepest thanks for your excellent courage and stalwart resolve in these dire circumstances. I could not have asked for a better crew." This was answered by weak applause. "We have become befouled by doldrums. Our quarry has undoubtedly suffered the same fate. We have the advantage! We can gain on them! But I have to put to you a severe task. In this hot weather, I know I ask much, so I shall reward as much as I ask. I need the sweeps run out and we need everyone able to scull us after our quarry! Everyone who takes a watch on the sweeps shall be given an extra ration of fresh water, an extra half meal ration at breakfast, and an extra half rum ration at night!" His grand speech was met with disgruntled grumbling and general comments of malcontent.

One burly hobgoblin, named Alexandr, called out, "Is that the orders of the green behind the ears land-hugging dwarf captain?"

"Secure that! It was his decision under my advisement!" bellowed Mr. Drake.

The raised voices set a match to the tinder. In less than a heartbeat, men and women alike were screaming and hurling threats at each other like feathers at a maid's coming out party. That is to say, things began to spiral out of hand until a woman's clear, resonating voice pealed one word in a volume to rival a thunderclap over the tumult. "PEACE!"

Everything froze at Wanda's word. She then spoke again, unaugmented by divine will. "Everyone is on the same ship, literally," she smiled. "We are all taken with the heat. And we all want to be quit of this voyage. If we make haste, we may overtake our foes and end our journey early. Focus your rage, hatred and frustration on those who forced us to drag you out here. Not your shipmates."

Suddenly, seeing that her words had silenced the animosity that seemed to be roiling in the heat, Vlados hit on an idea from his youth. "Look here!" he cried. "When I was a lad…" After the chorus of groans that began, he swiftly interjected, "Bear with me! This is relevant! When I was a lad growing up in the mining community where I lived, during the summer, the great forges never ran around the heat of the day. Thus, I suggest that the watches rotate to one bell after midday to one bell before midnight, and the opposite. So no one swelters through the heat of the midday!"

At the sound of more complacent murmuring, Vlados continued more softly, "I'm not here to drive you to an early grave. I am here to ensure thirteen daughters aren't taken to theirs. Now are ye with me?"

The chorus of assent was weak, but it was there.

It was seven more days before trouble again reared its head for the gallant crew of the Flamerunner. There was a sudden heavy drag to the scullers' oars, and the ocean began to seep up through the hull-boards into the hold. This sent the sailors into a panicked fit. Casks were destroyed and pitch applied until the mysterious leaks stopped. The damage, psychologically, had been done. The crew viewed this as an ill omen.

Vlados's officers still held their convictions with him, Sylethra being the most high-praising of him to all she tended with their maladies.

Among those who used to hold the day watch, now the watch that ended just before noon, Jacob, the stoic helmsman, was beginning to wane in his faith of his captain, though he still stood by him. Tandi, the quartermaster, proved dwarven loyalties were as strong as mountain roots, and gladly voiced her opinions to all.

The hobgoblin, Alexandr, was downright mutinous, seeking to find like-minded crew to take the ship and return her to port, "While we still can." He had managed to rally Argent Quanthee, the metal ephemorae, as well as Izzy Nunez, Menshirre Orran, and the Vitani Callath Bierntree to his cause.

The deckhand and rigging rat Jarrol, along with Glip Glip, both seemed determined to keep their heads low and not get involved at all.

The lookout Robert Marquis, the Vitani rigging rat Nespyran Oakroam, and the human deckhands Achmed and Fransisco Nunez, remained loyal to the captain of the ship.

The afternoon watch was even more bipolar. Those loyal to Vlados held less conviction, while those opposed harbored greater grief. Three seemed determined to just work and not involve themselves in any manner.

'Marc', the lithe young woman masquerading as a deft male rigging rat, Puraji, Brom, and Jetten the Monitorman, all threw their lot in with Vlados.

The Komodoman helmsman, Bargress, Mahar, and Gregor were content to focus on their jobs.

While a frightening six – the deckhands Jarrod, Lavarth, Ronald, and Henry, the lookout, Lawrence, and the Jaraguaman, Biq – all supported the seditious talk of Alexandr. This meant he had the ear and the hearts of eleven of the thirty souls on board. At least the thirty that everyone knew about.

A vengeful aquan remained aboard. It had an inner sense of navigation, and an awareness of how little land there seemed to be around, based on the taste of the air and the roll and sounds of the waves on the ship. He had worked pitch loose, and he had caused leaks for the crew's inconvenience. He could sense the unease of the mammals and land dwellers. Now, he felt, would be a good time to take a life.

It was shortly after the beginning of the afternoon watch, when Vlados had three sweating men crammed into his smaller cabin with him. Mr. Drake, Mr. Pallan and Crallick were all there to discuss the rising tensions among the ship's crew.

"Now then, Mr. Pallan, don't hold back, how bad is it getting on the afternoon watch, truly?" Vlados was saying, his strawberry blond beard dyed dark from perspiration.

"Six are blatantly talking disfavourably about ye, ser," Mr. Pallan informed him. "I got three ignoring everything but their work, and four we can count on."

"Ouch," muttered Vlados. "Mr. Drake?"

"That shite disturber has rousted up four to his cause. Two are biding their time. And six stay loyal."

"You know there is a very fast solution to this," Crallick began.

"No!" Vlados exclaimed. "There is a process, and I'll not have random acts of violence carried out without due course." His words had just left the air when a frantic tapping at the door came.

"Come," Vlados called.

The door swung open, jostling Drake in the process, to reveal a nervous rigging rat. Marc looked at the room of men, swallowed and spoke, "H-h-he's dead, sers. The mutineers tore his throat out while he slept."

"Who's dead, Marc? Who?" Vlados demanded.

"Deckhand Eli Puraji from Jherrim, ser. I found him when he didn't rouse for his shift. I came right away," Marc swallowed.

"That's fine now. Ye did right. Run to the surgeon. Get a saber from the quartermaster, and guard the surgeon," Vlados instructed.

"Aye ser," and she was gone.

Crallick grinned. "Now can I kill the hob?"

"Aye, ye can, but we got to make it a legal spectacle," Vlados cautioned.

Mr. Drake cautioned, "Aye ser, but I'm not sure how to safely go about that without firing up more resentment. If Ser Crallick can finish this in a quiet fashion, they might just go to ground for fear of similar reprisals."

"No. We are not cowards or assassins," Vlados stated dourly.

"I am a hunter. Pure and simple," Crallick growled.

"I'll call all hands. You can judge him then," Vlados said.

At the coming protests of his mates, he added, "We'll be armed. They will not. Will that assuage ye fear for me safety?"

They disassembled to fetch weapons and met back on the aftcastle, where Crallick stood apart from the rest, without anything other than his ringmail. At the rousing call of hands to the main deck, sluggish and grumbling men came together to glare at the gathered officers.

"Vlados, by what right do you drag us out into Asha's inferno of a hot box to listen to yer dwarvish whining?" Alexandr blustered.

Unable to contain his fury any longer, Vlados erupted on the insolent hobgoblin. "Ye bite yer festering tongue ye scabrous dog! What kind of a shite-eating worm kills his shipmate to make a point! Eli is dead for yer nefarious ends. Now ye've gone and roused up good Ser Crallick to take a stake in events!"

Scoffing, Alexandr blew back, "So what if I did? Not that I would! You're framing me to be sure. See what desperate tricks they fall to!"

"Shut up," came Crallick's quiet retort.

Billowing up on his own confidence, Alexandr drove on, stepping closer to the separated

Crallick. "Or you'll what? You elvish knight? I'm unarmed, what'll you do?"

It took three heartbeats for Alexandr to realize his folly.

One, the greatbow appeared in Crallick's hand, with an arrow nocked.

Two, the sing of the bowstring, and the powerful tug at his jerkin, blasting the air from his lungs.

Three, Crallick's mocking voice coming through what seemed to be a lengthening void, "That's knight-ranger, you arrogant shite, and I'll do whatever needs doing to solve things."

There was no fourth heartbeat.

For the rest of the crew, the shocking, bloody display held them all in a paralytic trance. Crallick walked over, among them. Nonchalant. He forcefully yanked his arrow out of the corpse. Then, with his foot, he unceremoniously shoved the cadaver over the side of the ship to the waves below. Then, with his back to the crew, he further admonished, "Think of raising a hand to hinder me in my quest to retrieve my daughter, and I shall deal with you no less kindly. Mark well my words."

With that, he turned, smiled broadly and asked, "I'm thirsty, who wants a drink?"

Feeling that this mad, half-drunk elf was not worth the fight, the entire crew, teetotallers and all, took an offered helping of rum.

After all the crew had a warm feeling in their

bellies, Crallick took their measure and addressed them again. "I fear the murders haven't ended with the death of Alexandr."

The raucous cries of horror rang out from the alarmed crew.

"Why would you say that?" Vlados asked sharply, not liking the direction that the relief was taking.

"Because Marc said that Eli's throat was torn open. Alexandr was strong, but for him to swiftly and silently kill a sleeping sailor without alarming anyone else, he'd have to choke him to death, not rip his throat open like a Nekomin or a Komodoman." Crallick looked back at Vlados, "Don't worry, none of the lizardmen have bits of flesh stuck in their teeth. They're innocent of this mess. But this means we have a stowaway."

Vlados felt his cheeks redden. "But, but…" he spluttered. "That means you had me execute an innocent man!" he roared.

The crew was in a rapt silence, watching the exchange, not sparing a breath.

"Innocent, my arse," Crallick growled. "He got in the way between me and my quarry. I would do it again in an instant!"

"How dare ye?" Vlados raged.

"I dare so easily, the Queen herself gave me the title!" Crallick snarled back. "And those were only matters of the kingdom. This is my daughter! Our daughters." A ragged breath later, he concluded, "Any questions?"

Chagrinned, Vlados felt his temper ease back, knowing that the passion that drove his once insignificant, drunk farming friend was the reclamation of their kin. He couldn't fault that. Also, how would he face his own if he couldn't claim the same reckless fervor to defy anything that would prohibit him from getting her back?

"All right. Ye have my leave." Softer, he added, "and my apology." To all, he called, "Watch well for an intruder, not a soul is to wander alone! All are to be armed until the murderer is discovered!"

Below decks, the Aquan blinked its understanding. It would lay low for a while. It had done well. Two land dwellers for the one kill. It flapped swiftly back into the hold to melt into the damp darkness.

***

Hullaboo stirred in his freshwater keg. He hated this ocean travelling. If not for the debt to Crallick, he'd have long ago left their company. He hated the salt in the air. It desiccated his skin and hurt his eyes. The nictating membranes did little to relieve the saline irritation. So he found himself confined, almost like hibernation, in this keg. A disturbance in the bowels of the hold jarred his awareness. He could tell that the bulk of the crew were up on the deck. None of their footfalls sounded like the flapping that quietly receded into the hold. Stealthily, Hullaboo rose his head so that only his bulbous eyes broke the surface of the water in the keg. He rotated slowly, not causing even a ripple. The salt in the air stung his eyes, blurring his vision. He couldn't tell if that had been a movement or a trick of the light. He sank back down into his keg.

Crallick left the sight of the crew, and after making what he thought was a quick stop, only two or three ladles of rum, he retired to his cabin. There he found Kittalae's ass stuck up in the air, tail wiggling furiously while she rummaged under the cots. His brow creased in amused confusion. He silently closed the door and waited for a few breaths while listening to her mutterings to herself. "Here, here, here, it has to be here."

"What has to be here?" he declared.

"Eeep!" With a start, she jolted upright, her head running into the ropes that formed the lower cot. Twisting, then throwing the offending things free of her hair, she scooted free on her derrière. "Umm... sorry, master, I'm so sorry, I lost your bow."

"This bow?" Crallick shrugged off the greatbow and placed it where it usually hung, on a peg that used to support a lantern.

"Uh, yeah." She sheepishly grinned, "That bow."

"I found it." Crallick sat on the chair behind

the captain's desk.

Kittalae swiveled to both watch him and to afford him a better view of her attributes. "How did you get it, Crallick?"

"Magic," he snidely answered, kidding, but not lying.

"Seriously?" she asked.

"In truth, yes," he replied.

"Really? How do you channel your magical energies? I commune with the elemental wood." Kittalae had a twinkle in her eye betraying the joy she felt at a perceived commonality with her master.

"Oh, I don't know. I just shape little forces here and there. I draw mostly from the light that I bound my sword and bow to. It allows me to reach into Etheria and retrieve them at my will."

"Oooo," Kittalae said, realization dawning. "I shall never again fret if they go missing. That is so convenient."

"I draw from wood to both impede my foes and make my passing easier."

"Simple tasks for wood," Kittalae smiled. "I do much more with wood," she winked with a tantalizing eye.

"Ahem, yes, well, I also draw from fire to burn my foes, keep my comfort, and clear evidence from my actions. I also draw from metal to hone my blades and strengthen my mail," Crallick concluded.

Kittalae watched Crallick sitting at the desk

for a while. Then she said, "You must miss her terribly."

"Of course I do! I failed her! It's why I'm on this hunt to get her back," Crallick snapped.

"I'm sorry, I was talking about your wife, not your daughter. Though I'm sure you're heartbroken over her too," Kittalae quickly clarified.

"Don't be ridiculous. I don't ever think of my wife. She's ten years dead. My only focus is on getting my daughter back!" Crallick glared.

"Of course," she said. She thought, *'My ass, my dear master, you are so distraught over the thought of failing your dead wife, you are willing to meet her in Chessintra's embrace to make sure you don't. The only reason you don't think of anything more immediate is due to your constant poisoning of yourself with your Flowwe-be-damned rum.'* "I assure you," she said, "I will do everything in my power to aid you in getting your daughter back."

"Hah!" he scoffed. "What can you do?"

Smiling, the half-demonic slave girl slid to her knees beside him. "More than you; more than anyone can possibly imagine. And my dear master, no one expects a simple slave girl, or concubine, to do anything other than pour wine, give pleasure and look pretty. I am a stronger ally than you can imagine." She gently kissed the back of his hand. "May I clean your armor, Crallick?"

Crallick thought long and hard before consenting. She was an enigma. That much was certain. He made a note to ask Wanda about her thoughts on Kittalae later.

Back above deck, the afternoon watch was well settled into its routine when the sails snapped full with wind. A cheer came up from the hands. When Mr. Pallan inquired from the aftcastle cabin, the report of the wind coming up strong was likewise well received. Right up until the moment the crow's nest called down, "Mr. Pallan, Mr. Pallan! Storm 'head to the north east!"

Wallace made his way to the aftcastle and gazed starboard. The sight chilled him to the bone, even in the tropical heat. As black as Chessintra's arse, clouds piled upon each other in ravenous eagerness, miles tall, and full of malice and destruction. A grey pall hung under those dreadnaughts. It was a torrential rain shadow. There were flickers of strobing light that played across the features of the malicious beast.

"Fuck me, Chessintra," he whispered to himself. Then, to a nearby hand, he instructed simply, "Better go wake Mr. Drake, Jacob, and the Captain. We're not likely to outrun this."

Chapter Eleven

"We shall raze the village true enough. Burn them all.
Eat your fill, cremate the rest. Bannathyr shall weep.
When Knights try to save them, we surround. Watch them fall"
Skywyn was ruthless. No winks would he lose of sleep."
Verse 12: Ballad of Ser Crallick Carnage-born

Crallick heard the commotion of sailors mustering out of their racks and rushing about the ship. Curious, he took his leave of Kittalae and headed up to the deck to see what the goings-on were for himself. Upon reaching the deck and taking a quick scan, he noticed Vlados at the back of the boat. He headed over to the stalwart dwarf.

He walked up to Vlados's left side, as Mr. Pallan was already at his right. "What's going on? Trouble?"

"Isn't it always?" Vlados grimly joked. Then he nodded to the horizon. "Think you can shoot that with an arrow?"

Trying not to laugh in spite of himself, Crallick admitted, "Oh, I could shoot it, sure enough. I'm just not sure it'd have any effect." When his jest met with no merriment, it dawned on him just how grave the men were taking the situation. This was further reinforced with Mr. Drake's arrival.

"Well, if it ain't Moredhel, Chessintra, or Asha, who haven't I pissed off to be buggered like this?" Drake named off the gods of fate, death, and fire as potential candidates for those he may have angered.

Hanging his head low, Vlados muttered, "How long until it overtakes us? I am correct in assuming we can't outrun it?"

Both veteran sailors barked dry, sardonic laughs. The pair replied, "No."

Drake said, "I dunno Pallan, you figure eight hours?"

"Only if we wait 'til it's nearly too late to reef the sails," Pallan objected. "More like six if we're playing it safe."

After a brief glance at each other, their eyes doing most of the talking, they mutually looked at Vlados. "Six, ser," came the unanimous appraisal.

"Just how bad a fix do you figure we're in?" Crallick asked them, sparing Vlados the pain of inexperience forcing him to ask that question.

One sailor glanced at the other. Then Drake began, "Well, ser, it's like this. When you get a storm of that scale," he gestured behind him at the front moving in, "we are not much more than a pile of twigs in the washbasin of the gods. You see, on one hand if we were closer to shore, where the waves come up to the shallows, we could bottom out and be shivered to splinters. Or capsized from unpredictable wave action on shallow outcroppings, be they reef, shoal, or rock. So we're kind of in a favorable position out in the depths, as we suspect we are. The drawback though, is there is no buffer betwixt us and the force of the tempest. The winds can truly run as Aarison's whim decrees, and the swells know only the bounds of Flowwe's bountiful bosom. What that means good sers, is that should we roll broadside to a swell, we capsize and sink. The slightest sheet of unreefed sail and we splinter anything from a yardarm to the mast, to hole the hull by the keel."

Looking shaken and more than a little grey, Vlados sat heavily down against the rail, "S-s-s-so how do we avoid certain calamity and doom?"

Mr. Pallan glanced back to the horizon. "Too large to try to flank it. I'm thinking it's best we heave to, and run with it. How 'bout you, Mr. Drake?"

Erik shook his blond head slowly. "Naw, mate. I agree with heaving to, but we should come about and run headlong into her. It'll shorten the time in the heavy water considerably."

"Mate, that ain't up to me. That's the Captain's call. Either way, I figure we can keep this girl afloat, don't you?" Wallace turned a keen eye to Erik.

"Sure we can. I'm just advising the safer course." Drake rose a hand up, "I'm not trying to get into it with you."

"I'm not suggesting you are, mate." Wallace nodded his chin towards the quaking dwarf.

Then added in a hushed tone, "This is just for our virginal captain there. For confidence, aye?"

Understanding came upon Drake. "Aye," he declared. "We can keep us afloat, either way."

Crallick sized the two men up. "How long are you figuring we'd be in a storm that large for?"

"Running headlong into it, probably a day, maybe a little less," Drake said.

"If we run with the storm?" Crallick then put to him.

"Well, then it becomes more of a marathon," Pallan added. "It may take as much as three to five times as long to get out of the heavy water."

"How much time do we lose running into the storm? And how much time do we lose running with it?" Crallick grimly asked.

"Huh," Drake snorted. "Running into it, we lose about two days getting through the storm. We have to backtrack those lost leagues, so that could be another day. Plus any repairs. Let's say five days. To be safe."

"Running with the storm will still run the delay of repairs to the ship. Plus there is the problem of navigation. We'll need to track our way back on course, no matter how secure our compass heading," Wallace conceded. "We may still run an extra two-three days behind."

"They'll suffer the same storm though," Crallick ascertained.

"Sure, but after it already hits us," Vlados noted the wild look in Crallick's eye. "And no, you're not even that good. If we were to run into them in the storm, it would be just as pointless as not running into them at all. Savvy?"

Crallick scoffed, "Yeah. I understand. I'll wager, they'll suspect they're being pursued; at least I would if I were them. It's always better to err on the side of caution than recklessness. They've demonstrated a resourcefulness that can ensure they would share that sensibility." Crallick looked at Vlados, "For our daughter's sake, run with the storm, Vlados. Trust me. Get your crew to do whatever they need to do to ensure we get through intact. We must run with the storm." With grim determination, Crallick strode off towards the bow entrance below deck.

"Where you going?" Vlados called after him.

"I need to check some tricks that I hope I have up my sleeve!" Crallick said before disappearing below deck.

Vlados looked at his two mates. "Well, you heard my boy, step lively mates. Let's get the Flamerunner ready for the storm."

Below decks, Crallick quickly found Wanda. She was taking some time with the ship's surgeon. The two women quieted on Crallick's approach.

"Excuse me ladies." Crallick paused, then continued, "Wanda, I need to talk with you for a moment."

"What did I tell you?" said Syllethra.

"Shut it," said Wanda, rising. "All right, let's go."

They walked across the tight companionway. They stopped just in front of the ship's arms lockers. Wanda could smell his musk in the heat of the mid-afternoon. She smiled in spite of herself. "So what was it you wanted to talk to me about?"

"I need you…" he started.

"Yes…?" She butted in, her anticipation getting the better of her patience.

"…to calm the seas around the ship. Are you that tight with your goddess? Can you swing that? The waves could get pretty intense," Crallick concluded, frustrated at her interruptions.

"Depends for how long, and how much they need to be pacified," replied a rather crestfallen and disillusioned Wanda.

"Oh, just so we don't break apart, and maybe for four to five days?" Crallick humbly admitted.

"Are you fucking kidding me!?" Wanda screamed. "I could manage a few hours maybe. Days?" She shook her head and took a deep breath, "When I decided to go with you, I figured I would be put to a strong test of faith. Never did I imagine it would be the whole journey. I'll pray on it and see what I can do."

"Thanks. I'm sure you'll do the best you can," Crallick said.

"Where you off to?" she asked of his swiftly retreating back.

"Contingencies!" was the only word Crallick called back to her.

Dashing through the companionway, under the main deck, Crallick burst into his cabin. "Kittalae! Kittalae!" Crallick cried.

Popping up to attention from where she was polishing his ring mail, ring by ring, Kittalae responded, "Yes Crallick? I'm yours to command."

Shaking his head at the alien sounding words, Crallick blew it off. "How in tune are you with the wood?"

"Very," she replied.

"If it were to splinter, or to leak, could you repair, or mend, or somehow get it to endure?" Crallick asked in earnest.

"Of course. Why? Is my master in trouble?" A look of concern tightened her youthful visage.

"We all are," Crallick pointed out the aft cabin windows. There could be seen the black horizon, and the increasing chop of the ocean. "There is a severe storm coming."

Kittalae smiled reassuringly. "Don't worry, my sweet master. I shall keep you safe." She put her hand on his arm.

Crallick never allotted any time to her comfort. He dashed back out to return to Vlados.

Crallick found him on the aftcastle. Vlados was watching his rigging rats reefing the sails tight. Casks and crates that couldn't be stored below decks were being lashed to the deck. Men were shoring up the companionways, and lashing tarps over the cargo hatches.

"Where were you?" asked Vlados, as Crallick ran up.

"Sorting out contingencies." Then at Vlados's uncomprehending look, he added, "Wanda is a cleric of water. I was just trying to figure out how much water she could effect if she put in a good word with her goddess. She's praying for it. Also Kittalae…"

"Who?" Vlados interrupted.

"My slave, Kittalae, she's some sort of woodtalker. She'll try to keep the hull intact." Crallick finished off, "I can entangle the helmsman to the deck to keep him safe while we run through this."

"I'm not sure that's a good idea, usually they just tie off the helm," Vlados began to protest.

"I think that would be a grand idea, master Ironfoge," came the deep, resonating timber of Jacob, the day watch's helmsman. "Many ships are lost because a rope snaps and there is no one to hold the helm while the ship breaches a wave and rolls. If I'm secured to the deck by Mr. Oakentree, then the helm is tied. We're sure'n to be in a safer way than all hands hiding below!"

Vlados nodded gravely. "Aye, all right, you made your point. Let the other helmsman know of the plan."

"Aye ser." Then Jacob relinquished the helm to a deckhand for a while.

Vlados and Crallick silently watched the approaching tempest, side by side, until the first curtains of rain began to pelt them, foreshadowing the oncoming deluge.

"Well, friend. It's been a pleasure," Vlados said.

"Shite of a dragon," Crallick grinned. "It has not. I've been drunk more often than not and scared the shite out of your staff more often than not. Pleasure, my ass. But thank you for your friendship."

Vlados laughed, "Ye got me there boyo. But you're welcome."

As the swells began to chuck the ship through steeper ramparts, Mr. Drake came up to them. "Excuse me, sers. Mr. Oakentree, would you be so kind as to lash Mr. Martine to the deck? Captain, please come below, there is no use for you up here."

"Thank you, Mr. Drake. You make safe as well." Vlados turned towards the hatch to go below. Foam plowed in massive geysers from the bow of the ship as the brigantine sliced down hard on a swell.

Crallick went over to the helm and waited for Jacob to wave him on. After Jacob leaned heartily into the lines holding the wheel in place, he called to Crallick, "I hope you lash me secure! This will be a ride of a lifetime to be sure! Good luck and gods bless you!"

Crallick grinned with assured grimness, "You'll be fine. Just make sure I am. Make all the prayers you want, just hold on, and don't drown!" the wind now was forcing the men to shout. The pitch and roll of the ship was making it hard to keep footing. The skies were so dark as to appear midnight, not five hours after noon.

After a brief concentration, Crallick invoked his channeling of life energy and caused vitally strong vines to erupt from the deck of the ship. Unlike his efforts against the Aquans, these held no thorns, only sure gripping bark. These tendrils bound Jacob securely to the deck and the wheel. Jacob was so secure, in fact, he could only nod his affirmation that he was all right. His words were breathed away by the gale as soon as they left his lips.

Crallick headed below.

***

By the end of the first watch of the storm, Jacob had done well, surviving the furious onslaught of wind and water, and pitching deck. He managed to get below, unscathed, when Crallick and Bargess the Komodoman helmsman got him down. Crallick was lost in thought when a swell rushed over the railing unexpectedly, taking him for a ride over the edge. It was only after Bargess had dug his massive clawed feet into the deck boards, that he grinned a toothy grin.

Through the pounding rain and the early morning gloom, Crallick clawed his way along the length of one of his vines with gritty determination. Hollered words being too much of a waste of effort, Crallick simply nodded. He recast his incantations of growth, entangling the Komodoman and the helm wheel further, then breathlessly made his way below.

"You alright?" asked a worried Vlados. "You took your sweet time."

Noting the worried faces of the slavegirl, and helmsman behind Vlados, Crallick blew it off. "Just wanted a quick swim. The water is a lovely temperature."

Vlados laughed dryly. "You are one crazy son of a…" he trailed off in a smile. "Be careful. Your daughter needs you," he finished instead.

There was little water making it in through the hull, however, the torque of the ocean on the keel was taking its toll. There was a painful groaning, almost splintering sound from the bowels of the ship. The keel, the spine of the ship, was beginning to fail.

Kittalae rushed through the ship, reaching out with her mind to touch the spirit of the wood. Running her hands along the floor of the hold, she, guarded by Crallick, sensed out weak stresses in the ship and soothingly, lovingly cooed to them, persuading and seducing them to bend to her will.

***

The next change of helmsmen went off without a hitch.

Mid-afternoon found all of the glass shattered out of Crallick's cabin. The shutters were reclosed, then lashed shut.

The two masts of the ship were creaking more than they used to but were hanging in. The deck seemed to be reinforced by all of the life energy that was being poured into it. The hull, likewise, under the careful ministrations of Kittalae, seemed to be holding strong. The greatest worry seemed to be the keel, which continued to groan and protest.

All of the sailors cowered in the hold, fearing for their very souls.

Wanda ensured Vlados she would unleash a divine miracle when she was called to it. This sent the dwarven Captain off grumbling in a fit of stress, not quite approaching rage. He muttered heretical and blasphemous slurs until his door slammed him out of sight from the others.

The second day's tension was alleviated by the drinking of rum and playing at an island game called Slapping the Bones. Lanterns swung in the gloomy hull. Demoralized sailors prayed to any god they could think to invoke.

Those prayed to Aarison to calm the winds.

Some prayed to Flowwe to calm the ocean.

The desperate prayed to either of the Thetwin goddesses of light and dark. Jyslin to help them survive, and Chessintra to not take them too soon.

The dour mood of the trapped sailors did not go unheeded. The silent and stealthy aquan waited in the depths of the bilgewater, hiding in the subflooring of the hold. Fresh seawater flooded in regularly. The aquan began to plot to see how it could send these trespassing mammals to their doom.

The eye of the storm passed about an hour after midnight, on the third day. This held an uneasy truce for the sailors and their jailer storm. Wide-eyed, Vlados surveyed the devastation. The deck had been stripped of everything not nailed down. The aftcastle and helm were a veritable jungle of vines. The foremast had fared better than the mainmast, which had snapped halfway up. The tail end of the storm soon set upon them with renewed vigor and rage.

It was the fifth day that the waves seemed to be cresting the highest peaks. It was then, the aquan decided to act. Deftly and stealthily, he ascended the ladders, up to the main deck. He didn't bother to close the hatch behind him. That wouldn't matter. He decided to crawl along the deck to the wheel of the ship. The vines were alien to him as he tried to make his way to surprise the one sailor on watch. Using a coral knife, he shredded the rope. This caused the dark mammal to grunt with surprise, and his muscles to bulge.

Jacob was alarmed. There was no reason that rope should have given way. The strain on him, the wheel, and the rope had been all lessened by Crallick's vines. He furtively glanced around him, all the while the renewed strain on his muscles kept dividing his attention. Too late, he saw the familiar fish-face of the aquan interloper. The saboteur drove a coral blade at his arm. Coral shredded its way through muscle and tendon, flaying his forearm to the bones. Jacob felt the strength leave his hand, as the muscle failed. By the god's, if he lost the helm, all would be lost.

Below decks, Wanda began to pray fervently, inspired to calm the seas to the best of her ability.

Jacob let go of the wheel with his left hand, praying that the vines would hold for the moment he needed. He grabbed at the flailing aquan in his left hand. He felt the knife plunge into his shoulder. He drove the aquan's head to the place where the handholds of the wheel disappeared into the brace for the helm. With a satisfying crunch, the wheel that he had spent so many hours guiding, did its part, crushing the aquan's skull into a makeshift block to prevent the wheel from spinning out of control.

Jacob's eyes began to swim as he desperately held on to the wheel. He would not fail his crewmates, was the last thought he would remember.

The pitch of the deck grew more rhythmic and less volatile. Some of this was attributed to Wanda's furious chanting coming from the bow of the ship. She was crying tenants and adulations to Flowwe until she was hoarse. Sunlight began to stream in through the cracks of the shuttered portholes and aft windows.

Crallick and Vlados went above deck first, in order to lead the crew to assess the damage, and to relieve Jacob.

A grisly sight greeted the once cheerful and relieved survivors of the storm's fury. In front of them lay the splintered carnage of shivered masts and yards, a deck swept clean of all traces of occupancy. And on the aftcastle, still clutching the helm wheel, was the rigor rigid Jacob, eyes staring a-bow, and foot braced against the crushed skull of the aquan who helped keep the ship true to its course.

"Jyslin damn it," Crallick said. Tears quietly welled up in his eyes as he gazed upon the sight of his former friend's last heroic moments. Crallick solemnly bowed his head and turned from the scene. "I'll be in my quarters. Figure out how off course we are. Get us back on track, Vlados. I want to quit this floating coffin and get back on dry land. I want to kill this Eli piece of shite."

"Yeah sure," Vlados quietly said to Crallick. "I'll let ye know what is going on as soon as I have everything shored up. Send yer girl up if ye would. I need her feel for the wood."

"Sure." Crallick wanted to be alone anyway. He'd stop by the rum barrel first though.

Their foremast was now the tallest mast on the ship, so that is where they stationed the crew.

Mere hours later, Lawrence Marley was singing out, "Land ahead! Big coastline! I think there be sails anchored off it too!"

Mr. Drake had Jerrin run down to collect Crallick from his cabin. The lizardman and the Vitani-blooded warrior seemed to have a good bond.

Jerrin returned to the deck, rubbing his jaw. "Crallick's drunk, and not handling the loss of Jacob well, I fear."

Vlados glanced over at Kittalae, who was working mystical energies over the mast. "Lass, sorry to put this on ye, but can ye…"

"Do not apologize," Kittalae countered, interrupting the dwarf's platitude. "He is my master, therefore, my responsibility."

"When we get his daughter back, I'll wonder what she'll have to say about that," Vlados mused dryly.

Kittalae found Crallick right where Jerrin had left him: in his cabin, with a decanter of rum in his hand, glass long forgotten, swilling the amber liquid in long draughts from the vessel. At her entrance, he glanced up. "What do you want?"

"To please you, and make sure you don't make a fool of yourself," Kittalae smiled soothingly.

"Fine then!" Crallick drunkenly growled, yanking at the draws of his breeches. "You've ogled me oft enough. Have at it then! Do whatever girl!" he fell back against the cot, slopping rum over himself in the process.

Smiling bemused care, Kittalae reached for his breeches and tugged them closed. "You've seen my appreciation for you. That is good, Crallick. You are drunk though, and our first tryst shall not come to pass with the aid of my demonic charms, nor your chemical fortitude." Wrapping her arms around him, she dragged him upright into her embrace. "Forgive me master, but I shan't grant that request just now. We can wait on that."

Crallick mumbled something unintelligible against her breasts. She dragged him over to the chair and dumped him in it. "They've sighted land, Crallick. They want you topside. The villain's ship is also in sight."

This plea got through the rum-induced haze of the man. That couldn't be? What were the odds? He managed to splutter out "Wanda," before succumbing to the rum.

***

Crallick awoke, violently heaving his intoxicating gastric contents over the side of the rail. His head throbbed, his throat burned. His mind was clearing. He could hear Wanda telling Vlados, "He'll be lucid soon. The toxins will be flushed soon enough."

Whoosh; another gout of vomit projected out to the ocean in a greenish brown coloured broadside.

Wryly, Crallick straightened, collected himself, and turned to face the gathered onlookers. "All right, anyone fancy a kiss?" he puckered his lips for effect.

With somber satisfaction, several of the sailors ran off to puke at the notions put into their imaginations from his sinister play. To Crallick's dismay though, Kittalae strode up to him and kissed him purposely on the lips, her tongue briefly sweeping the inside of his mouth. This caused several other sailors to join their shipmates in their gastric distress.

Then she stepped back and asked him directly, "There, now isn't that better than rum?"

Gasping slightly, Crallick agreed, "Yeah, that was nice. But you're too young…"

"I'm yours," was all the argument she provided.

Shaking his head free of all the polluting thoughts, Crallick turned to Vlados. "Where is the damnable ship?"

"Just yonder," Vlados pointed.

Crallick checked out the anchored vessel. It too, looked in rough shape. Then he took in the verdant jungle beyond it. White strips of sand created a border to the undergrowth, to separate the aqua sea from the shoreline. A dark green mountain range rose in the background. This gave Crallick pause. The extent of the mountains was such as to suggest more than a big island. He glanced at the veteran sailors.

"This isn't an island, is it?" he asked.

Drake simply shook his head.

Pallan agreed. "Nope, ser. It doesn't look like that at all."

"Okay," Crallick looked back to the panorama before him. "I figure we take their ship. Then when they have nowhere to retreat to, we go inland and take them. Thoughts?"

Vlados sighed heavily. "Well, I suppose it's an inevitability. We're going to have to take them on sooner or later. They're bound to have a larger crew than us. It'll be tough."

"We can take all of the launch boats over to their galleon and board her from the anchor chains, nice and quiet. Kill a number before they can raise an alarm," Mr. Drake commented.

"Good idea," Crallick approved. "Even if they've landed some on the shore, we should be able to keep it quiet. I'll be first aboard."

It took only half an hour for the crew to be split up between four launches. There were five souls manning each boat. They left behind Mr. Wallace Pallan in charge of the Flamerunner until they would return. He was left with a skeleton crew of ten men. Among this number were counted the surgeon and the quartermaster.

In Crallick's launch, he had Kittalae, a rather diminutive tree froggle by the name of Glip-Glip, Jettin the monitorman who had watched his back in Jamtown, and the Amarallan Brom Corr, who he had first met in Marahaven.

Vlados's launch followed close behind Crallick's. In it, he had chosen the eagle-eyed Carib native Lawrence Marley, the two brothers Fransisco and Izzy Nunez, and the Monitor lizardman, Menshirre.

The first mate's launch contained Hullaboo, who was so happy to be smelling fresh water in the air, as well as three human deckhands: Gregor, Jarod, and Jaroll Hawthorne from Bannathyr.

The last launch was commanded by the massive Komodoman Bargress, who carried Wanda with him, as well as Mahar from Jherrim, Lavarth from Amral, and Ronald Noble.

Crallick took a stiff pull on a flask of rum he had stowed in his jerkin. He felt the warmth and burning comfort fill his mouth with cane sugar and spices, then the burn ran down the length of his esophagus as he swallowed. The comforting crutch radiated out through his limbs. When the boat nudged the side of the massive ship, Crallick leapt over to the hanging anchor chain and drew himself up the length of the Chess's Blight's hull. The black lacquered wood was rather difficult to scale, but still, he beat all but the tree froggle to the top. Glip-Glip called out "Kree kree" a few times at the empty deck. There was no answer of any sort. By the time the other three launches had tied off and disgorged their crews aboard, an ashen Crallick was coming back up to the main deck.

"Well, how 'bout it lad? Save any for us?" Vlados joked, hefting his hammer jauntily. "Did you see the girls?"

When Crallick was slow with an answer, Vlados began to move forward, "What is it, what's the matter?" Panic was welling up in the dwarf's anxious face.

What wasn't slow was Crallick's hand snapping out to snare the dwarf roughly on the arm. "No!"

"Bugger that," growled Vlados, trying in vain to pull free of Crallick's iron grasp. "Where are they?"

"Not there," growled Crallick back, matching the dwarf's vehemence. "They're gone. The whole crew is ashore. They surely don't care what happens to their ship but I'm telling you, there is not a living soul aboard, other than us. Let's get to shore, now. Have the Flamerunner send over the crew, this ship is in much better shape than the Flamerunner."

"You're right," Vlados began. He half-turned to Mr. Drake, "Signal Mr. Pallan with those instructions." As he felt Crallick's arm lighten its tension, Vlados reversed his momentum and dropped his weight down and away from Crallick, whom he actually caught flatfooted. Tearing free of Crallick's grasp, he bolted down into the hold of the ship. There was a chorus of "No!"s and "Stop!"s that followed his departure.

The first thing that assailed the dwarf's senses was the bouquet. There was an acrid stench of stale, long-standing urine. The acid wrenching putrescence of half congealed vomit followed the initial wave. All the while was the pungent, heady odour of feces, some stale, some fresh. Mildewed and mouldy hay covered twelve iron-barred cages, six aside. Vlados sank to his knees, the pluck and vigor leeched away from him through his nose alone. A sob wracked his core, as he thought of his daughter in these squalid conditions. An urge to wretch began to consume him, fueled in part from the stench of vomit; his shoulders began to shudder. Vlados wept openly.

"I told you not to come down here," came the quiet admonishment from behind him.

"Bugger you," Vlados choked out. "How can you even imagine your daughter in this shite?"

"I don't need to," Crallick said. "She etched her and Bekka's names on the hull."

Vlados choked and puked.

As his breakfast joined the slurry of effluvia on the hold deck, Erik came down the companionway ladder, holding his nose. "Don't worry, they'll have this clean before we get back, sir," he said in a vain attempt to dignify his captain's distress. Then to Crallick, who motioned him to leave, he said, "They're on their way with the Flamerunner. They'll tie her off, and begin transferring cargo over."

After Vlados could hear Erik's footfalls no longer, he sobbed out, "They'll pay for this Crallick. By all the gods, they'll pay. They'll pay for what they've done to our daughters."

"Yeah," Crallick agreed. "We'll kill every last one of the blighters. I promise you." Then, tucking his arm under Vlados's shoulders in a mockery of what Vlados had done for Crallick for nearly ten years, Crallick helped the vomit-messed, sluggish dwarf to his feet, and helped guide him out of this twisted misery.

Up on the deck, the sea air revitalized the dwarf. The rest of the crew, having been forewarned by Mr. Drake, had the good sense to give the two fathers their space. Crallick fished his rum flask out. He offered a shot to Vlados. "To the hunt?" he toasted, and swilled the amber potable down his numbing throat.

Vlados grabbed the flask and tilted it up, pouring a generous helping into his mouth. With a gulp, he cried out, "To killing every last one of the fuckers!"

Chapter Twelve

"Pyrotha veiled the village with streamers of red.
Vexed Knights heard screams of anguish and smelt cooking pork,
Then Crallick gave the orders that filled them with dread.
"It's a trap, we all know. Time to take the hard fork."
Verse 13: Ballad of Ser Crallick Carnage-born

The crews, having sense enough to swallow their own opinions, clambered back into the four launches and made for the sandy shore. They marked a point on the beach where the overturned humps of six much larger launches lay on the beach, dragged up from the high tideline in the sand.

Eli and his crew had obviously landed here. Something kept gnawing at Crallick's rum-dulled intuition. This was too easy. Why would Eli abandon his ship? Take his entire crew ashore? It didn't add up. Unless... His thoughts came quicker all of a sudden. "Vlados!" he called across the distance between their boats, loud enough, he figured for the others to hear him as well. "Expect resistance on the beach!"

Vlados grimly raised his hammer in acknowledgement.

In his own boat, those not rowing got weapons accessible for those rowing, then got their own weapons ready too. Crallick imagined the same was happening across the small flotilla.

Crystal blue waters flew by, under the boats. It was so glassy-clear and beautiful that Crallick could see the ocean floor. There was light aqua coloured sand, punctuated by blossoms of vibrant coral. Fluttering leaves of schools of fish danced in tidal winds. The poetry of the serene scene was violently ruined when about fifty men broke cover from the treeline, running forward and shouting.

When their defiant yells failed to change the course of the four longboats, the fifty men raised pistols and crossbows, and let loose a volley of shots and bolts.

Of the first volley, only four crossbow bolts found their marks. Pistol shots whizzed like angry mosquitos, and the later firecracker pops that followed were the extent of their influence. The crossbows, silent, save for the hissing of missed shots, were more effective. Crallick's own boat had two victims. Jettin had a quarrel bite into his right shoulder as he furiously sculled the oar he handled. Brom Corr, working the other oar, cried out as a bolt careened off the paddle of his oar and ricocheted into his left thigh. "Of all the damnable luck!" he bellowed.

Vlados felt like he had been punched brutally in the side. He looked down to see blood seeping from around the tail end of a bolt. It was buried square into him. *'Damn,'* he thought. *'This is a shite way to start a rescue of my daughter.'* Jaw clenched, uttering not a word, just a massive exhale, he snapped the protruding part off. "Pull hard lads!" he yelled.

Mr. Drake's boat was the only other boat blooded by the first volley. Jarod had a bolt graze his right hip, giving him a torn side, and a scare. Immediately he began invoking the name of Moredhel, goddess of fate, begging her to keep him in her plans for a while yet.

The four boats ate up the distance to the shore in a hurry. Those not sculling grabbed whatever ranged weapons they could find and returned fire, just as the shore's forces let loose with another volley. Their volley was much smaller this time, as pistols took a while to reload.

This volley, though only twenty-four crossbows strong, was just as effective as the first. Four bolts, again, struck flesh.

Crallick's launch received ineffective attention from the shoreline defenders.

Vlados was spared further punishment. However, Izzy Nunez's brother, Fransisco, was killed mid-joke, as he rowed. He was opening his mouth to finish a Jherrim word when the bolt slammed through the back of his skull and erupted as a perverse mockery of his tongue. Izzy screamed. The monitorman, Menshirre, went to grab up Fransisco's suddenly impotent oar, only to be rewarded by stopping a quarrel with his left forearm.

In Erik's boat, Gregor was the unlucky one. As he stood to take a shot of his own, he felt his left foot go numb. He discharged his own pistol, then fell to the boat. "Blighters shot me!" he groaned, looking dumbfoundedly at the quarrel that had severed the nerve and locked his ankle into place.

Bargress's launch had been tailing the Captain's, just off to the side. So far, they had been fortunate, but when Wanda insisted she be given line of effect to try to strike back with a spell, their luck ran out. Wanda was halfway through casting her spell when Bargress noticed a quarrel streaking towards her head. Having no desire to see magic go horribly wrong in such close proximity, Bargress lashed out his tail with a grunt. Taking the bolt in the meat of his tail, he simply fixed upon who would pay for that insult. He hafted his spear, and with monumental strength, let it fly.

That volley from the longboats, though much smaller in number, found three marks, and promptly ended them. Crallick's greatbow drove a shaft through a man's right shoulder, severing his brachial artery and causing the shattered fragments of bone to pierce his lung. The man was swiftly unconscious in a maroon patch of blood-soaked sand.

Bargess's spear lanced through a defender's spine. The man never felt his death.

Erik Drake's pistol rang out. The shot left the barrel, rich with the stench of black powder. It flew, sunkissed, through the tropical sky, over shoals of fish, over the white foamy surf, the creamy sands, entering the throat of a statuesque man with a very nice hat. Upon hitting the man's throat at such speed, it malformed, spinning into the man's spine. This caused it to ricochet down through his torso, puncturing a hole through his lung, kidney, colon, intestines, and rectum, before punching through just beside his anus. The man gurgled once, shat himself, and then unceremoniously dropped amongst the cries of "Captain? Captain?"

There was just time for the defending shore party to fire off one last volley as Crallick, Vlados and the rest of the Flamerunner's crew beached their boats in the clear beach surf. As they scampered, leapt, or just plain flung themselves out of their craft amidst the devastating shots and bolts, Vlados cried out "Have at 'em lads!"

Crallick leapt from the bow of his launch, firing one last shot from his bow that flew wide, before dropping it into the surf to call his greatsword to his hand. He knew his bow would be all right. All he would have to do later is call it to him, and the etherian enchantment would draw it through the plane of light to him. He began his rush towards the closest foe.

Kittalae followed her master, grabbing a discarded oar as she left the boat. She followed him closely as they made their way up the beach.

The sight was both horrible and beautiful in her demonically formed thoughts.

Jettin, who had followed Crallick into Jamtown, rose from his feet to again follow Crallick into harm's way when he abruptly sat back down. He had been punched firmly in the chest. It was impossible to draw a breath. He tasted iron in his mouth as he looked down to see a bolt stuck through his heart. He never saw the shot that took the back of his lizard-hided skull off. He pitched backwards, convulsing, as his nervous system desperately tried to hold onto life, and then he was still.

Brom Corr pulled the quarrel out of his leg, then gracelessly fell over the side of the boat into the surf. Dragging himself low in the water, he pulled himself close to the beach to begin his run at the enemy.

To say Glip-Glip could fly would be poetic. What the little tree froggle could do was leap many times his height with a single bounce. He also could rub darts on his toxic skin, and throw them with vicious accuracy. He jumped from the stern of the boat, landed just five feet away from a sailor from Chess's Blight, and promptly killed him with a scratch to his cheek from a tossed dart.

Hunkering down in the bow of his launch, Vlados, nursing his grievous wound, fired his crossbow into a blond boy of no more than sixteen years, who held a brace of pistols. His shot nicked both the aorta and esophagus, causing a violent crimson gout to erupt from the wound where it passed through the boy and his mouth.

Menshirre hefted a harpoon, then let it fly. He never bothered to watch his cast. Instead, he dove into the water to get a boost of speed from his muscled tail. That loosed harpoon took a defender square in the abdomen, pinning him to the sand like a parody of a butterfly collector.

Lawrence Marley took a load of shot to his left arm while in return, he fired his own pistol into the heart of the offender. As he clambered over the side of his craft, he spat, "Chessintra take ya bra'."

Izzy, still distraught, was rocking his dead brother in his arms, when Fransisco, even in death, proved to be a saving grace for his brother. Fransisco took a bolt into his back that would have surely slain his brother. Izzy lost all reason at that point. Standing tall, he yanked his brother's pistol, then fired it and his own, before charging forward into the growing melee. Neither shot amounted to anything other than noise, but they did serve to bolster Izzy into action.

Eric, having discharged his pistols, dropped them in the boat. Drawing his cutlass, he leapt forward from the prow of the boat to charge headlong into the fray. He was followed by Jarod who shot and missed with a small crossbow, but then swiftly clambered after the first mate.

Hullaboo leapt with his powerful legs to send him sailing through the air. A bolt pierced his thigh shortly after his launch, so when he landed he crumpled in pain. This didn't help the victim of his pounce, however, as Hullaboo's spear devastated the man's belly.

Gregor Titus's day quickly went from bad to worse. First, his shot missed. Second, when he went to go over the side of the boat, a bolt took him in the calf, causing him to topple. He cracked his head and lay, dazed, in the bottom of the boat.

Jaroll Hawthorne lobbed a flaming flask that shattered amongst three shoremen. The burning poultice erupted and sent two diving to the sands, and immolated the third. He then blanched and sat back down in the boat as his breeches became very wet, very swiftly, as though he were a babe not yet out of swaddling clothes and peeing himself freely. The intense pain and the telltale hole in his pants told him a very different story.

Bargress's launch had the unfortunate luck to have landed at the focal point of the enemy's fire. His left shoulder was grazed by a bolt as he launched a second spear at their adversaries. This time he failed to find his mark.

Wanda's incantation was cut short by a bolt through her throat. As she squeaked out a desperate plea to her goddess, she had her chest explode with the force of a horse's kick, compressed to the size of a thumbnail. This instantly shattered her sternum, driving shards of lead and bone into her heart and aorta. A bolt ruptured her lung. A third and final blow, that she scarcely felt, rent through her uterus and exited her lower spine. So committed to her divine worship, her dying breath actually managed to complete her prayer. The life-giving waters of eight enemies of Flowwe were drained from the blasphemers and poured into those servants most in need of them. Her goddess was a just goddess.

Mahar never even got the chance to get out of his seat. He was shot from behind, still holding his oar, intent on getting them to shore safely. The bolt created a small tent on his shirt, by his left breast. He swooned and passed, almost immediately.

Hurling a throwing axe, along with Amarallan curses, Lavarth leapt the gunwale of the boat to go tearing across the beach, only to have a bolt skewer his right thigh, causing him to stumble into the surf.

Cowering behind everyone else, Ronald Noble propped his pistol on Mahar's still shoulder, aimed, and squeezed the trigger. With a gout of smoke and a sense of worthwhile pride, Ronald watched a sailor drop into the sand.

By the time the melee on the unnamed beach had reached full swing, fifteen of the original twenty of the Flamerunner's crew had made it to shore. They had done incredibly well, all things considered. The defenders, once numbering fifty, now seemed closer in number to the mid-thirties. Those numbers, mind you, kept reforming into disciplined fire lines. That is, of course, until the beachhead was made by the attacking force. Then all thoughts of ranged combat were tossed aside, and melee weapons were drawn. The onrushing mass from the Flamerunner barreled headlong into troops trying to ready their melee defense.

Crallick, leading the way for the crew of his launch, parried one strike, before reversing his blade to sink it deep into the side of an unsuspecting adversary. The blade only stopped when it caught hold of the man's spine. Crallick drew it out with an accompanying gout of effluvia.

Glip-Glip, beside him, slapped an opposing sailor in the jaw, his toxin immediately sending him to the ground in convulsing death throes. A second man fell this way when, unthinking, he tried to drag Glip-Glip away from his friend with his bare hands.

Kittalae's oar seemed to writhe about with an entrancing life of its own. As she casually jogged beside her master, the oar lashed this way and that, sparing her incoming blows from her master's enemies.

Brom, eager to revenge himself upon one who may have injured him or his mates, leapt over the slain bodies of those poisoned by Glip-Glip to drive a cutlass towards the throat of one of the beachholders. This frenzied assault was batted aside with practiced ease.

From the prow of the launch, Vlados wearily cranked his crossbow, locked it, set the bolt, took aim and fired. A nekomin dropped off his graceful feet; Vlados's bolt driving home where the nekomin's heart was.

Menshirre, charging along, swept his cutlass low and had it come up in a spray of gore as it severed a man's leg, at the knee. The victim fell hard, darkening the crystal sand with a garnet finish.

Izzy Nunez, out of his mind with rage at the loss of his brother, stomped his boot into the head of that fallen man, breaking his neck with a satisfying crunch of vertebrae, before launching himself, cutlass first, into the defending line. He did so, heedless of personal harm. Thus, his accuracy was uncanny. He drove the tip of his cutlass through the windpipe of a shocked goblin, who never really had time to realize his peril before it was already over.

Marley, meanwhile, found himself embroiled in an even struggle between himself and another islander. Matching each other blow for blow and parry for parry, the two danced in a graceful and perilous ballet.

Erik hit the first line so hard that both he and the defender were staggered, and heaving mighty breaths, unable to do much else.

Beside him, Hullaboo was in his element. His spear flashed here and there but was unable to break through any defenses. Likewise, no defender was able to get a blade on the dashing, jumping, hopping, and jabbing froggle.

Jarod used the deep wound in his hip to lure in an opponent. The gullible mark soon found himself skewered upon a darting and very lithe blade.

Jarrol Hawthorne tried to flank the fore defenders, but instead found himself flanked in turn. It was all he could do to keep hungry swords from feasting upon his flesh.

The Komodoman Bargress locked blades with a warrior, who leered in his face. Only seconds later, that leer, along with the rest of the face, was torn free of the skull by the helmsman's brutally toothed jaws. His opponent fell screaming into the sand, writhing and convulsing in excruciating pain and panic.

Lavarth and Ronald teamed up to distract and disembowel a defending sailor.

Kittalae's oar swept back and forth like a living serpent. It kept all comers at bay.

Brom Corr coughed and grunted as a blade snuck in under his guard, and slid into his right armpit to pierce his lung. Meanwhile, Crallick parried a brace of daggers that tried in vain to cut through his feints and parries.

Glip-Glip, finding no one around him, took the opportunity to leap behind those harassing his fellows in the front lines.

Vlados set about reloading his crossbow. His haggard breath coming in short spurts.

Menshirre battled his adversary. No blade from either side finding purchase.

Izzy, incensed, turned from his fight and blundered right into the fight between Marley and his opponent, only to deflect a mistimed swing from his sudden intrusion, just to have it bury itself into the side of Marley's brain. Marley staggered, sagged to his knees, then in an uncomprehending shudder, sat down on his buttocks and dully looked around the battlefield.

Erik ran into little resistance as he and his opponent both frantically drew ragged breaths after their collision.

Jarod, Jarrol and Hullaboo all held their own, staving off rebuts to their own assault. Gregor, still dazed in the longboat, vaguely wondered where he was and what was with all that clamor spoiling the warm sun.

Bargress took a biting welt into his right chest as a cutlass furrowed a trench into the thick scales over his ribs. This opened a pinkish-red valley that oozed blood and caused pain with every breath.

Ron Noble ducked under an assailant, shoving him aside, only to realize too late that he had tripped the man into the blind quarter of

Lavarth. Lavarth let out a blood-curdling scream as a hatchet chopped down between his shoulder blades and his spine, renting muscle, ligaments, tendons, and bones alike. The fissure tore through the man's aorta and ended Lavarth's existence with a vibrant spray of vital fluids over the beach, the sand acting as the wicked artist's canvas.

Braving the slaughter, the crew of the Flamerunner continued to fight their way up the beach. Every yard seemingly came at the cost of another quart of blood.

Crallick grimly went about his business, no more harried than a maid selecting a dress for a ball. He stepped purposely to his right, reversed a swing of his greatsword, and amputated the left leg of the man he had just stepped by, removing it at the hip. This set him up to follow through, swinging forward to drive his serrated blade home into the right side of another defender. Crallick's once green clothing was becoming more and more burgundy, as spatters, gouts, and jets of his opponents' blood bathed him.

Coming up on Crallick's right-hand side, striding forward to the space vacated by the blade of her master, Kittalae interposed herself between another foe and Crallick. She thrust her oar at his chest. Her foe didn't really pay attention to the blunt weapon, being more concerned with the toxic skinned tree froggle nearby. She imagined his surprise as the suddenly magically morphed oar pierced into his liver in a gruesome spray of black gore. The oar shortened and fattened to get free of the falling cadaver on its own accord.

Brom was wheezing heavily and coughing up blood. He forced himself to run at the next line of defenders. They had arrayed themselves in a skirmish line, five abreast. Forcing himself to focus, Brom targeted the last man on the outermost side of the engagement. This meant that it would take slightly longer for him to become surrounded and overwhelmed. Brom launched himself forward, stiffening his right leg ahead of him. His foot landed squarely on the man's knee with a crunch of gravel caught in a mill wheel. As the man toppled and fell, Brom ensured that he fell chest first onto his dagger. The man began to vomit blood onto him; Brom hastened his death with a quick strike of his cutlass to the temple of the dying fellow.

Glip-Glip hopped along the back of the frontline of the shore defenders. He found a man whose shirt had come loose from his breeches and flapped sloppily as he fought a massive form in front of him. With a happy "kree-kree", Glip-Glip patted the naked flesh of the now convulsing sailor. As the body spasmed to the ground, a bull froggle appeared, which looked gargantuan from the three-foot tree-froggle's point of view. "Kree!" called Glip-Glip in his cheerfully tenor voice.

"Hello yourself," Hullaboo replied. "You stay clear of me now. No touchy!"

"No touchy," agreed Glip-Glip. Then he turned to find another quarry.

Vlados's strength was waning. He slipped as he cranked the winch for the crossbow. It snapped through to its fired position. Dejectedly, Vlados began cranking the crossbow back again. Gods, he felt so tired.

Menshirre grabbed a descending strike with his scaled claw, reversed the blow, and thrust it deep into the bowels of his aggressor. As the man began to bellow, Menshirre silenced him by extending his neck, opening his jaws, and clamping his teeth down on the disemboweled man's windpipe.

Screaming like a wailing spirit, Izzy disregarded all form and finesse that usually goes with wielding a cutlass. Instead, two-handed, spurred on by his grief-fuelled rage, Izzy cleaved a man from his hip to his groin, sending grey-pink loops of eel-like intestines puddling the beach around his victim. He dove forwards, trying to find a way behind the defenders to wreak more havoc.

Erik and the other man looked at each other for long moments. "You're as solid as an Amarallan," huffed Erik.

Nodding, the other man said, "You get a head of wind on you like one too."

"I'm from Drakespire," Erik said.

"Wyvernhold."

They nodded and stood silently while the tumult raged around them.

Jarrol broke free of the front line to rush forward. He saw Brom taking on a skirmish line by himself. It wouldn't do to leave his mate out to dry alone. With a war cry to let Brom know help was on the way, he charged the other end of the line. A scruffy Nekomin hissed at his charge. Jarrol batted away the Nekomin's feeble parry, then he changed the angle of his thrusting sword, and drove the tip into the hollow of the neck of the scruffy thing. The tip of the blade sliced over the sternal notch, and dove, as though a kingfisher seeking the heart-fish. His blade came out with the smell of iron, and scarlet spray.

Noticing the rising struggle deeper inland, Hullaboo leapt the forty feet to dive his spear towards the midst of the skirmish line that was fast turning into a front. The surprisingly nimble, but heavily muscled orc deftly stepped aside, and Hullaboo's spear point struck nothing but sand.

With thrusts and parries coming at swifter periods, the momentum of Jaroll's duel took a life of its own. Faster and faster until it deteriorated into unplanned thrashing, the outcome of which would be decided by either fate or chance. Well, one of the goddesses must have been pleased with him, Jaroll decided, as his blade failed to meet resistance and buried itself to the hilt in the opponent's chest. His cocky well-being was short-lived, however, as the man fell away, twisting his cutlass half from his grip. Then, with the torque on his elbow, there came a brutal eruption of pain and a spurting flow of blood, as the dying man took his elbow clean away as he fell. Jaroll fell too, screaming, and crying in pain.

Gregor had lucidity come back to him with a start! He bolted up in the bottom of the boat and felt the lump on the side of his head. Then he remembered they were trying to storm a beach. He took a quick stock of himself. Shot in the left calf; he tied that off. He'd limp, but he'd manage. Knot on side of the head, nothing to be done about that. Next, he grabbed his dropped sword. Finally, as he got out of the boat, he marked his surroundings. He noted the captain, looking ashen in the bow of a nearby boat. That wasn't good. He hurriedly limped his way over.

Bargress lumbered through the fray without bothering to use his sword. Instead, he tore a man's right side free of its fleshy moorings with his own claws. The fearful image of the blood-soaked Komodoman roaring and flinging bits of carrion away like slobber drooling from a hungry mastiff's mouth set terror in the hearts of friend and foe alike.

Ronald Noble was finally stymied when his less than noble tactics were sniffed out and foiled. Coming for a deft strike on the flank of a defender, his motion was caught in their peripheral vision and his target pivoted on one foot, carrying them out of the reach of his blade.

The man caught the unsuspecting Ronald's arm and pulled, adding to his forward momentum. All that acceleration made Ronald's encounter with the man's sword very abrupt indeed. With the force that launched the blade into his chest and the air out of his lungs, Ronald twisted to the side to try in vain to save his life. This had the undesired effect of slicing the blade through his lungs. Ronald's eyes rolled back into his head and he collapsed, unseeing, into a darkening patch of sand.

Nursing his stump of an arm, Jaroll wondered why he felt dizzy, and then the world went topsy-turvy. It wasn't until his body rolled into view that he realized the grave state he was in. Then without closing his eyes, sight left him. His mouth felt dry. Then nothing.

Bargress, roaring, frothing at the mouth, raging forward, locked his sights on the five men who fired bolts and shot at him. He deftly evaded three of the missiles, only to have a bolt imbed itself in his chest. It shot a trough through the scales on his left leg. Staggering, he kept coming.

The three remaining men in the skirmish line focused their fury against the massive froggle. Hullaboo dodged one strike, parried the blow of another, and grunted in pain as a third struck home. Noting the limp in the froggle's right leg, the defender waited for the shift in weight, then sank his cutlass into the right thigh's already weakened flesh. Hullaboo dropped to the ground.

Crallick silently charged across the reddening beach to the side of his friend. Standing over Hullaboo, he drove a bolt of fire into the face of a man who seemed intent on cleaving Hullaboo's head from his shoulders. The man wasn't even able to scream as his vocal chords were immolated almost instantly, and his brain parboiled in his own skull. Crallick's sword kept another blade from falling onto the fallen froggle.

Kittalae followed her master, dutifully staying in his shadow. As he deflected a sword with his own, she snuck her oar-turned living spear into the liver of the oaf who had the gall to assault her master. She smiled bitterly as he slid free of her serpentine weapon, spilling more blood slick ichor onto the once pristine beach.

Wheezing heavily, his arms feeling heavier with every passing moment as oxygen starved-muscles cried out for relief, Brom kept soldiering on. He managed to side-step a man focused on the fallen Hullaboo, and he drove his own cutlass into the man's kidney, his body weight, more than his muscle, driving the point lethally home.

Two springing leaps sent the three-foot tall Glip-Glip sailing to the rearmost group of enemies. They were still using missile weapons and were frantically reloading. None of them saw, until it was too late, the flying blue and yellow tree froggle. The man pounced on was fortunate enough to have his crossbow up. Screaming, he tried valiantly to keep the slimy creature from touching him on his skin. Glip-Glip's rather non-toxic tongue slobbered all over the man's face, sending him into hysterics.

Menshirre ran heavily along, trying to close the distance between the former front line, and the missile shooting Chess-spawn in the back rank.

Izzy heard a plaintive cry from behind him, spun around, and saw two vile defenders still threatening his crew. For all he knew, they were the ones who had killed his brother. He grabbed one by the neck, taking him totally off guard, locked his hand in the man's sword arm and proceeded to use the man to run through his mate. The shocked and flat-footed man simply gurgled up blood as the slender blade struck through his neck, slicing out the other side. Izzy giggled.

Vlados managed to raise his loaded crossbow and fired ineffectively at what he thought was a member of the abductor's force. Blearily he took note of Gregor approaching.

"Seen better days, Captain?" asked Gregor.

"Yeah," breathed out Vlados. "I'm afraid they killed me."

"Aww, Captain, now don't ye be saying that. We've got your daughter to fetch. Ye don't want to be disappointing her, now do ye?" Gregor prompted.

"Now that's just not right," Vlados grumbled.

"Now, I'm not saying ye have to be a hero or nothing, just hang in there." Gregor knelt beside the dwarf. "Now let me have a look at ye."

Vlados let himself lay back in the boat. He sprawled across the seat. As he felt Gregor tugging at his shirt, and the clammy hands sending jolts of pain through him, he gazed up at the sky and thought about what a perfect blue it was. Vlados smiled.

Gregor, meanwhile, was not enjoying the romance of the scenery, nor was he casual. His frenetic, jittery hands tore Vlados's shirt off, then fetched a dagger from his boot. He ran his tongue along it to clean the old gore from it, then drove it into the wound, pushing the bolt out through Vlados's back. When he heard it hit the bottom of the boat, he withdrew his dagger. He poured rum into the wound, then frantically pulled out four of his black powder bundles for his pistol. One by one, he emptied them into the leaking wound. Once he finished, he leaned forward and whispered, "Vlados, mate, I'm truly sorry for this."

Jarod leaned into his swing and drove the man's own parry into the man's trunk. He then headbutted his nose. As the man staggered back, reeling in pain, he felt Jarod slice his side open. Then he tasted the alkaline flavours of the beach's sand as he crashed to the ground.

Hullaboo used his spear to regain his footing.

"You alright?" Crallick growled.

"Yep, yep," Hullaboo then swelled his throat and erupted into a foghorn-esque bellow that rolled the length of the beach, matching Bargress's roaring from the other end of the skirmish.

Drake and his opponent had exchanged names, and to keep up appearances, were batting at each other's weapons, perhaps not entirely convincingly. The two fellow countrymen parlayed as the violent struggle went on around them.

Roaring the whole way, and oblivious to his wounds and pains, Bargress rushed across the beach and leapt upon the two end crossbowmen, taking them unawares as their fear and concentration had been split between the toxic tree-froggle and the massive Komodoman. One he only knocked back, the other was more grievously wounded. His left hand had fortunately found the man's throat, and claws left it a tattered ruin.

Bargess took a blow to the side of his head as a man, instead of drawing steel, chose to smash his crossbow down into his skull instead. All that accomplished was to break a perfectly good crossbow. The man Bargress was on was bleating like a wounded sheep. He clumsily fished out a dagger and dropped it in to the sand.

Glip-Glip fared well with the defender he was grappling with. However, the pain that erupted in his back, followed a breath later by the report of a pistol, did not entirely signify the end of his fortune. The shot passed through his side and into the chest of the man he was struggling with. Nevertheless, he let out a baleful "Kree!"

The poor sailor locked in Izzy's giggling grasp struggled, twisted, and finally managed to turn to face Izzy. The wild-eyed countenance he beheld made him lose all hope of reconciliation. Izzy giggled again, "I have a short point to make. I hope you get it."

Feeling the gentle pressure in his belly, the man cried, "No!" With a sudden surge of adrenaline, he tore away and began running up the beach.

The last five defenders rushed their fallen companions, leaping over the corpses to stab and strike and thrust at the Flamerunner's crew. Most of the blows were ineffective, being either dodged or parried. Two fell through the defences.

One sought out the flesh of the already wounded Hullaboo. The blade opened up his throat pouch, sending mucous and air blowing back at the attacker. Other than pain, and disrupting his bellow, Hullaboo's pouch did exactly what it was designed to do. It made him look bigger. It also took an otherwise lethal blow into a sack of skin.

Kittalae was the other victim. She held up her oar crosswise to deflect a blow. The ship's hatchet cleaved the oar in two, along with her left wrist.

She screamed. Her senses assailed by the most intense pain she had ever experienced in her life.

Upon hearing her scream, Crallick dropped any pretense of calmness he had for these proceedings. Hissing out arcane syllables, he vented fire at the one who hurt his girl. His sword rent the torso of the other in front of him. Both dropped. One immolated, the other simply adding to the charnal colouring of the beach.

Kittalae threw what was left of her oar at another Chessintran sailor. It burst into scores of flying splinters that accelerated far too swiftly to their marks. He died on his feet before falling in a gory heap amongst the dunes.

Brom Corr sliced open the tendons on the wrist holding his opponent's blade. The blade fell to the sands. Corr wheezed, "Do you yield?"

Glip-Glip finally caressed the cheek of the man he was tussling with. There was a brief spasm, then he focused on the one who shot at him.

Vlados erupted in a sweat. Then his numbed brain registered the smell of burning sulfur and… pork? Mmm. He would be hungry, if not for his damn belly ache. He groggily lifted his head to see Gregor having lit a bit of black powder that was on his tummy. *'Oh no,'* his mind screamed. Then there was searing, excruciating, burning, stinking, and screaming. Contrails of smoke whisped out of his body. Gods, why couldn't he just lose consciousness? That seemed so appealing. But no, the goddess of fate had it in for him today.

Izzy, calmly for one deranged, fished out his pistol, loaded it, then aimed at the fleeing sailor and fired. The figure took three more footfalls and collapsed in a snowy plume of sand.

Jarod flanked around the man who cut at Crallick and liberated him from his head.

Hullaboo drove his spear deep into the defender who stood against him. The man's ribs split and snapped as the wide-bladed spear point rent through them, then with a twist, sundered the man's lung before withdrawing to the air.

Bargress filleted the man he knocked prone under him, his back legs kicking repetitively until there was little more than ruined meat staining the sand.

Menshirre devastated the final opponent he faced with a ravening draw of his blade across the offender's throat. So coated in blood and gore was he, you could no longer tell the monitorman's original coloring.

Wanda gasped an alarmed breath. One she never thought she would ever draw again. She sat upright. Her spell had gone off. Sadly, instead of providing a healing mist for allaying the wounds suffered by her comrades, it poured all of its power into restoring her fluids and healing her tissues as a whole. She still felt a wreck. In the distance, she could make out the dying sounds of battle, and the cries of the wounded.

With a rather cocky and sheepish grin, a final defender dropped his blade into the sand and coyly said, "I surrender mate."

Crallick strode up to the surrendering man and drove his serrated blade through the man's midsection. "I don't care," was his dry response. He then took a moment to gaze around the once beautiful, now quite grisly beach. It looked like a child had dumped buckets of red paint over a white canvas, then added splotches of brown and maroon. There was one stranger talking to Mr. Drake. Marley was sitting curiously in the middle of everything. Of the twenty men he had set out with in the launches, a mere thirteen besides himself remained upright.

Crallick marched over to Drake. "Who's your friend?" he growled.

"This is Armon Faulk of Drakespire, in Amaral," Erik explained.

"Good to meet you," Armon began.

Leveling his sword point at Armon's throat, Crallick warned, "Shut up. I'll talk to you when I want to hear you, not before." Then to Erik, he lightened his tone slightly. "What makes you think we should keep him alive?"

"He felt their mission was shite. But being the only rational man in a crew of zealots meant he kept his head down and prayed for deliverance," Erik explained.

Nodding, Crallick said, "Fine, but he's your responsibility, and he only lives if he tells us everything he knows. Not now, mind you, I have to take stock of our resources and check our wounded. Later." He put his hand up when Armon seemed about to speak again. Then he walked away, bellowing at the top of his lungs, "Everybody, listen up! Collect yourselves by me. We'll take stock of how fit everyone is, and figure out our next step."

It took a while for the groaning, limping, and bleeding lot of them to gather. Once together, mind you, Crallick could easily see things were direr than he had anticipated.

He had come through the battle unscathed, just like so many times before. Only Izzy Nunez and Erik Drake could likewise make this claim. Although, Crallick noted, Izzy seemed a little unhinged for some reason.

Glip-glip, Menshirre, Jarod and Gregor all had minor wounds. This gave him a fighting force of seven men.

The remaining seven, he held serious reservations over.

Wanda had been shot three times through the middle of her torso, and while she claimed divine healing had saved her and that she was fit, he had his doubts. Besides, Wanda was one of the only members of his team that knew anything about the mysteries of the body, and how to heal the damnable thing.

Bargress had Crallick feeling a little more at ease after he explained to Crallick that the gouge on his left leg, puncture to his tail, and cut on his left arm were all healing swiftly, and in a day or two you'd only notice the discoloration of the scales. Nothing more. Crallick decided to trust the Komodoman and he added him to the combat-ready list he was compiling in his head.

Hullaboo's mangled right thigh was seriously hindering his mobility and stability. His torn throat made him sound like, to use his own words, "I have a frog in my throat." He enjoyed the human saying so much that he was still chuckling to himself for a good while later. Binding and reinforcing the leg was the only option to allow Hullaboo to continue on. So it was done, and Crallick added one more to his beleaguered band.

Brom Corr sat down heavily and waited patiently, wheezing and spitting blood. On examination, Wanda suggested he go back to the ship for the surgeon to take care of his lung. His impaled leg was an annoyance to him and hobbled his movement slightly, but the real threat to him was the collapsed lung. He grudgingly agreed to wait behind to get treated.

Once they had noticed that Lawrence Marley was still sitting with a smile on his face, some ways off, Wanda and Crallick moved over to check out what was wrong. Coming up on him, it was soon very apparent that he was in serious shape indeed. The cutlass, still imbedded in his skull, glinted in the sunlight.

"Oh my goddess," Wanda breathed. "Are you feeling okay Lawrence?" She was amazed he was still conscious.

"Ire," he said. "Just enjoying the sun. I have a bit of a headache."

Crallick said, "Just relax, my man. We'll take care of things." Then, in a hushed voice, he said to Wanda, "Get the surgeon over to the land to treat our wounded. Then she can figure out who and how to move them."

"Agreed." Wanda looked back over her shoulder to Lawrence, "Shouldn't we tell…"

"Absolutely not!" snapped Crallick. "Just make sure he doesn't lie down. Maybe have Brom hang with him."

"Okay," Wanda said.

They got back to the others and explained how bad Lawrence was. Crallick enforced the importance of not telling him about it. Brom agreed to babysit the wounded look-out. Then Crallick turned an appraising eye at Vlados.

"You aren't going anywhere shot like that," Crallick softly said.

"Bugger you," Vlados spat, "the Plains of Feyarth take you. I'm getting my daughter back."

"You'll need to be alive to do that my friend," Crallick advised, ignoring the slur and insult.

When Vlados again seemed about to protest, Crallick hastily added, "Besides, I need someone back here to make sure our escape is good to go. And I'm as good a farmer as I am a sailor."

"Yer no good a farmer," Vlados grumbled.

"You're right," Crallick said. "You're a much better sailor than a tavernkeep."

"Bugger you again," Vlados sighed. He was very tired, and even the argument seemed to be taking a toll on him. "Fine. Yer right. Damn ye. I'll stay."

Kittalae piped up. "Master, I'm fine, just need to cauterize my hand. I'm so sorry I got damaged, I'll be better next time."

Crallick looked affectionately at the lithe young woman, "No, you stay too."

"No Crallick! I can't protect you if I'm here. You need me!" she seemed so distraught that Wanda's heart went out to her.

"Crallick, let me pray over her. If I can pull one more miracle out of my butt, I'll let her go with you. If I can't, then she'll stay with me. I'd rather you have someone watching your back who truly cares about you."

Under the combined pressures of the two women, Crallick conceded. "Fine, you have until we're ready to go."

So he had, including himself, nine to take on thirteen. Well, he had gone up against worst odds. And if Wanda could work her miracle, they would have ten.

"All right, Armon, now let's have you tell me a story, and make it rich in detail," Crallick finally addressed their Amarallan prisoner.

Chapter Thirteen

"Let them burn, let them burn, let the wee children burn
The hamlet is lost to Amaral's mighty troop
Let them burn so the tide of battle we may turn."
Through cries and screams, he forced his head never to droop."
Verse 14: Ballad of Ser Crallick Carnage-born

Armon began his tale to the gathered crew of the Flamerunner. "I'd been working out of Wyvernhold in Amaral. Then about three years ago, a bunch of us veteran sailors were approached to crew a ship, the Princess Grace."

He sat down on the sand, leaning his back against a palm tree of sorts. "The first thing we thought was odd was that they had us help dry dock the Princess. We then took her name, and put some kind of black varnish on all of her wood. There were some gaunt priestesses wandering around with their shaved heads all glistening with silver. They had poured metal onto their scalps, or some shite. In any event, they were there all mumbling and praying, and generally creeping us out.

It got worse when we re-blessed the ship the Chess's Blight. Who names a ship after the goddess of darkness and death? Let alone her bad mood? Well, they then took all the lads out for drinks and pleasant company. That was when we first met Eli.

He was flanked by two Komodomen bodyguards, and there was a Nekomin concubine who was massaging his feet. He called out to the sixty of us, 'Hey lads, who here wants to undertake a voyage never before attempted? When you get back, you'll get wealth, fame, and pleasures beyond imagination!'

Well, naturally all us low-born were excited to have a taste of the high life. Also, you see, we were tasting heavily the wine and spirits. As such, we all pretty much joined in without him really having to sell it very hard. Our pay had already been handsome without leaving port, so we could just imagine our rewards."

He glanced around the blood-soaked beach, scoffed, then continued, "Now even though I'm sure you don't feel it, these boys weren't the villains, just victims, like you. The true villain is up in the interior somewhere. But I'll get to that. The next day Eli had told us to make her ready to sail and to meet him in Marahaven in three months time. He had to travel by land to see if he could collect a few things before joining us to make our expenses lighter. We supplied the Chess's Blight, then made way two months later. After we arrived at Marahaven, we took on some cages and five, I think, young women. All were very attractive, and all were very young."

At Crallick's dangerous gaze, Armon quickly

added, "They were also unharmed."

"Go on," was all Crallick had to say to menace Armon.

"We then set sail, against the tide, to Jamtown. Eli, who had boarded in Marahaven, needed to get some slaves there. We presumed they would be gifts for someone. The way he had gone on about sacrificing what was dear to explore new untold vestiges, we naturally figured new civilizations might require tributes.

When he returned from his shopping, he had a chain of eight virginal looking slave girls. We had a hold full of breeding stock, and a crew of sixty horny and lonely men. Suffice it to say, after the storm and the examples of what would happen should someone touch his 'meat', we arrived here with only fifty souls of the crew left."

"Examples?" asked Drake.

Swallowing hard, Armon's voice grew tight. "Eli wanted his tributes to be unspoiled. He keelhauled four men, crucified two, and drew and quartered a final man. No one much felt like thinking about our cargo after that. The storm took three."

"Too bad," Crallick growled. "What about your arrival?"

"Well," Armon continued. "We arrived early morning. Then came the order that we were to all make landfall. Most of us thought this preposterous. The captain delicately put to Eli the risk of that action. Eli seemed not put out in the slightest by our fears. 'Worry not. For that ship is as safe as Chessintra's womb.'

None of us common folk were too sure about just how safe that would be, but neither would we argue. He armed us all to the teeth, and he and his men girded themselves out for war, it seemed. Then they gathered the women, chained them in a train, and took them ashore. This left the Blight empty at anchor. Damn foolish, I thought. I told our captain as much, but he just hushed me.

Eli then told the captain to hold the beach at all costs. There would be a thousand dragons for any who survived. Thusly motivated, the greedy blighters fired as soon as they saw you leaving the Blight."

"Back up a bit," Crallick said.

"To where?" Armon asked.

"Just before you're ordered to hold the beach. Did you happen to hear anything about where they were heading? Or just taking a stroll randomly into the jungle?" Crallick worked his grip on his greatsword like a dog worried a bone.

"Hmmm..." Armon thought intensely. "Well, there was some discussion from his scouts. They were trying to figure out the lay of the land, particularly to the northwest. While they never said directly where they were going, they did face that way and talked at length about water, lack of paths, inclines, dragging mewling women, and other possible hindrances to their journey."

When Crallick seemed about to say something, Armon cut in. "Eli and his Nekomin mage did mention something about a temple in the skeleton of the world. That is probably the last thing I can think of that might be of any help. Was it?"

"Was it what?" Crallick looked for clarity.

"Helpful?" Armon pressed.

"We'll see," Crallick grumbled. "We'll see."

Turning to the collected group, Crallick addressed them. "All right then, we have an idea of where these pieces of filth are heading. We know they will be slowed down by their victims. We also know that they will not kill their victims until they reach this temple thing. Is there anything else I'm missing here?"

"This sacrifice may have something to do with Asha Trixiaxi." Wanda spoke up after a moment of low murmuring amongst the gathered companions.

"Wait a minute?" Crallick put out suddenly. "What makes you say that? Were you not the one pointing out this hokum about Chessintran magic and the Malefecorum? Why would you muddy shite now with this?"

"Wait, wait, wait," Wanda said. "I know what I proposed earlier. However, I don't deny that. After all, it's still relevant." You could see the thoughts coalescing in her mind. "The Malefecorum can steal the will of any of the greater servants and bind them to its will. The month of Chessintra would be the Haunting. Still three months away. We're at the last days of Pyrois, the flame. Asha's month, her purification, is next month. And anyone want to hazard a guess as to her greatest servant?"

The two men from Amaral and Crallick all choired the answer, "Dragon."

"Well?" Wanda pressed.

"It makes sense," admitted Crallick. "Armon, where did they head inland, did you see?"

"Yes," Armon pointed north, up the beach a way, to where a copse of strange trees invaded the white track of sand and seemingly walked right out to the ocean bay on wispy roots. "There seems to be a low swampy river that they followed inland."

"Right then. That's where I'll start tracking them from." Crallick purposely spun on his heels and strode off towards the location. He hadn't gone more than twenty strides when he heard the none-too-quiet crunching of sand behind him.

He turned.

What he saw rent his heart. Ten weary, bedraggled, battered and yet determined companions held arms and were dogging his path. "What in Jyslin's great grace do you all think you're doing?"

"I'm following my master," Kittalae pronounced.

"Your hand?" Crallick cautioned.

"Better." She held aloft a wooden, yet seemingly prehensile left hand. "Wanda used her attunement to water, and I used my attunement to wood to produce a skeletal and living new hand to replace the one I lost. It might even be agiler than my former hand." She winked. "Want to find out?"

Sighing, Crallick muttered, "Not the time. But, fine, you can come."

Hullaboo hopped up. "I owe. I go."

The rest of the crew pushed Erik forwards. He obliged. "Well ser, it's like this, they all want payback for their lost mates. We all want to get your daughter back, as well as the Captain's." Glancing back over his shoulder, Erik then looked back at Crallick. In a lower tone, he finished, "Besides, if we stayed, we'd have to listen to Vlados complain incessantly about his injuries and the fact he's travelled all this way not to be there to rescue his own bleeding daughter. Getting eaten by a dragon seems a fairer proposition."

Laughing, Crallick shook his head. "Fine, you made a good point there. You are all wyvern-stung crazy, but thank you. Let's get going." Then he noticed Armon, "Wait, why you?"

"I know you've been grievously wronged, ser. I seek to make right my part, no matter how insignificant," Armon said.

Nodding, Crallick conceded, "I know a thing or two about honour, especially laden with guilt.

I shan't burden you with it. You are welcome to redeem yourself."

"Thank you, ser!" Armon swiftly rushed ahead to catch up to what was now the vanguard of the inland bound expedition.

Crallick pulled out his flask, and in the scorching afternoon sun, drew a long pull of fiery amber rum. Glancing skyward, Crallick softly prayed, "Amalae, darling, wherever you are, know I'm coming. Hang on, my dear. Just hang on a little while longer."

The group moved north along the beach. In a short time they came to a saltwater delta that choked an egress of an inland river. Mangrove trees greedily clutched at any bit of dry land they could. They kept it from the ocean's devouring waves. It was an uncanny and seemingly unnatural alliance of wood and earth against the water of the ocean. Kittalae cringed at the unintuitive matrimony.

Deep brown bark sheathed the tendril-like roots that fed the slender boles that then rose anywhere from fifteen to thirty feet above. The leaves of the mangroves were a rich emerald, cut in twain by a thick rib. The underside was a paler green. The effect of the breezes blowing through the trees was to send flickers of the two shades pulsing through the river. There was a serene beauty to the place. The river water was its own semi-opaque shade of green. Black organic soil lined its banks. There was a rich dank smell of sweet rot, mixed with floral perfumes from water hibiscus and lilies.

As the group slogged through the mire in the shallows of the river, sweat slaking their clothes to their skin, Crallick, among a few others, kept scanning the water nervously for disturbances that seemed out of place.

Vines and creepers climbed up the trees, vying for any light they could feed on. There was vicious competition going on all around him. Crallick knew that animals weren't the only things willing to kill another to live themselves.

By the time the sun dipped below the horizon and the tips of the trees were dripping the blood of the end of the day, the thinner rooted mangroves were beginning to give way to more majestically buttressed cypress trees.

These trees had heftier roots, and much thicker boles that rose even higher. Their canopy sported broader leaves as well. Alien hoots from unseen animals, and cries and screeches from unseen birds, haunted and mocked them on their passage.

When the night became too dark to safely find purchase with their feet, Crallick found a spot of slightly elevated ground. He navigated over and instructed the others to set up camp for the night.

He pulled his ring mail off and set it aside. He was then interrupted by an eager pair of yellow eyes gazing bewitchingly at him belonging to

Kittalae. "Hey, can I help you with anything?" she winked. "Anything at all?"

Wearily looking up at her, he grunted. "Fine. Find grass that looks like this," he held up a broad blade. "Pick all that you can and bring it here."

Flashing him a dazzling smile, Kittalae scampered away to her task.

"Great work boss," Erik said, walking up. "You found their campsite."

Crallick gave him a look that suggested where he could go if he doubted his abilities.

"We found a fire pit, and four privvie holes," Erik concluded. "Are you sure we want to rest now?"

"Yes," Crallick stretched his aching muscles. Their aches suggested they thought he was going soft with his age. Perhaps they were right. "This is a marathon, not a sprint. No point exhausting ourselves to catch them, only to be too tired to kill them. Right?"

As Crallick let the question hang in the air, he watched Erik mull over this notion. Erik nodded, "Okay, I see your point."

"I'm so glad. Now go and organize the watches for the evening." Crallick leaned back against the tree. He idly wondered why he wasn't being harassed by mosquitoes.

Around midnight, Kittalae woke him with bales of grass. "Sorry, dear Crallick. I gathered all I could carry. Now what am I to do with them?"

Shaking the webs of sleep from his mind, Crallick shuffled into a sitting position, then grabbed his ring mail coat. One by one, he wove blades of grass into his mail, covering each ring in turn. Catching on swiftly, Kittalae joined him at his task. As they emptied the first bale, she smiled sweetly and said, "This is the first thing we've really done together."

"No, we stormed a beach together," Crallick corrected.

"Alone, I mean," adjusted Kittalae.

"They're here." Crallick nodded at the eight sleeping forms lying in little groups on the mound.

"They're asleep, and we're under the moonlight." Damn, her master was making this hard.

"So?" Crallick asked.

Kittalae leaned in and sweetly kissed him. "I'm sorry, my dear Crallick, but you are quite dense." Leaning back to relish the disjointed look she had plastered on the older half-elf's face, she added, "Why are we doing this anyway?"

"Two reasons. First, it dulls the glinting of my armor. Second, it muffles the sound of the metal." Crallick finished the rest of his work in silence.

Kittalae never pressed him further.

***

That morning, the camp arose to howls and screams of agony. Every one to a man, froggles and lizardmen included, leapt up slapping, pinching and holoring at the hundreds of stinging irons that were piercing their flesh. Bright red-orange ants were swarming over everything. This sent the lot diving into the river. The two froggles' tongues were quickly washing over everything, turning red-orange as they accumulated ants by the score off themselves and everything their sticky appendages could reach.

"This land just keeps getting better and better," growled Crallick as he pulled a drowned ant out from the front of his loincloth.

With a twinkle in her yellow eyes, Kittalae whispered playfully, "Need anything kissed better, my dear Crallick?"

He simply glared at her, "Let's move out."

Pouting at his lack of humour, or sense of flirting, Kittalae threw on her own clothes that she had doffed in the water to shake out the dead ants.

Miserably, full of bites and grumbles, the group resumed their trudge through the cypress swamp. Away from the mounds, a new bother that was easily recognized came to annoy them. The thrum and whine of tiny wings, followed by itchy nips at their exposed flesh, identified their tormentors. Mosquitoes. By the time midday rolled around, the land had started to rise and the clouds of mosquitoes had begun to thicken. Heat was scorching their bodies dry of sweat and they had no real shelter from the sun. They were hiking through meadows of a long-bladed grass that was a ruddy purple in colour. The fields were punctuated with trees that had thorny spikes running the length of their branches and trunks. Wide leaves drank in the sunlight. Skull sized bobs of white fleece dotted the ends of several branches. The red grasses under several of these silk floss trees looked to be capped with snow.

As they climbed longer into the day, the fields gave way to massive banyan forests. They were mixed with strange baobab trees. Massive trunks the size of small cottages grew from between the taller, but twisted and gnarled root and trunk systems of the banyans.

Evening fell as the music of the evening birds and hidden animals rang through the forest.

Ahead, up the side of the root of the mountain they were slowly gaining on, Crallick could see several glowing points of light, betraying campfires. '*Sloppy*,' he thought, then he grinned evilly. Crallick sat and drank some rum. Thinking back, he could barely recount the last time he was part of an expedition like this one. He had been twelve years younger. He shook his head. He was getting too old for this shite.

He offered to take first watch. The rest of the group slumbered. Erik and the others, wiser now, had picked the campsite after making damn sure there were no ant burrows hidden in the grass.

Crallick touched his fellow watchman, Kittalae, on the arm. "Stay here. Stay silent," he ordered in a no-nonsense tone of voice.

She nodded her obeyance. Suddenly he was strangely glad she was his slave, and couldn't argue or disobey. There was something to be said for unquestioning loyalty, even though it was questionable in the manner in which he had acquired it. Nevertheless, he stole away into the night to scout out the route to the enemy camp.

Moving faster and more silently than he could do if encumbered by the others, he made the fringes of the enemies' camp in a few hours. His keen sight told him everything he needed to know.

The first thing that met his eyes were the number of plant-based dwellings in the clearing. The marauders had obviously taken over a local tribe's village and hadn't had time to construct permanent buildings. There was a path leading from the far side of the village into the darkness. A conical mound in the distance belied some plinth, or ziggurat, or pyramid. Some religious temple; the site of Eli's intended sacrifice, Crallick mused.

There were sounds of laughing, crying, and rutting coming from the village. Crallick's blood curdled in his veins when he saw what he thought to be children, being bent over rails, tables, and lain on the ground to be raped by their marauding captors.

So galled by this barbaric behavior, Crallick found his bow in his hand. He hadn't even been aware he had called it to him. His eyes hardened. He had some time to kill.

Deftly scrambling up a banyan tree, Crallick laid out upon one of its tremendous branches. Aiming his great bow, he nocked an arrow, drew taut the string, slowly inhaled, and loosed the arrow with his exhale. Silent, the dark shaft shot through the night. A wet thud told of it finding its mark. Through and through, the arrow entered and exited the chest of a mailed figure with a bastard sword and shield who was pointlessly standing watch. His body flopped lifelessly to the ground.

Sighting again, Crallick marked a Vitani, with a bow of his own. This target was scanning the trees. The almond eyes widened in fear and realization when they fixed upon Crallick, who let fly another arrow. This arrow took the Vitani in the throat, choking off his cry of alarm.

A scream, followed by raucous laughter, caught his attention. A goblin-blooded man was stretching a naked and diminutive woman under his corded mass. Onlookers pretended to ignore, or jeered the mongrelman's sport. With a feral growl, Crallick let fly an arrow that tore through the man's spine, heart, and sternum. This stopped the man's thrusts dead with an epileptic spasm.

The victim began screaming anew, terror seizing her wits, as blood bathed her in a crimson wash. This inevitably drew attention. One of the first responders was taken off his feet as a missile drove through his ribs, to collapse his lung.

At this juncture, Crallick thought it best to make his escape. As he fled, unseen, through the forested slope, he managed to bloody his foes twice more. One he shot through the liver, leaving him consigned to a long and agonizing death. Who knew, if the human victim was unlucky, he may find him again tomorrow. The other died from the arrow destroying his brachial artery. The arrow caught him in the right arm, tearing it clean away. This left the exposed artery to spray the surroundings with his vital lifeblood. The man staggered all the way back to the village, only to collapse in the warm embrace of Chessintra.

Crallick got back to camp to find a small but irate contingent of his friends waiting for him. It was five hours past midnight.

"Just where have you been?" Erik bluntly asked. His burly arms were folded across his chest.

"I went to reconnoiter the village ahead," Crallick cooly stated, unslinging his bow from his shoulder.

"What village?" Hullaboo asked.

"The one that Eli's marauders took over for themselves." Crallick handed his bow to Kittalae.

"No one knew where you had gone," rumbled the massive Komodoman, Bargress. "We were concerned."

"My sla... Kittalae knew where I went," Crallick unshouldered his quiver of arrows.

"She didn't say where you had gone," said Erik.

"Good," Crallick smiled. "I told her not to. The last thing I needed was to have a half dozen of you crashing after me in the bush and getting me killed."

Erik's jaw tightened. "Come now, Crallick, I don't think we're that incompetent."

Shaking his head, Crallick conceded the point. "Fine, you might not be. But I just wanted to do some careful scouting, and get back. That is all."

Erik glanced at Bargress. Bargress shrugged. "So be it," Erik said. "What's done is done. Well, tell us what you found."

"There is a village of humans, I think. Jaragua sized. Eli's host was harassing them. I noted ten of them. One of the Komodomen, the Nekomin, and Eli were nowhere to be seen. I killed four and wounded one while I made my escape. There are six left, plus the three. Nine in total. We'll press on to the village at first light. It will take about an hour to get there. Once there, we'll kill them all, save the village, and save the girls, though they must be sequestered in a hut, because I couldn't see them. There was a distant shape that looked temple-like beyond the village. I'm guessing that is where the sacrifices are to take place. Any questions?"

"Nope." Erik smiled grimly at the news of the upcoming task.

"Go share the information with everyone. I want everyone thinking smartly. We'll leave in an hour," Crallick concluded.

"Your pride is your downfall, my fleshy friend," said Bargress after Erik had headed off.

"Excuse me?" Crallick asked.

"You are easily one of our best warriors and you could have denied us that asset while you satisfied your personal curiosity. Had you been compromised, we may not have had the martial strength to rescue the maids. Consider your end objective the next time you choose to heedlessly risk yourself." Bargress paused, then politely added, "Ser."

Stunned at the rebuke of his rashness from such an unlikely source, Crallick mutely nodded.

Kittalae spoke for him. "He's sorry, you are right of course, and it surely won't happen again."

Pulling his lips away from his teeth, Bargress nodded. "Rest well, good hunter," he said, then pounded away to Glip-Glip and Menshirre.

Crallick looked up at Hullaboo, "Nothing from you?"

"Nope, nope," Hullaboo licked his eyes to moisten them. "You'll be fine, if not, I rescue your daughter. I owe you." Then he limped off to join the other non-mammalian members of Crallicks group.

Crallick took a swig of rum from his flask. He leaned his head back against a bole of a banyan tree. He watched Kittalae fuss about, making him a breakfast. She was squeezing ripe looking red berries into boiling water. He lost consciousness.

He awoke to a gentle prodding. "Sweet Crallick," Kittalae cooed.

He hocked phlegm through his nose and throat to spit it into the dirt. "Huh?" he grunted.

Wiping away a strand that clung to his mouth, Kittalae flicked the mucous away with her fingers. "Drink." She gave him a hot beverage.

Crallick swilled it down with three long draughts. This was when he noticed the gathered company, all waiting and watching him.

Erik spoke for them. "We're all ready. We've collected weapons, armor, and we're leaving supplies here. We've bound and reinforced all injuries as best as we can. We're ready to go ser."

Crallick got to his feet and nodded. "Excellent," he said. He glanced around at his assembled group. He had to remind himself not to call them troops, as they weren't trained soldiers and assuming them to be so would get him killed, as suredly as it would see them perish. He took stock of them.

Glip-Glip wore no armor, had a harness and belt, and at some point during their trek through the swamp, had collected a hollow reed, which he had fashioned a blowgun out of. For ammunition, he had a pouch full of thorns harvested from those strange silk-floss trees. He had a dagger as his only forged weapon.

Gregor Titus was wearing a leather jack. He had fashioned a wooden shield. His cutlass was hanging from his hip.

Jarrod Pajmahr likewise wore a leather jack and had a cutlass. He still had his pistol, and had a brace of hatchets slung to his belt.

Izzy Nunez had only two cutlasses.

Hullaboo had his longspear and his harness. He too, chose agility over being fettered by heavy armor.

Armon Faulk had been outfitted to defend the beach. He had a cuir bouilli jack, leather greaves, and vambraces. He also had a pistol and a cutlass.

Bargress Trothe held a brace of pistols in his belt. In addition to his naturally gifted weapons and armor, the Komodoman held a wooden shield and cutlass.

Menshirre Orran wore leather over his scaled hide. He wielded a cutlass and a crossbow. There were only a dozen bolts for it though.

Erik wore a leather jack, but he had vambraces and grieves. He had a cutlass, a hatchet, and a pair of pistols.

His sweet Kittalae was the only other member to be wearing anything resembling heavier armor. She had used her magic to cajole pieces of wood to form to her lithe figure. She still had a spear and Crallick knew she also had her spells.

Sighing heavily, he felt obligated to give some sort of speech. They all looked so damned eager to get themselves killed. Had he ever looked that fucking naïve? Ah well, Jyslin save them all.

"All right you sorry sons of bitches. Some of you may know that I served in the elite Bannathyr order of knight-rangers. Just because you are fighting alongside me now doesn't make you warriors. I want each one of you thinking for yourselves out there. If you don't, you'll die and there won't be a damned thing I can do for you, except piss on your grave after I've toasted your passing."

There was scattered and slightly nervous laughter.

"I'm not kidding. No heroism. If you think you've got into a bad situation it'll be because you have. Get the bloody way out of it as soon as you can. There is no excuse. If you make a mistake there will be no need to apologise, you'll be dead. If you find better gear, take it and use it. This is the real shite. That play at the beach was a dress rehearsal. This is the performance." Taking a deep breath at the stunned faces, Crallick idly wondered if he had overdone it. Bugger it all. "Okay, let's go!"

With those final words, he turned and headed towards the village at a brisk pace. Fast enough to cover ground effectively, but not so fast as to tire himself or the others out. His ten companions fanned out on their own volition, creating a skirmish line that ate up the distance swiftly.

Two hours into their march, Crallick found the man whose liver he had perforated. Thick, blackish slobber ran down his chin and his wide eyes darted to and fro, panic-struck at facing the final moments of his life.

Crallick paused briefly. He lowered himself to a knee. Then, lifting the man's chin with a gauntleted hand, he softly asked, "Where are the girls? You aren't long for this world. You may as well leave with some dignity, and a good deed to barter Chessintra with."

"Bugger you," came the feeble spat reply.

Crallick wasted no more time with him. Snapping his neck, he glanced over to Gregor. "Here's some mail, and a bastard sword. Take them."

Gregor doffed his jack in favour of the chain mail shirt. He then hefted the bastard sword. He felt the blade's heavier weight. "Ok, I'm ready," he said to Crallick who was patiently waiting for him.

The next ten to twenty minutes passed swiftly as Crallick took the opportunity to advise Gregor what to expect when wielding a heavier blade.

As the sun crept higher in the sky, Crallick's skirmish line got into position to where he had left the village the night before. As he had predicted, the forces left behind were far more vigilant than when he had literally caught them with their pants down last night. Crallick could see five guards, as well as the injured warrior who was propped up with a crossbow.

Much to his disgust, Crallick also saw that the tiny women of the village had all been stripped naked and lashed to a series of posts in the center of the village. There was a pile of lumber that was fashioned to form the base of a bonfire. Tinier children were tied to fences, behind which stood four of the guards. The men of the village were nowhere to be seen.

"Shite," mumbled Erik as he moved up beside Crallick. "What do we do now?"

"I'm thinking," Crallick muttered. He drew his flask. Shaking his head, he tried to resolve what he was about to propose to a group of untrained amateurs with a snort of rum. He was off his rocker.

"Who had ranged weapons?" he asked.

Erik said, "Well, Bargress, Jarrod, Armon, and myself all have pistols. Menshirre has his crossbow, and Glip-Glip has that blowgun. Why?"

Crallick sighed heavily. "So with my bow, we only have three silent ranged options. And all of the shots can't miss their targets."

"Obviously. Or you'll kill a child," Erik agreed.

Mocking Erik, Crallick said, "Obviously, or they'll kill the women by fire as well."

Erik paled at the admonishing of his oversight of that major factor in the upcoming fight. All of those women tied to the structure in the middle of the village. "Sorry," he mumbled.

"Shit, don't be," Crallick said. "You aren't trained for this. I'm sorry I laid that on you, my friend." Crallick then turned to Glip-Glip. "Psst. Glip-Glip! Come here. But not too close."

Glip-Glip obliged. In a soft high pitched voice, he asked, "Kree?"

"Can you get to the south flank really quietly and take out those two guards without alerting anyone?" Crallick asked.

"Kree!" came the confident reply. And before Crallick could advise Glip-Glip on what the signal was to be, Glip-Glip had stealthily hopped away into the branches of the surrounding trees.

Cralick rubbed his now quite rough stubble on his chin. Sea-faring hadn't helped with his hygiene. He motioned Menshirre over.

The monitorman came to him swiftly, "Yesss?"

"Take out the northmost guard. If you can," Crallick said.

"What will be the signal?" Menshirre asked.

Snorting, Crallick said, "Either on my mark, or at the commotion to the south. Savvy?"

Flaring his nostrils, Menshirre said, "Your mark means what?"

"My target will drop. I have the two in the middle. When one drops, you fire." Crallick would have killed for just one man from his old unit.

Turning finally back to Erik, Crallick concluded his loose battle plan. "You take everyone else, really quietly, and get as close as you can. When things go wrong, you get as close as you can to the enemy. Put pressure hard on them. Make as much noise as you can. Keep them from hurting anyone else. Got it?"

"When things go wrong?" Erik looked to clarify.

"Oh, I promise you, they will," Crallick groaned. "Just get on it," he added when presented with Erik's disapproving look.

Crallick hoisted himself up a tree. It was one of the strange baobab trees with the massive trunks. The foliage at the top provided an excellent sniping blind. Calling his bow to his hand, he pulled an arrow from his quiver. He nocked it and sighted down its length. He panned back and forth until he located the target he wanted to drop first. Finding it, he inhaled, ready to let fly with his shot. Then things went wrong.

Glip-Glip obviously had made it to a position he liked, because the guard to the south slapped his cheek as if stung by a wasp. He then convulsed into a seizure, flopping to the ground. This had the undesired effect of setting the children tied to his fence into screaming wails of hysterics.

The northern guard took that moment to look over his shoulder to the south. The quarrel took him in the back of his skull. This sent those children into wails of terror.

The eruption of noise caused his skirmish line to charge forwards towards the center of town, ignoring their own safety. The distant wildlife and birds quieted in the sudden din of the ill-executed fight. Crallick's shot missed wide of the target as he had bolted to the side towards the convulsing man to the south. At the sound of the arrow striking the wood of the hut behind him, he started, glanced back at the vibrating arrow, and then looked into the forest from where it came.

The three frontrunners of Crallick's skirmish line met with immediate disaster. Armon tripped over a cord stretched tight between two huts. He fell flat on his face. Other than a bruised ego, he was unharmed. The real damage was a spray of lantern oil that fountained out of a suspended cask above the bound townswomen. Crallick cringed in mortified terror with what happened next.

"Ser Oakenshield!" called out a voice from the city. "I know you're out there! I recognize a fellow knight-ranger, just like me!"

Unable to contain his indignation, and against his better judgement, Crallick yelled back. "Bugger you! We're nothing alike! I would never serve Chessintra as you! I serve only Jyslin and the Queen!"

"You sure about that?! The only difference that I see is that I'm open about who I send to Chessintra! I'm also younger, faster, and not so vulgar as to take trophies from my kills!" Crallick was scanning the village to try to find the source of the voice, as he was sure the other ranger was doing to the forest. Unless... No! Of course not! The ranger would be trying to echo his voice off of a hut. That meant he was in the forest too.

"No. I don't have to tell you that any more violence will result in the death of the townsfolk. Chessintra will have your daughter either way!" the gob-buggered ass continued. "We can have a nice sit down and no one else has to get hurt. Just the sacrifices. Besides old man, you can barely draw the string on your bow. Just admit it, you're too old for this shite."

Crallick realized he could see him. He narrowed his search at the thought, also he simplified his body movements. Damn, he still couldn't find the guy.

Glip-Glip, meanwhile, sent another guard into seizing convulsions, leading to a noisy death heralded by six screaming children.

That simple turn set off a powder keg of actions that culminated into a six-second hell that ended the entire altercation for the village.

First, the elven ranger said, "Too bad." Then he fired a flaming arrow into the village square.

This marked him as two trees over from Crallick. As he drew back his bowstring to quickly load and direct his next shot at Crallick, Crallick shifted his aim and fired at him. The arrow was devastating at ranges of over two hundred yards. He was merely twenty yards away. The arrow holed him through his torso, spinning him to the right, and knocking him clear out of the tree. The arrow didn't kill the ranger, but Crallick was pretty sure the sickening crunch of the guy's neck finished the job for him at the base of the tree.

Jarrod fired his pistol, along with Bargress's pair. The trio of shots rang out into the tied form of a child, the chest of the guard, and the trunk-fashioned hut behind them. Both the guard and child jerked and went still.

Jarrod took a crossbow bolt to the abdomen. He doubled over in pain, vomited blood, and fell. That shot had come from the wounded man who had been left with the crossbow. He had made his last shot count. Menshirre made sure it was his last shot with a bolt of his own.

Erik's shot went low, blasting the skull of a captured child into shrapnel that did little to bother the man cowering behind the other five children.

The man, aiming a return shot at Erik, never saw the Bull froggle's swift leap and spear pointed descent, not even when the spear entered the top of his skull, driving through his brain, rupturing the palate, diving through the man's throat, and into his chest cavity to cause a massive eruption of blood to come frothing forth. The man's sagging to his knees prevented further damage. This was lucky for Hullaboo. Hullaboo knew it was very hard to pull a spear tip from a man's pelvic girdle once it got snagged in those bones.

Izzy cornered the last guard, who shielded himself with a child of no more than six years. The guard smiled, "Now I know you Bannathyr types! You won't risk a child. Right! Let's talk."

Izzy simply said, "You killed my brother." Then he drove both of his cutlasses through the man's chest; right through his makeshift shield.

The guard garbled out something about "You beast."

Izzy's cold eyes never left the dying man's. "You put me in the position, you coward." Then he yelled, "Clear!"

By the time Gregor and Kittalae reached the pyre, eight of the twenty women were alight, screaming endlessly as their skin sizzled and popped. The stench of cooking and burning pork was rich in the air. The two of them did their best to try to pull free those women that they could. By the time Crallick had climbed down rather shakily from the tree, the tiny ant bites bothering him more than the two healing ribs, the women were either safe or dead.

Before anyone could stop her, a woman, seeing her child dead on a rail, dived back into the bonfire consumed with grief. She was soon consumed by the fire.

Crallick sighed heavily. The wails of those immolated had died off. The wails of those grieving were rising up. Erik came over to him.

"Hey, Crallick. We got through that really well, don't you think?" Erik asked.

"Tell that to the nine women and three children. And then tell that to the fathers and husbands of those dead," Crallick glumly answered.

"I meant our forces," Erik quietly said. "Look pal, I know you try, but you can't save them all." He tried vainly to reassure Crallick.

"Once, I could have." Crallick stretched. He listened to his vertebrae crack into place. "Damn it, Erik, I missed a young pup of a Bannathyr knight-ranger just twenty yards away. Ten years ago, he would never have even been alive that close to me unless I had wanted him that way." Crallick's voice was torn somewhere between grief, desperation and frustration.

Bemused, Erik gave a sidelong glance at the crumpled form at the base of the tree. "No offence Cral, but you're being a little hard on yourself. He's dead. You're not. We're still going to save your daughter. Also, we saved most of the children and women of this village as a bonus."

"He's right, master," Kittalae said, coming up to them. "Sorry, I mean Crallick."

Snorting back a laugh, Crallick said, "Fine, and don't worry, I'm not upset at you. Get everyone over here. Have them strip whatever gear we can. We have to quickly find out just where they've gone, and how far we still have to go."

The men of the village were found tied up in two of the huts. They were in pretty bad shape. Several of them were beaten and some bore nasty cuts. All of them were malnourished and dehydrated. When they were let out the men, all of whom were under four feet in height, rushed to find women, children, or both. Some succumbed to sobbing and wailing. Others chattered amongst themselves, presumably about Crallick's men. They were all nut-brown, and lean. There was a fierce pride in their eyes. They clearly didn't like what had just befallen their village.

Crallick and his team were scrawling in the sand their rough approximation of the surrounding lands. They were also divvying up the spoils of the dead. Then Izzy nudged Hullaboo and pointed.

Tentatively approaching the group was a cluster of six women, trailed by peering and quietly chattering children. The men were keeping a focused gaze on them with strange weapons at the ready. Even though they seemed armed and ready to defend themselves as best they could, they were content to let these brave volunteers go forth in some gesture of peace.

Erik whispered to Crallick's right ear, "What are they anyways? They're too thin for dwarves and they're half the size of a human. They are not ugly enough to be Boggles. Fairies?"

"No. Now shut up." Crallick stepped forward, aware of his team tightening hands on weapons, and of Kittalae gently coming up behind him. He lowered himself onto one protesting knee. He opened his hands, palms up, and spread them away from his body. He smiled without showing any teeth. Although for the life of him, he couldn't remember how to make the rest of his face not seem hard.

One of the women was carrying a large, clay vessel that sloshed with a rich brown liquid in it. The liquid steamed and gave off an earthy, heady aroma. Crallick groaned inwardly, knowing what was likely to be expected to come next. Sure enough, one of the other women was carrying a bunch of clay cups. A different woman took a cup from the cup-bearer, and while the cup-bearer handed out the cups to Crallick's team, she dipped hers into the liquid, then drank deep of it. This display was to prove to Crallick the safety of the beverage. All it truly proved to his paranoid mind was that she was willing to die for the good of her tribe. Wait, village. It was a bad assumption to think that these folks were tribal. Crallick watched for any telltale signs of distress. Then after long moments, he helped himself. The rich liquid was warm and rejuvenating. Everything seemed to come into clearer focus. It was good, though it had a bitter taste to it. The rest of the group were murmuring to themselves about their own experiences of the beverage. The consensus seemed that it needed something to sweeten it. Other than that, it was amazing.

Kittalae had been deeply involved with one of the local women, and soon came over with a bit of a sheepish grin on her face.

"What is it?" Crallick growled, hiding his rum flask. He drank some more of the brown liquid, now enriched with some rum. Oooh, yeah. Much better.

"Well," Kittalae giggled, "I've been getting the hang of their speech. This drink is coffee. It comes from these." She held up a branch with some red berries on it. "They pick them, then dry them in the sun, then prepare them like tea."

"Great." Crallick looked hard at her. "I care, why?"

"Because for saving their village, the elder has decreed you are entitled to five hundred of those coffee plants. Also, three wives are yours for the taking." It was impossible for him to tell if she was blushing under the red pigmentation of her demonic skin. But she couldn't hide her amused smile.

"No."

"You don't want to insult them," she cautioned.

"No."

"You could say it's your custom to only accept one," she advised.

"No."

"You could say you'll pick after you return from the temple," she offered.

Crallick gave a low guttural growl in concession.

"The temple is only half a day's hike up the slope from here. The path is easy," she said. "They were very helpful once I said you'd be honoured to take a wife with you."

Glaring at his slave, one violation already made of his ethics and vows in order to save his daughter, Crallick resigned himself to have to suffer at least another before this trial was over. Swallowing his pride and his rage, he said first to Kittalae, "Well then, I suppose you did well getting us that information." Then to all, he cried out, "All right everyone! Get the lead out of your balls! Let's go get those girls back!"

With that, they gathered up their gear and swiftly began moving up the path that led to the distant looming ziggurat.

Chapter Fourteen

"Crallick's Cradle Knights stormed the Amarallan flanks
The hamlet turned to ash and they wept with blood
Crallick and his nine finest sent the drake their thanks.
Spears and arrows struck home. Drake's fire began to flood."
Verse 15: Ballad of Ser Crallick Carnage-born

The full heat of the day was upon them when they left the village to ascend the slope to the mountain temple. Not even the biting flies bothered to buzz noisomely in the heat. They followed a path of heavy flagstones that was choked over with vines and leaves. Mosses also deadened the sounds of their footfalls.

There were telltale signs of a recent passing: indentations in the moss; scuffed bark on vines; occasional broken twigs among the floor litter. All were clues to some group of not-too-concerned travellers coming this way.

Crallick noted with a wry smile a small thread of yellow fabric from Amalae's skirt, placed notably higher than her waist. His daughter was alive. She had to have placed it there to be easily spotted.

Crallick led his now slightly better-equipped band through the rainforest. He paced them by a good ten yards. He had instructed them to keep each other in line of sight, but easily several yards apart. He had explained that they were tracking a mage who could easily destroy a ten yard radius with one strike of a battlefield geared spell. That sobering thought quelled any misgivings the band may have had with Crallick's expertise. He had also explained with his leading so far forward of the group, should anything horrible happen to him, they would have time to react and either avenge him or save themselves.

Birds called in different notes and timbres from high in the canopy. Strange little animals likewise chattered and screamed in the distant branches. This backdrop of noise had cropped up as the sun fell steadily towards the west. The midafternoon gloom of the canopy shade did little to relieve the heat. Just enough for the bugs to begin chirping, biting and buzzing again.

The forest's choir abruptly stopped its harmony. Crallick stiffened in surprise at the subtle change in his environment. He crouched down and glanced around nervously. As a hunter, he knew what this meant for the wildlife of his homeland. He guessed, against hopes, that it was the same for the wildlife around here. Back in Bannathyr it usually meant the presence of a predator. Anything from a wolf, up to a marauding wyvern. As for what it could mean here – who knew?

The sudden deep thrumming of wingbeats sent an echo of a memory running to him from his past. The steady, rhythmic tempo and the force of the wind change coming from those wings could mean only one thing.

Dragon!

The solitary word chilled him to the bone in ways that no other foe had ever sent fear running through him. Ironic that the servants of fire could chill someone with fright. Crallick had just enough time to yell "Dragon!" and drop to the ground. Then the approaching wings were overhead and then past. The suction of the great passing wyrm caused the trees to sway and groan and creak like so many tall blades of grass moving in a spring breeze. Beams of sunlight pierced the under canopy of the rainforest. This caused a strobing effect that sent Crallick's band running to and fro, trying to avoid being caught in the open. Some trees with boles as large around as small huts cracked in protest of the torque set upon them from the rushing gale of the passing dragon.

Crallick took a quick stock of those hiding amongst the trees with him. There was Erik, Gregor, and Armon, all who hailed from Amaral, a nation who employed dragons in their elite airborne cavalry. They would be acclimatized to the presence of the massive predators, though not one of this size. Crallick guessed they wouldn't freeze up.

Menshirre and Bargress were both lizardmen, so their kinship with reptiles should keep them able.

Hullaboo and Glip-Glip were unknowns to him. As was Izzy. In fact, Izzy's unstable emotional condition was of great concern, though Crallick hadn't dwelt upon it. Up until now, if Izzy wanted to get himself killed while avenging himself upon as many of his brother's killers as he could, that was his problem. But now, with the complication of the dragon... to say it changed the field a bit was an understatement.

Kittalae's familiarity with elemental magic was hopeful. She shouldn't be too shocked by the elemental fire beast. Her demonic heritage should likewise give her an ability to handle supernatural encounters with a certain coolness and acceptance. These were all best-case scenarios.

In short, Crallick mused as he called his bow to his hand, they were buggered.

Wordlessly, Crallick raised his bow skyward. That great beast had been hunting. For what, Crallick had a sinister idea. Nevertheless, the wyrm should likely pass again as it searched for its prey. Crallick's peripheral vision caught the others pulling ranged weapons from their belts, sashes, and pouches. This day was about to get very ugly, very swiftly.

Crallick thought back to the last time he had fought a dragon. The leather cloak that laid across his shoulders from the wing of that beast gave him some small comfort. Of course, he had dealt with that much smaller dragon with a crack team of Bannathyrran knight-rangers. Two of those men never saw the end of the battle. Now, almost a decade and a half later, here he was, older, slower, and with untrained men, facing a dragon easily twice the size. The maelstrom inducing creature passed overhead again. The great wyrm was readily over one hundred and twenty feet in length by Crallick's guess. The searching pattern meant that it had picked up the scent of prey nearby.

Crallick grinned savagely. At the very least, that meant that his crew would at least spare the maidens from their fate for the scant moments that it would take the creature to devour them. Bolstered by this thought, Crallick steadfastly raised his bow to the heavens, waiting with bated breath for the third pass.

As the approaching gale grew in volume, Crallick let fly with his first shot. This was key. If he could bloody it right off the bat, he could surely give a morale boost that could give his doomed party a fighting chance. His arrow bounced harmlessly off the dragon's armored underbelly instead of into its armpit, where he had been aiming. Damn it all. He glared balefully at his bow, as though it were the cause of betrayal to his shot, and not his own eyes.

Alerted to the threat within the trees, the great wyrm Pyryathan slowed her passes with several mighty back-beats of its majestic wings. She snaked her head back and forth, looking for the diminutive mortals that she could now smell. Living in this part of the world, she had become used to the scent of reptilemen, humans, halflings, and other beasts of the rainforest. But coming to her mountains lately had been new and tasty smells. The canopy stymied her efforts to find her prey. She began to lower herself through the foliage to get a better look under the ocean of leaves.

A huge reddish reptilian head crashed its way delicately through the trees and into view. Upon seeing the monstrous visage, there was a general hue and cry of panic and alarm. Fortunately this clamour was accompanied by a volley of missile weapons launching up towards the incoming threat.

Crallick was again foiled by blurring vision that caused his arrow to glance off the mark. He shook his head in frustration, not quite putting together that the heat, combined with the alcohol consumption and the morning exertions, coupled with age, were producing a debilitating dehydration that was taking its toll on him.

Menshirre let fly a bolt from his crossbow that stuck into the dragon's right foreclaw.

Drake, Faulk, and Bargress all focused their pistol fire on the beast's belly. Armon Faulk's pistol backfired. It destroyed itself and severely burnt his hand in the process. Bargress's shot wasn't as dead-on as it needed to be, so it careened off into the sky. Erik's shot found its mark, shivering a scale and burying itself into the dragon's skin.

Glip-Glip's neurotoxin laden dart from his blowgun pierced the dragon's right foreclaw with no small amount of luck. While not causing much in the way of physical damage, the slight twitching denoted the effects of the toxin.

Kittalae, however, did something altogether unexpected, and quite probably battle-turning. She saw the beast moving towards the group. She saw it forcing its way between the trees. Her yellow eyes blazed, she darkened her features in supreme concentration and bent the will of the forest trees to her own. The trees around the dragon began to writhe and lash out, their trunks twisting into manacle-like loops to anchor the dragon in place. Two twisted around its right foreleg and one around its right wing joint, impairing its ability to stay aloft. Two others, further back, bound its left hind leg and its tail.

Spread out like that, it became quite the dangerous roof on an impromptu house of horrors.

Hullaboo, Izzy and Gregor, all lacking missile weapons, hurriedly made their way up the boles of several nearby trees in an attempt to reach the ensnared dragon.

The dragon tried in vain to free itself from the trap. After yanking its trapped limbs, and clawing at the trees that held it fast, it gave up for the moment. It spied the climbers. It inhaled and gouted forth an eruption of flame from its gullet.

Gregor saw the glow in its mouth. This gave him barely enough time to hold up his shield. He felt the blast of heat wash over him, then scant moments later, he was drenched in the vomiting flames. They cascaded over him, his shield, and the tree, immolating as they went. He felt the taste of ash in his mouth, and it took him a moment to realize that it was the shield that saved his life by forfeiting itself to the fire. His eyes hurt terribly from both the intensity of the light, coupled with the dehydrating heat. He was sure he would die. Blisters rose up on the reddened flesh of his forearms and on the calves of his legs. Wood charred and splintered around him. Glowing hot embers sparked and fell from the tree. In spite of all these harrowing conditions, Gregor managed to maintain his hold aloft in the now burning tree. Gritting his teeth against the pain, he continued to climb.

Crallick rubbed his eyes. He listened to the cry of Gregor's pain. Shaking off the dehydration-induced blur in his vision, he leveled his third arrow at the great wyrm. He loosed the arrow as the glow from the flames died away from its throat. The bladed arrowhead sped through the air. It lanced deep into the dragon's neck. Crallick knew from experience that fighting these great predators were marathons, not sprints. Other than from a tap-room's boisterous braggarts, he had never heard of a quick fight with a dragon. Grimly he fished another arrow from his quiver.

Kittalae was hiding amongst the roots of a massive tree. She was focused on directing the restrictive efforts of the rainforest on keeping the dragon bound in place. She sent more trees in to lash onto the mighty beast. She tried to drown out the elemental wails of anguish as fire began to consume the one tree, and embers fell to the undergrowth to take light and begin to smoulder in the damp undergrowth.

Glip-Glip felt more at home than he had felt for many a night. His sticky foot-pads helped him swiftly scale the trees to almost level with the deep ruddy beast. He glowered at it through bright yellow eyes. He leveled his blowgun to his mouth. Glip-Glip then rubbed a thorn on his skin and slipped it down the reed. He filled his lungs with air, then exploded it out through the tube, sending the small dart whizzing to the dragon's left hind leg. It spasmed. Glip-Glip let out a "kree" of happiness. This was easily the biggest thing he had ever hunted. Ever.

Bargress and Erik swiftly reloaded their pistols.

Armon, realizing he had no working pistol and no working trigger finger, wisely hid behind a tree.

Hullaboo leapt from branch to branch, devouring the distance to the dragon swiftly.

Izzy was likewise making good progress, though it would take him a while longer than the froggle to get to his enemy.

Gregor, sobbing, forced himself to pull himself upwards. When he lifted his left hand to grab a branch, he watched in horror as the skin sloughed away, cauterized to the trunk of the tree. Fighting back tears and a sense of impending doom, he struggled onward.

Menshirre's crossbow failed to hit his mark effectively. The bolt skittered harmlessly off the dragon's scaly underbelly.

Pyryathan watched with contempt the little morsels. They crawled and stung at her. A sting on her throat felt upsetting. Also, she was feeling pins and needles in her foreleg and hind leg. She noticed a lizardman with a human by the base of a tree. One was cowering. Maybe it would demoralize the others if he died. She spat a bolus of flame to their tree. Conveniently it should maybe kill one of the infernal tree-spirits that were forgetting its place in the cosmic wheel. After all, wood should never challenge fire.

Whether or not it was the goddess of fate, Moredhel, or the goddess of luck, Zereah, smiling upon him, but Menshirre noticed the blaze reaching for him in barely enough time to dodge from danger. He desperately leapt forwards, rolling over himself to allow the momentum to carry him as far as it could. His quiver of bolts was upended, and his roll sent bolts scattering this way and that.

Armon Faulk felt, rather than saw, the flames. They erupted into the tree behind him. The bole of the tree charred and began to kindle. The blast of flame and heat charred the back of his neck, shoulders and back. His helm saved most of his hair. He screamed as his leather armor was boiled into his skin.

Armon's scream of pain was not the only roar to escape the conflagration. A large striped cat took flight from under the roots of the tree. It yowled its anguish as flames licked its orange furred hide.

With the cacophony of violence erupting around him, Crallick's panic calmed. His heart at peace, he faced the winged doom, took aim, and let his fourth arrow fly. The dragon deftly swatted it away with its dominant foreclaw, only to realize that it wasn't responding as deftly as it had hoped. Crallick's shot buried itself into the beast's palm.

The Pyryathan's cry of surprise at this insult was cut off in her throat, as a tree began to tighten aggressively around her neck.

Urgently, Kittalae tried to drown out the elemental chorus in her mind, as more trees became engulfed in flames. She continued to choreograph their deadly assault on the dragon. No longer was she content to merely hold it in place, now she sought to strangle the life from its body.

Thorn from pouch. Roll on skin. Insert in reed. Fill lungs. Fire blowgun. Hanging precariously from a high vantage point in a canopy was nothing new for Glip-Glip. However, taking on a creature of such magnitude was befuddling for the tribal tree-froggle. He couldn't fathom if his poison was even bothering it. The last thorn he fired stuck into the membrane of the beast's right wing. Well, he would have to hope he was having some effect upon it.

Bargress and Erik continued to fire on the dragon's belly, hoping that their focused fire would have some effect. Their two shots seemed to do little more than crack a couple of scales.

Menshirre picked himself up and quickly began scavenging for as many of his bolts as he could find. May the gods spare him this horrible day.

Making decent enough time in their climbs, Izzy and the wounded Gregor were closing in on the massive dragon. Izzy was climbing furiously, madness clouding cowardly thoughts of self-preservation. Gregor, meanwhile, was far more tentative in his ascent, fear and pain providing such a cocktail of nerves that he was practically drunk with his own wretched mortality. He climbed as though already dead.

Hullaboo landed on a branch close to the beast's neck. He aimed his longspear and *thrust*!

Unfortunately, the choking trees got in the way of his strike and he only dug a furrow into the side of a tree. "Garrum!" he muttered in indignation.

Armon Faulk stumbled through the forest floor, trying to get to another location to hide. Unbeknownst to him, Pyryathan's eyes were very good. She tracked his flight and sent another ejection of flames to seek out his flesh. Fortune saved him this time by allowing him to trip face first over a root that sent him rolling down a trough-like ravine, thus sparing him the roaring flames and only costing him a broken nose for his troubles. He lay at the bottom of the ravine and wept.

Crallick's fifth arrow. He paused to pass over it with an incantation. His firebolt spell was useless. His entangling spell was a pittance compared to whatever it was that Kittalae was performing. No, he had other tricks. He transformed the head of his arrow into a frost mine. As soon as it impacted with something it should detonate, causing ice shards and freezing temperatures to blast everything in a five-yard radius. He figured everyone was still clear of the beast. He couldn't see the camouflaged Hullaboo, nor the deft Glip-Glip. He shot the arrow, aiming for the beast's neck again. For only the second time in this fight, his aim was true to the mark. The arrow buried itself against the neck of the creature. The resultant blast of frost and ice caught its head, neck and forelegs in the blast.

One wing also came under the ravaging blast of the spell. Ice crystals and frost coated the surprised beast for a moment.

Crallick knew the chilling effects wouldn't last long, especially in this heat. But hopefully it would slow the beast down somewhat.

Pyryathan felt cold unlike anything it had felt before. When it washed down her gullet and chilled the fires of her breath glands, a massive belch of steam was all that would muster forth from her tormented lips. She was no longer having fun with these strange, tasty smelling creatures. There was one golden shining to that horrible blast. It had weakened the tree holding her neck, so when she had yanked her head back in response to the blast, it had torn her neck free of the bondage.

Kittalae's hold on the dragon was weakening, she could tell. She tried to squeeze every tree that held it, to keep it in place. She was getting very tired, very quickly.

Glip-Glip saw the mighty beast rear up in agony, with steam roiling out of its mouth. He aimed under the upturned head and fired into the roof of the dragon's mouth. His mind-numbing dart found its way into the creature's mouth and buried itself into the soft palate of the roof of its massive maw.

Brain freeze! Brain freeze! No, not exactly. There was something numbing her mind. She couldn't think clearly. She was beginning to panic. Something wasn't right. Her coordination was off. Her balance. Her vision. Breathing was getting hard. Pyryathan felt something she hadn't known for many ages. Fear.

Bargress and Erik loaded their pistols. They were breathing heavily and taking shelter behind different tree trunks that were about twenty yards apart. They had noticed what had happened to Menshirre and Armon and had no desire to repeat that mistake.

Menshirre fired one of his salvaged bolts into the now drooping right wing of the great beast. It tore through the membrane and flew out of sight.

Gregor missed a handhold. It was a numbing sensation to realize that he was doomed. Not devoured by a dragon as he had envisioned, but sent crashing to earth due to a misplaced hand that broke away a branch which had his life attached to it. Panic clutched at his throat as he felt gravity pull higher and higher on his back. As he fell away from the tree, he felt a branch tear through the seat of his pants, cruelly gore his rectum, tear along his peritoneum, and de-glove his scrotum from his testes. The burning pain lasted until another branch snapped his left arm like a twig and sent him into a spin. Two breaths later, he folded backwards with a grinding crunch at his belly when his back met the root system of the massive tree. Mercifully, he could no longer feel anything below his chest.

Izzy launched himself forward with a bellowing scream, driving both of his cutlasses into the back of the dragon's head. He had aimed behind the horns that crowned its head with a lethal tiara. The blades bit deep, and one lodged in a suture of the beast's skull.

Pyryathan never felt the blades bite, nor the weight of the man. She was beginning to violently thrash about, terrified of the sensations and the loss of feeling.

Hullaboo glanced his spear pointlessly off of the chest of the now thrashing monster. He could barely keep his balance, so violent was the throes of the beast.

Armon looked up from his vantage point at the bottom of the ravine. He had a good long view of the calamity about to befall them.

It began as a series of splintering cracks that shivered the tops of half a dozen trees. Then it escalated to the mad drop of the several ton creature plummeting through the forest.

Kittalae screamed in protest to the wails of the injured wood spirits in her head. She threw her hands up to her head as she became disoriented. Swift reacting Crallick, not anticipating that much of a response to the cold, but knowing never to second-guess quick changing battlefield conditions, had begun to run as he saw the seizures start to wrack the dragon. Dashing by Kittalae, he reached out and grabbed her roughly up and tossed her over his shoulder. He'd worry about apologies later if he made it. He then flung the two of them free of the creature's growing shadow.

Glip-Glip's sticky toe-pads made riding out the thrashing tree an easy enough task. He knew he was fortunate enough not to be on one of the trees that were trying to hold the dragon. As his perch swayed back and forth through yards of space, he watched in awe as the massive dragon fell away below him.

The rest of Crallick's party were not so lucky. For ill-fate struck them all.

Menshirre found himself rolling to safety again. His crossbow lay crushed where he had dropped it. He felt his shoulder dislocate painfully as his pell-mell tumble took him into the path of a tree's root system.

Bargress had almost all of the life crushed out of him as he ran over to his good friend and shipmate, Erik, and violently tossed him to safety. He had been upright when the wyrm's mass came down upon him.

Bargress's life-saving throw sent Erik sailing through the air, only to have his flight arrested by a tree trunk. His armored left shoulder took the bulk of the abuse.

Izzy rode the beast all the way down, hanging on for dear life. He screamed unintelligibly for the whole ride. On impact, his chin bounced off the hilt of one of his cutlasses, causing him to bite off the tip of his tongue. He also broke the thumb of his left hand.

Hullaboo's fall through the air was rough, but he managed to land on the back of the dragon. Unfortunately for him, the spines that crowned the vertebrae on the back of the great monster broke his right leg at the knee. He howled in pain, then mercifully went unconscious.

Armon was sure he was free of the falling dragon. As it turned out he was. The shadow that persisted to fall across his ravine, though, was a tree. The tree dislodged from the dragon's fall, likewise joined the trend and allowed itself to also fall. The bole thundered down with almost the same intensity as the dragon. As sure as Chessintra was here to take him, Armon cried and wet himself. When the dust and earth began to settle, Armon choked and sputtered, still very much alive. There was just enough room in the now compressed earth at the sides of the ravine to allow Armon to ride out the collision. He gingerly touched the tree. "Thank you for not killing me."

Pyryathan had lost all sense of direction. Even up and down eluded her perception. Then she couldn't seem to make one wing work. Gravity decided to assist her higher, albeit fuzzy, brain functions at least with the problem of up and down. She was falling. Her eyes could see, but her body couldn't feel it. It was terrifying. She watched trees loom skywards all around her.

There was even one that seemed impossibly close. She heard, as though through a distant cave, tiny screams and cries. Then came the resounding impact.

The ground met her mass with a shuddering whump. The crushing collision shattered her jawbone, dislocating the mandible and driving one of the spurs of bone into the temporal lobe of her brain. Her neck broke over a rocky outcropping. This had the small mercy of a short jolt of pain, then nothing but a brutal headache. The bole of a tree that had once tried to tie her neck in place revenged its prior destruction by gallantly spitting her through a mighty lung. Thus, a simple tree managed to accomplish what many a noble knight had merely dreamed of: the lancing of a dragon to win the day. No other part of the great beast was undamaged. The concussive forces ruptured internal organs, blood vessels, and torqued bones to their breaking point. She expelled everything left in her body.

Flames belched forward from the final vomit of her breath gland. This immolated a thirty-yard stretch of rainforest and set the last of Menshirre's bolts alight. He had barely cleared the area of vomiting flames himself. His tongue was flicking out of his mouth so rapidly, it had the appearance of a permanent pink proboscis. He was desperately venting excess heat.

Armon had dragged himself to the top of the ravine. His head crowned the lip that was facing the broken tail of the dragon. Black fecal matter was cascading out of the wrecked rectum. His pain-blurred mind thought there must be a joke there somewhere. This caused his face to tighten into a weak smile. That was the last smile his face would recognizably make. For the next breath witnessed a yellow jet spray forward. The pungent draconic urine smelt of rotten eggs. It burned with both heat and acidic potency. Armon screamed as the lips and side of his face burned away in a chemical nightmare.

Again Crallick found himself on the surviving end of a dragon fight. *'Just great,'* he mused. *'Another adventure no one will believe in the pub.'* The grizzled veteran took a moment to go around and to secure the scene of the carnage. His first order of business was to approach the mighty beast while calling his sword to his hand. Then, seeing Izzy close to where he wanted to be, he said, "Move."

Confused and in severe pain, Izzy took a few long moments to figure out what Crallick wanted. Finally he saw the look in Crallick's eye, and the way he was gripping the sword. Izzy nodded and scuttled away, abandoning his own cutlasses in the dragon's skull.

Crallick laid his head over the back of the dragon's occipital notch, a groove that accommodated the dragon's neck vertebrae while it flew. Before he slid his sword home into the hindbrain of the majestic creature, he spoke a short parting phrase in draconic speech.

"Asha carry you home to the great furnace."

He sank the blade to the hilt with a very intense effort. He growled and huffed and roared as the ligaments, cartilage and tendons all resisted his efforts. Then with a pop and sluice, his blade penetrated the membrane that held the dragon's brain. The last foot of his blade sank in as though he were slicing through an overripe peach.

This chore completed, Crallick glanced over to Izzy. "You okay?"

Izzy smiled a bloody-toothed grin. "Just lucky Crallick. I only think I hurt my left thumb. Might have bit my tongue too. It feels swollen." There was an uncharacteristic lisp to his words that made what actually came out of his mouth sound like: "Wust ducky Cwallik. I onwy pink I hurt my weff tumb. Might of bit my tongue too. It fells swowwen."

Crallick half grinned. "Probably. Well, you did good Izzy. Help out will you? Check around for the rest of our crew. Try to get as many together as possible. We need to take stock before we press on."

"Aye, aye ser," came Izzy's sharp reply.

Glip-Glip jumped from a tree to the crown of horns atop the fallen dragon. "KREE KREE!" he chirped as loudly as he could. Which was disproportionately loud.

Crallick looked over to the small poisonous froggle. He did some mental math. "You okay Glip-Glip?"

"Kree!" Glip-Glip's very wide smile was almost contagious.

"Were you using your poison?" Crallick was beginning to smile himself.

"Kree-glip. Kree!" Glip-Glip nodded frenetically, then opened his mouth and pointed to its roof. "Kwee!" he said with his finger stuffed inside it.

Nodding his understanding, Crallick said, "Great. Now get off our kill so we can butcher it safely. Savvy?"

With a wet double blink from his nictating membrane covered eyes, Glip-Glip 'kree-kree'ed' his understanding and hopped down. Crallick noticed he seemed none the worse for wear.

Kittalae leapt upon his back, hugging him with wild abandon. This was so unexpected and disorienting that Crallick almost called his blade back to his hand, even though it was still buried in the dragon's brain.

"Whoa! By the furnace! What's all this about!" Crallick startled.

"We killed a dragon! We killed a dragon! We killed a dragon! We're alive! And we killed a dragon!" She was rambling. Her breasts were heaving against his back and he was beginning to feel… well, it had been so long, he wasn't sure what he felt. And damn it, she was so young! She kissed the back of his neck. Her tail coiled around his inner thigh.

"Kittalae! Enough!" Crallick barked. He was really beginning to feel uncomfortable. This was no time for romance or any other such foolishness.

Kittalae fell away, stammering, with tears welling up to shimmer the surface of her smoldering yellow eyes. "S-s-s-sorry master, I was just so caught up with the joy of it all. I-I-I-I'm sorry."

More softly, Crallick said, "Look. It's not your fault. No need to apologize. I just need to concentrate on the mission at hand and you can be quite the distraction when you put your mind to it. Okay?" He figured that was the best he could do to comfort her.

"Oh. Okay then." She wiped the back of her sleeve across her face. Then she looked back to him with a devious smile; the kind only one born of sin and lust could make. "So then, master, what can I do to help?" She dripped way too much honey on her words to let him know this wasn't over by a long shot.

"Find anyone who needs help and collect them in one place. Try to help them as best you can." Crallick glanced over to Glip-Glip, "You hop back up a tree and keep a weather eye out for anything coming in to scavenge, other than us. Savvy?"

"Sure, I'm on it," said Kittalae as she ran off, her tail swishing lightly as she went.

"Kree," agreed Glip-Glip, who promptly hopped back up into the trees.

"Crallick! Mate! Over here!" called Erik's voice.

Crallick leapt into action, scrambling over the corpse's topography to the other side. Sliding down the side of the dead beast's ribs, he landed beside Mr. Drake. "What's wrong?" he huffed. "You okay?"

Tears left pale clean streaks down the anguished ashen face of the Amarallan sailor. Erik choked out, "I'm fine. Bargress. It's Bargress. H-h-he saved me." As Erik's voice fell to sobs, he simply pointed under the dragon, where Crallick could barely make out one Komodoman hand limply thrust out from under the weight of the dragon's chest.

Crallick took in a breath. "My goddess," he swallowed. He had to play this right. He didn't want Erik to lose his shite. Not here; not now. He had seen things like this before. He remembered back to the other dragon he had fought. Hollister had presumed they had won the day when the last arrow had struck the beast and it began to fall. He had given a triumphant cheer and had raised his hands in victory… only to be buried under the red drake's carcass.

"Look. Erik," Crallick roughly grabbed the other man's unkempt chin, twisting it to meet his gaze. "You know how you apply pressure to a wound?"

"Wess." Crallick's grip on Erik's mouth was causing the cheeks and lips to bunch up oddly.

"Well, Bargress is wounded badly, I'd say. But right now he has all the pressure he needs. He's either dead or being kept stable. Either way, he's best off right where he is. This will be the location for all our injured. Go and let everyone else who is helping know this. Then help out yourself. Got it?"

"Oi, oi saw." Erik spat when Crallick released him, then he added, "Thanks Cral."

"Don't sweat it, my man. After all, you're the one helping me through this shite. Don't forget that," Crallick grimly reminded him.

Crallick thought he heard his stomach rumble but then he dismissed it as the accompanying abdominal trembling didn't occur. He waited a moment. There it was again. A low "rrrrrrr."

Shifting to the balls of his feet, Crallick padded into the forest, towards some of the burning trees. Nestled in the gloom of cypress roots, its golden eyes flickering in the firelight, was a frightened orange cat. It continued to rumble its discontent balefully at the flames.

"Just great, Jyslin," Crallick rumbled himself. "What fresh buggery do you plan for me now?" Then a little louder, he growled at the trapped striped cat. "Well now, that was a pretty stupid place to hide. Some master assassin you turned out to be." Based on the size of the head, Crallick deduced that the cat would be about two and a half feet long. About the size of a full-grown lynx; or a teenage cougar. Both made decent hunting cats if you had time to train them. As for this feral cat? He would probably just savagely attack him, or flee into the undergrowth. Either way, Crallick had a soft spot for animals... well, ones that weren't either trying to kill him or his supper. "Hope you make the right choice, big guy," Crallick said, as he unfurled his dragon cape and laid it on the ground to create a path for him. He leaned across and gathered up the black and orange ball of furry fangs and claws that furrowed and dug their way into the rings of armor. Crallick could tell this was a desperate need for purchase, and not anything aggressive. Just fear. Nevertheless, he was rewarded with dozens of tiny red jewels beading his skin under his clothes. Growling, Crallick admonished, "Hey now, take it easy. I've got you." Crallick dragged the cat free of the tangle of cypress roots. Once he cleared the other end of his cloak, he tried and failed to detach the rumbling feline. Sighing, Crallick gathered up his cloak, wrapped the beast in it, and began staggering around the field with an extra hundred pound weight hanging off of his front. He idly mused if this was what his wife had experienced with Amalae during her pregnancy. With that, he thought maybe he could understand some of her griping.

Lumbering around, Crallick watched the others gather by the fallen Bargress. Menshirre's right arm was hanging in an unnatural way from his chest. Hullaboo had been dragged back by Erik and Izzy; his leg was loosely flopping along the ground.

They had led Armon, recognizable only by his clothes, to rest against the side of the great beast. His face and hand had been rendered unrecognizable by nasty burns. One eye was milky-white in its lidless socket. The other eyelid was fused solidly over the other orb.

Gregor was nowhere to be found. He was presumed under the dragon, like Bargress.

Kittalae used her wood-speaking talents to great effect. She fashioned form-fitting sheaths for Hullaboo's fractured femur.

Erik and Izzy held down the violently hissing Menshirre and brutally relocated his shoulder with a gut-wrenching pop.

Noticing the tumour-like bulge on Crallick's front, Kittalae came over to ask him, "What's with the weight gain? You didn't eat the heart of the dragon did you?"

"No," Crallick said simply, then added, "Why, does it give strength, or powers in battle? I remember our mage was very interested to get some the last time I fought a dragon."

Kittalae laughed, "No, master, it's a virility enhancer."

"A what?" Crallick was dumbfounded.

Pointing at his crotch, she purred, "It makes this undefeatable."

"Oh," Crallick said, then actually laughed. "That dirty old Vitani fuck! We all thought he was needing it to make potions of fire resistance, or flasks of fire, or the like."

"Nope. That's the blood and the breath glands respectively. He just wanted to impress the ladies." She winked, "I'm sure you wouldn't have needed it anyway."

"Heroism? Strength?" Healing?" Crallick was desperate to give his old friend the benefit of the doubt.

"Brain, muscle, and bone. Now what's under your cloak?" Kittalae asked.

Crallick pulled the cloak away to reveal the large orange and black ball of fur.

"Mrowr," it yawned and blinked golden eyes at her.

"Oh my master, you are a good man," she smiled at him. "It's beautiful. What is it?"

"A cat," Crallick growled. "And I'm not that good."

"Of course not, master," she demurred. Putting her hands behind her back, she swayed slightly, "I figured it's a cat. What kind?"

"Furnace take me if I know," Crallick shrugged. "I've never seen one before. It's about the same size as a young cougar. It's a couple of feet long. Feels about a hundred pounds. I figure it's pretty much done growing; maybe another six inches and twenty pounds. If it bonds well, I may have a decent hunter."

Kittalae had noticed one of the cub's paws. She felt that her master was underestimating the cat's growth. However, he was the hunter and it was not her place to challenge him. She simply smiled. "Well then, your good deed shall be well rewarded. Shall I take him off your hands? That will free you up so that you can try and help the others with Bargress."

"Great idea." Crallick was beginning to wonder how pregnant women had the back strength to walk around with an extra hundred pounds on their stomachs.

The idea was better in practice than in application. They ended up with the yowling and crying cat having to be pulled off complete with Crallick's armor and cloak. Kittalae sat with the cub, stroked its head, and spoke comfortingly to it while the now topless form of her master set her imagination alight.

Crallick joined the others at carving out the lung and bone around the area with Bargress buried under it. As they revealed parts, they bound and compressed him so as not to cause his injuries to be too disrupted.

Night was falling by the time they had him free. That night would mark the time when the veil was most receptive to souls and offerings. This night in the Haunting held no moon. Chessintra would be hungry for certain. Crallick was becoming more and more restless. "Look, we'll have to leave those who are too injured here. We'll butcher the body when we return. We have to get going. Now. The girls don't have much time. I can feel it."

Hullaboo spoke up. "I can protect our trophy and friends! Yes-yes. Garrum."

"That's great. We'll be back for you as soon as we have the girls," Crallick tried to reassure him.

"Good, good. I am eager to meet your daughter and Vlados's too." The bull froggle licked his head, "Garrum."

"Okay, see you soon," Crallick concluded.

"Bye-bye," Hullaboo waved. Then he gingerly hopped with one leg to the top of the dead dragon's back, carrying his spear with him.

Crallick grimly led his now much-diminished band of six into the gathering gloom of the gloaming.

Chapter Fifteen

"Crallick's bow spotted the drake's wing, taking its flight.
The falling drake found Hyrophon's triumphant head.
Crallick's men braved tooth and claw to end the vile fight.
Greatsword to the neck, Crallick ensured the beast was dead."
Verse 16: Ballad of Ser Crallick Carnage-born

Night had completely cloaked the party by the time they had reached the foot of the monolithic ziggurat. Torchlight glimmered in the cool jungle evening. A baritone chanting cascaded down from the pinnacle of the pyramid structure. The chanting was underscored by soft weeping and occasional shuddering sobs.

Crallick knelt at the foot of the vine-covered stonework and watched silhouettes moving against the night sky. From his limited vantage point, he could barely make out how many there were. He could see six static forms; he presumed those were almost half of the prisoners. There were three bodies moving about. He stopped watching as he heard Erik come up behind him.

"So Cral, how do you want to play this?" Erik asked in a hushed tone.

Shaking his head, Crallick confessed, "I'm not sure. They have a superior tactical position for starters. Secondly, in our order, we never usually had to rescue so many victims. Also, casualties were always second priority. Our primary goal was to make sure the bad guys died and were never able to commit atrocities again. So I'm kind of open to suggestions right now. I've never had to make sure all thirteen hostages survived, while killing all the bad guys, and then also making sure my untrained team survives."

Erik scoffed. "Well hell, why not make it easy on yourself then? I don't think you can raise the bloody bar any higher, do you?" Then he gently put a hand on Crallick's forearm. This had the desired effect of pulling Crallick's attention back from the top of the monument to the gods.

"What?" Crallick hissed.

In answer, Erik jerked his head to indicate that Crallick should follow him back. Then, staying crouched, Erik edged his way back into the undergrowth.

A scant moment later, one that felt an eternity to Crallick, he forced all his will to pull away from his position to follow Erik back to the others.

A short way back into the rainforest, the group were clustered about, readying their weapons and waiting on Crallick's orders to finally confront the villains that they had chased halfway across creation to catch.

Kittalae had cast some sort of enchantment upon herself. Her once scarlet and smooth complexion now was browner in hue, and was roughly ridged. The same roughening on the back of her good hand left the impression that this transformation was complete. Her spearpoint had been rubbed down with mud so there would be little reflection from it. The orange and black cat blended into the bladed ferns of the undergrowth really quite well. It was the slightly luminous golden eyes that betrayed its location at the feet of Kittalae.

Glip-Glip's blue and yellow markings seemed remarkably muted in the gloom of the night. His bar-like irises were dilated to almost circular dimensions. He rested only six feet above the ground in a low crest of cypress roots. His blowgun and satchel were still readily available at his side. His dagger had also been smeared with mud.

Izzy had taken it upon himself to smear the loam that he had found all over his face, hands and arms. He grinned wickedly at Crallick, his teeth seeming all the brighter against his once tanned, now filthy face. Those teeth, as well as the whites of his eyes, gave a ghoulish tone to his countenance. His cutlasses remained sheathed. His shirt had been traded for the armor from Armon. The cuir bouilli was darker than his linen shirt and offered more protection.

Menshirre had spent the time in the clearing taking sap from a freshly wounded tree he was suspiciously close to, and using it to stick ferns to the front of his breastplate. This rendered it all but invisible. Along with his naturally brown and green mottled skin, he easily had the best camouflage of them all. Except for maybe the cat.

His crossbow had been replaced with Bargress's pistols. He was finishing the loading of his second one. The first was already tied into his sash. His cutlass was darkened with sap and soil.

And that brought him around to Erik. He was glittering slightly in the dark with his chain mail armor. His pistols had already been loaded. His cutlass remained sheathed. He was standing just to the right side of where Crallick entered the little clearing. He relayed in a hushed tone to the others what Crallick's expectations were of himself.

Crallick helped himself to some of the tree sap and the loam and began painting his face. "Look, I'm open to suggestions. I have a pretty good idea how this is going to go down. I just don't like it." He then took a swig from his rum flask. The last drop fell to his tongue. Just great.

Erik started the suggestions rolling. "Two of us provide a distraction. Draw them out. We fight them off as best we can. The rest of you grab the girls; get them to safety, then save our asses. Good, huh?"

"So who commits suicide as bait with this one?" Crallick growled.

"Why, you and me of course," Erik grinned. "We may actually last long enough to be saved."

"Of course," Crallick sighed. "Next?"

"We rush them as hard and fast as we can. Kill 'em as fast as we can. Then try to save the girls after," Izzy offered.

"The girls would be sure to die swiftly. Also, we don't know how deeply staggered they are up there. Not knowing their disposition is a bad thing," Crallick grumbled.

"Dispo…what?" asked Izzy, screwing up his features.

"Location," Crallick clarified.

Glip-Glip offered a string of words and chirps and gestures.

"Thanks, I may use some of them," Crallick said.

"I think I can hear the chanting rising in volume," warned Kittalae.

"Thanks, all," Crallick quickly rushed out. "Okay, it's time to get this started. Here's what I want to see happen. Erik, from your idea, you'll head up the front. I'll come with, but I'll be out of sight…"

"Great," Erik interrupted.

"We're approaching the east side. Menshirre, you take the north side. Izzy, you'll take the south side. Kittalae will go with him…" Crallick continued, undaunted.

"Why, Crallick?" Kittalae interrupted this time, with a hint of a pout.

"Because he'll make a scene, and that should let you get to the girls quicker. Your job is to save the girls. As many as you can." Crallick was beginning to get frustrated with the lack of rum and the availability of interruptions. There would never have been this kind of discourse in the order. Shaking his head, he finished, "And Glip-Glip, you're the fastest in this terrain, so you can take the far west approach. If all goes well, we'll meet at the top, kill the bad guys, avenge those who have suffered at their hands, and save my daughter. I mean the girls. Now let's move!"

Under the cover of the night and the chanting rhythms, the group melted into the darkness. Moving swiftly, the much smaller parties all reached their points of ascent.

Crallick, meanwhile, had noticed two things he had overlooked. Firstly, he had no idea how to tell when they arrived at their locations. Secondly, he hadn't told them when to go. Shite, he was getting too old for this kind of shite when he forgot simple shite like that. Crallick then realized a third oversight. A low rumble betrayed the presence of the cat behind him. Jyslin preserve him. He couldn't train a hunting or war cat right now, and as sure as death's throne room, he couldn't cat sit right now. "Stay," was the one command he gave the beast.

"Where?" asked a confused Erik, who thought the order had been for him.

"Not you," a frustrated Crallick tersely replied. "The cat."

"Ah. By the way, how will they know when to go?" Erik mused out loud.

Scoffing to himself, Crallick thought that Erik was a good man. A smart one too. "We lead the attack."

"How do we know when to go?" Erik pushed, only partially satisfied with the answer.

Crallick was about to say "We guess," when a young woman's blood-curdling scream cut through the night. "NOW!" Crallick declared instead.

That command had been issued to the back of Erik's head. Upon hearing the despondent scream of anguish, he had begun his reckless charge up the slope of the ziggurat. One pistol drawn and his sword out, Erik Drake pumped his legs furiously up the stairs of the massive temple. He knew Crallick wouldn't be far behind him.

Menshirre had been waiting for what he felt was too long when the pitched voice pierced the night and his patience. He charged up his side. Both pistols were in his hands, and bale light was reflected in his eyes.

Izzy and Kittalae had been arguing when to go. The scream had Izzy paint a clear picture to Kittalae that, "For every scream you hear tonight, that is another way you have failed your duty to your master." Though truly a cruel thing to say to the young woman, it had the magic effect of sending her flying into action. Izzy had to sprint to catch up. As it was, he only drew even with her by the time they crested the top of the temple.

Glip-Glip had already gone halfway up the west side of the ziggurat when he had heard the scream. He doubled the efforts of his already stair-devouring hops.

The crown of the temple was an expanse of stone that held grooved troughs leading away from twelve sacrificial plinths, three to a side. They surrounded a central raised dais with an altar upon it. This too, had grooves for a nefarious run-off.

Each of the plinths had a fresh set of cast iron manacles that had been run through much older metal rings. These manacles arrested the wrists of eleven struggling, nude girls. Several of the girls at the northern side were sobbing or crying.

The twelfth plinth also held a nude girl. However, she no longer held the strength to struggle. She stared in shock at the slippery purplish mass of her intestines that had slipped free from her abdomen to lie in a pile at her feet. She had once been an Amarallan, of no small beauty. She had been athletic, blonde, and now her blue eyes watched in astonished horror as any hopes of knowing womanhood lay at her feet.

The altar held the thirteenth virginal victim. Also nude, she laid spread-eagled upon the stone, arms and legs all bound in a lewd display. Looming over the spayed sacrifice was Eli.

Eli had doffed his furs and cloak. He stood resplendent in diabolically intricate tattoos that painted his corded torso and arms. His metal cod and greaves glimmered a molten gold in the torchlight. A black tome floated on dark motes of energy scantly feet away from him. The tome itself was unremarkable. Only a foot and a half by a foot in its dimensions. Perhaps an inch thick if you didn't include the thickness of the covers.

Eli's gaze was unfocused and sweat glistened upon him. His tumorous voice resonated an ongoing chant, while almost mindlessly, he drew a black metal dagger across the back of his left forearm. Blood, as pure as the virgins, welled up and wept down his arm. He then turned and pointed to the west.

A Komodoman lunged his jawbone blade into the delicate belly of a calico nekomin maiden. Her discordant yowl was cut short as she vomited blood and bile through her nose and mouth. Her head sagged almost immediately as her body convulsed and then hung limp from the column.

This latest violent display shocked the rescuers from their grisly reverie at this macabre scene. Yelling, howling, chirping, screaming their rages, they descended upon the perpetuators of this taboo sacrament.

Erik discharged his pistol at the closest foe: a human man, in his forties, who held a wicked looking double blade. His shot took the man in his right knee. The man cried out in surprise and almost lost his footing outright.

"Take that, you buggering freak!" Mr. Drake advertised his presence over the shot and the chanting.

A far stealthier Crallick was taking aim at Eli. He was most certainly not going to miss like with the dragon. Not this time.

Izzy barreled headlong into one of Eli's Komodomen, his white teeth and silver blades flashing viciously in the torchlight as he delivered savage blow after savage blow towards the eight-foot-tall lizardman. The flurry of blows managed to open up gashes on the reptile's right side. He sundered the scales on his arm and hip on that side.

While Izzy drew the attention of the massive guard, Kittalae quietly drifted over to one of the plinths, then fished out a small sliver of wood from a pouch on her belt. Placing the splinter in a crack close to the metal ring that held the chains, she whispered a few words. Thus calling to the wood spirit within the splinter, she woke it. It grew. First doubling in size, then by a factor of ten. A resounding crack had the metal ring fall free, and the olive-skinned human girl collapsed into her arms.

The young woman asked something in Jherrim-ga. Kittalae shook her head without comprehension, and simply pointed down the side of the temple. The naked girl quickly found her feet and began to scuttle down the side of the terraced structure. She would have collected more than her fair share of cuts and bruises by the time she reached the bottom in the dark, but she would also have her life.

Glip-Glip's foe never stood a chance. One moment the Komodoman was licking the face of an untouchable sacrifice whilst murmuring what he planned to do to her corpse as she wept uncontrollably; the next, a stinging insect took a chunk out of his right side, just under the armor straps. Seconds later, his sphincters lost all tone and evacuated everything not held in place by tendons and ligaments. His eyes were glazed over before his seizure finished. Also, he died before he hit the ground.

Giggling hysterically, the girl he had been tormenting thrust her hips forward to urinate upon him.

This confused poor Glip-Glip, and for a moment he though maybe he had nicked her with his poison. However, he relaxed when he saw no further signs of loss of control.

Menshirre shot both of his pistols at the slender Nekomin mage. Unbelievably, she dodged one outright, and melted the other slug out of the air so that only little bits ineffectively singed her robes.

"Oooooh, bad luck to cross a black cat, my friend," she sarcastically hissed at him.

Tamilla, having devoted all her life to the worship of Chessintra and the study of her arcane arts, put that training to good use. From all of the floating stuff in the air, she rearranged their order by Chessintra's will, to form a globbet of acid hanging, suspended, waiting to launch itself towards her foe. The transparent shimmering sphere of liquid elongated slightly as her will propelled it towards Menshirre's head.

The orb struck with a liquid splash. That's when the chemical burning began. Everywhere that Menshirre had been dampened by the cool bath erupted in a fast-acting potent acid. His arms, which he had thrown up to protect his face, dissolved to the bones and clattered to the ground. Bands across his face melted to the skull. His eyes were left vacant sockets. His neck eroded through his wind pipe. With only his spine to keep his head aloft, it flopped forward. There was surprisingly little blood for such a gory demise. The acid saw to that. It cauterized vessels it burnt through. In the end, the only thing to pass through Menshirre's mind was, "What, water? Is she going to bathe me to death?"

Cholo had spent many of his years as a mercenary. As of late, he had begun to tire and was becoming concerned about his mortality. So when Eli had come to him with promises of ageless vitality, he decided to take on one more contract. Up until now it had been a milk run for him. Easy money, with a vault-load of perks at the end. Now, shot by some upstart Amarallan merc, he resolved to make him pay for crossing paths with him. Maneuvering so that the dragon-lover was between him and a girl, Cholo feinted at the man's head.

As Drake lifted his sword to block, the man reversed his swing, allowing the back blade of his double sword to sweep towards his quarry in an obvious move. Drake fell for this as well. He swung his own sword down to counter.

Halting his swing, Cholo tugged his blade back, so the sweep of Drake's block met with no resistance and carried through wider than he intended. This gave Cholo the opening he needed. He thrust forwards, into the other man's chest, spitting him into the girl behind him. "I now pronounce you dead and meat. You may kiss the bride... after the sacrifice," he chuckled grimly.

Erik felt himself being forced back against something soft and yielding with the force of the blow. This buggerer was talented. He could barely keep up. He heard the girl stifle a sob from close to his ear. Vaguely, he remembered she had been a pretty mortani lass; all dark skin, eyes and hair. He could now barely keep away. His breathing was now a serious effort.

As Eli's chanting reached another feverish crescendo, he pointed south. The Komodoman kicked Izzy away, then savagely eviscerated the guts from a hobgoblin maid.

A third line of blood began to weep from Eli's arm.

Ignoring the grunt from Erik, and the shortened cry and sizzle from Menshirre, Crallick reminded himself to focus on what he could control. Nothing more. He inhaled steadily and let fly with his arrow. With uncanny despair, Crallick watched as his aimed shot was shot out of the air by a fire bolt from a torch. The Nekomin witch had set up defenses against missile attacks. Jyslin, why could nothing ever be easy? So be it. He drew another arrow and incanted it with the seeds of flames. *'Let's see how the furry bitch likes this,'* Crallick grimly thought.

"Sorry," Erik muttered to the sobbing girl behind him. She was uncomprehending. He continued, more for himself than for anyone. "I'm inappropriately close to you and I'm trying to rescue you and just got you hurt. I'm sorry. It's my first time trying to rescue anyone"

"How touching," snarled Cholo, who, while amused at Erik's rambling, didn't notice him fishing out his back-up pistol from where it was mashed between him and the mortani maiden. "Now shut up, I'm waiting for my cue. Carry on your romance in Chessintra's court."

"After you," came Erik's dry comment. He then jammed the barrel of his pistol into the man's jowly throat and squeezed the trigger. The upward slant of the barrel caused Cholo's head to blossom and mushroom into a brilliant pattern before spraying his skull's contents everywhere in a five-foot radius.

At the violent death of the girl, Izzy roared at the Komodoman. The Komodoman laughed in return, and easily began parrying every strike that Izzy could throw at him. Izzy kept up, however. His feverish rage would not allow him to relent.

Dodging away from the gushing stream of feces and gore, Kittalae swiftly repeated her splinter trick on the next plinth. This held a young pygmy woman suspended so that her feet dropped a couple of feet before landing on the stone. Once down, her alert and fear-heightened eyes took in the scenario. She needed no explanation and was running furtively towards safety as soon as Kittalae pointed out a direction.

Kittalae then started to the three columns on the west side of the ziggurat. She hoped she'd be able to save all three of them.

Glip-Glip hopped to the top of a plinth that held a female tree froggle. He kree'ed and chirped merrily to her while he launched a dart towards Eli, planning on ending him like he did the dragon. He uttered a "Kirrup!!" of anger and dismay when a bolt of flame from a torch incinerated his wee dart. That wasn't good at all.

Looking to the west, Tamilia knew from the chant that one would have to sacrifice soon. There was a tree froggle atop the plinth with the virgin froggle. Smiling in predatory glee, she limited the scope of her fireball, but concentrated the heat. She let it fly. It blazed across the night to impact squarely on the plinth. Glip-Glip had seen it coming and had leapt for his life. The female froggle turned to ash, her two webbed and padded feet that fell to the ground were all that remained of her.

Izzy's rage met with brutal undoing as the toothed jawbone that was wielded by the Komodoman tore savagely through his left thigh. Three flaps of his quadriceps hung petal-like and crimson as though a jungle flower blossomed in his leg after the strike. He felt his resolve falter slightly. Was this the beginning of the end for him? Was his pain going to subside? So be it. He'd try to make it glorious.

Crallick launched his flaming arrow into the back of the Nekomin. Its flaming wake traced a line back to his position. That was no matter. The arrow had been true to the mark, piercing her heart. The flames had ignited her fur and robes. As her caterwauling began, Crallick couldn't help but feel like his old self again. Damn, he was good.

Erik kept chewing on his tongue to try to stay conscious. His ragged breaths seemed ineffective. He kept tasting iron in his mouth. He mumbled something in delirium about how he had always wanted to get attached to a pretty girl, but he was sure he hadn't meant it in this way. And the goddesses of fate and luck shouldn't be so damned literal.

Desperation rooted in pain caused Izzy to feebly swing his cutlass up, only to have it caught by the clawed fist of the Komodoman. Izzy spat in its eye.

Upon reaching the western columns, Kittalae repeated her trick on a struggling dwarven maid.

She was sobbing that she had to get to her friend Amalae, or she'd never survive her rescue. Amalae's father was a crazy drunkard and very scary.

Placing a comforting hand on her shoulder, Kittalae soothed, "I know he is. Who do you think is rescuing you? Now don't let me get into trouble and run down and hide in the south side of the temple. Okay?"

Sniffling, the dwarf agreed and stumbled off.

Scared out of his proverbial tree, Glip-Glip peeked back over the top of the ziggurat. He saw the dire straights that Izzy was in. He saw Drake's misfortune. He saw Kittalae's endeavors. He couldn't see anyone trying for the man leading the ceremony. So, keeping as low to the ground as his agile and small body would allow for, Glip-Glip began to stalk towards the man in the middle of the temple carnage.

Realizing his Nekomin mage was the cadaver burning on the temple roof, Eli threw a throwing axe into the chest of an aquan girl. This split her sternum, and when the axe fell back out with her convulsive jerk, it was accompanied by a warm spray of arterial blood.

Dropping his bow and calling his sword to his hands, Crallick yelled, "Would you just stop it? It's over! You can't finish the ceremony. I've slain the dragon, I've slain almost all of your men! If you don't stop, I'll add you to the list!" Crallick was menacingly striding forwards while uttering these words.

"No you won't!" Eli countered. Then he continued chanting.

"What's the point? You no longer have any servant to control!" Crallick persisted.

"You think there is only one servant? Fool!" Eli barked a short laugh. "Besides, my mistress has more important designs than what can be impacted by a good-loving knight-ranger of Bannathyr."

No one noticed, in the heat of the exchange, the tiny froggle's eyes widen in alarm as something didn't feel right. Nor did anyone notice the dark shimmering of ancient evil magic as the ziggurat's harnessed power drank the life energy from Glip-Glip. Even Glip-Glip felt no pain, he simply weakened and became still, then was no more.

Kittalae released another girl. This one was a fire ephemorae. She fled to the south to join the other girls.

With his sword firmly gripped by the Komodoman, Izzy watched with a detached hysteria as his arm was rended from his body at the shoulder by one massive cleave. Blood began spurting from the open and jagged gash where his arm had been. His left arm stabbed his remaining cutlass at his nemesis. This too, was ineffectual.

Crallick began to pick up his speed towards the maniacal priest. "Stop this now!" he raged.

"You can't kill me even if you want to, my desperate friend," Eli grinned as he fished out another throwing axe. "You know my ship that I abandoned? Chess's Blight?"

"Yeah, we seized her!" Crallick boasted.

"Well that's convenient!" Eli practically chortled. "That lacquer I sealed her with is a 'salve of souls'. Should my life energy leave, then every soul on that ship shall accompany me to Chessintra's throne room. You would be willing to commit mass murder, my goodly knight ranger?" As if to punctuate his point, Eli let fly an axe that split a Vitani's face in two, just to the right of the impaled Erik.

With a feral growl welling up in his guts, Crallick charged. A mere five paces into his charge, time seemed to dilate for him. An acute awareness of his environment seeped into his being.

Kittalae was freeing another girl. A tiny jaragua lizardman.

Izzy had just been disarmed by the Komodoman. He was beginning to fall to the stones, his blood coming with all the other effluvia.

Erik was trying to stay conscious.

The cat was creeping into the edge of the pools of torchlight.

Finally he noticed an unearthly, grave chill seeping through his bones; as though something was trying to sap his life energy through the soles of his feet. Then he perceived her: flitting around the edges of his vision, whispers on the cusp of his hearing, scents at the perimeter of his olfactory sense, a tickle at the back of his taste buds. She was like an idea he could barely grasp.

Her intentions were clear: malice and amusement. She had black skin. Crowning her head was darker hair that bore no luster. Silver teeth decorated her smile. Her eyes were silver orbs with black irises. Or perhaps they were only pupils. It was impossible to say. Her hushed and melodic words reached out to him, "My dear sweet Crallick. You have grown so cantankerous over the years. I was beginning to suspect you would drink yourself across my threshold. Instead, I see you back reaving souls for my halls like a demon possessed. You even sent me a great dragon. My servant Eli is right about some things. I reward those who are good to me. And no, a mere knight-ranger cannot undo my plans. However, he finds himself erring with two things. First, his importance to me is not so much. And second, I don't want your soul yet. You have too much work to do yet. Keep your life energy. May Zereah smile on you."

With that registering as nothing more than a phantom of a dream, Crallick felt the draining effect fade away with the ghost. The next heartbeat took him into the hallowed sanctuary. This put Eli right in his wheelhouse.

"Last chance you sick…"

"…or you'll what?" Eli interrupted. "You're a knight-ranger. Champion of good. Kill me and innocents will die." He turned his back to Crallick and aimed at the sacrifice Kittalae was freeing.

The way Crallick saw it, innocents would continue to die if this gob-hole lived. "I'm retired," he growled as he drove his serrated blade to the hilt through Eli's tattooed spine. There was a pulse of malicious energy that radiated out from Eli.

Eli twitched on Crallick's blade, spasmed, and spat out globs of mucous-filled blood. No utterances left his body, only fluids.

Kittalae had worked her way over to where Erik was impaled. She began trying to help him off of the girl and made sure the invasive blade came with Erik. She kept apologizing that she wasn't a healer like Wanda, but she'd get him back to her as soon as she could. Kittalae was so wrapped up with her task, she never saw the Komodoman bearing down on her with the raised jawbone.

In a dark orange blur, the cat leapt on the Komodoman's head, its fangs deeply sinking into the back of the lizardman's throat. As its hind legs raked the length of its prey's back, leaving wet sticky ribbons, its front paws clung to the armpit and shoulder, hooking claws deeply into the flesh. There was an audible grinding crunch as the vertebrae in the Komodoman's neck broke and then severed the spinal cord. The whole pile of fur and scales fell into a noisy heap only feet behind a terrified Kittalae.

"Oh my God! Skyurr save me!" she screamed. Then when she saw the red smeared face looking up at her, rumbling contentedly, she added, "Oh. It's you. Well uh, thank you...." Then after regaining her breath, she concluded with a "Good kitty."

"Daddy?" Amalae wasn't sure she could trust her judgment. "Daddy? Is that you?"

"Yeah, my sweetheart. It's me." His foot forced Eli's body off the blade with a meat tearing squelch. The stench of iron and offal hung dense in the jungle air. "Daddy's got you." His blade rose and fell four times against the chains. Each strike producing a shower of sparks and a severed chain. He bent to gather up his daughter, who scurried away as far as the altar top would permit her.

"Oh daddy, I'm sorry," her almond eyes were wide in repulsion. "I know you've just gone through the furnace for me, but please..." she swallowed, "have you seen yourself?"

"What in Jyslin's creation are you on about, girl?" Crallick's temper was quickly rising. His adrenaline from the day's battle not quite ready to give up its foothold in his body yet. "I haven't seen you for nearly a year, and I've been worried sick!"

"I know. I know..." How could she tell him just how foul he smelt, and how much gore was covering him? Instead, she tried to change tact. "But," she blushed for good measure... "I'm naked daddy."

"Oh." The uncomfortable awkwardness of the realization slowly pounded through his brain. "OH!" Quickly, a baffled Crallick swiftly searched around and came up with Eli's fur cloak. "Here," he roughly shoved the article at his daughter.

"Thanks daddy." She then put it on. Armored with this, she gingerly hugged her father. "Thanks so much." They stood in their fond embrace for long moments.

Kittalae meanwhile, had busied herself with securing the rest of the area. She had all the girls except for Amalae in one place. The injured mortani woman was with Erik, holding the sword blade in place. The cat had finished eating its fill of kill and was rubbing up against the back of Crallick's legs.

"Quit it," Crallick growled at the beast after the third bump almost knocked him and his daughter over.

"Is that ours?" Amalae asked, curiously.

"Apparently," Crallick conceded.

"I thought you didn't like pets," Amalae was confused.

"I don't," Crallick sighed. "I saved it from a dragon so it got confused and started following me around. It's too old to really be trained for anything useful." Glancing down, Crallick mumbled, "I don't even know what kind of cat you are."

"The locals call the striped cat a 'tiger'. I think they are afraid of them," Amalae reported.

"How do you know that?" Crallick asked.

Scoffing, Amalae replied, "With you as my father, you didn't think I wasn't learning all I could so I could try to escape?"

Crallick laughed. "Good girl. Now let's get going."

Izzy Nunez had bled out before Kittalae could get to him. The bodies were left on the crown of the ziggurat of death. This somber tribute to Chessintra was nothing more than thanking her for not taking them as well.

Dawn's grey hues were drifting through the canopy by the time they had made their way back to the fallen dragon. They had found the broken body of Gregor, who had passed some time in the night. He had fallen about ten feet too far away. By the time Hullaboo had found him while relieving himself, it had been too late.

The girls helped the broken-legged bull froggle hobble along. A few others carried a stretcher built from a cloak and some thin branches that held Bargress, who still seemed to cling to life. The blinded Armon was led by the arm through the path back to the tribal pygmy village.

At their return, the cannibal halflings rejoiced at seeing the return of one of their own. Crallick was promptly given the chieftain's favorite daughter to wed. Erik pointed out that they were far too outnumbered and too weak to argue.

"Just take the damned bride, and annul it at sea if you can't deal with it," He said.

The several long days back to the coast was made a little easier by the throng of pygmies who brought along supplies, the bulk of the butchered dragon, and trading goods. Such as the red energy-giving Jewel of Jyslin, as Crallick called it. The natives called it coffee. They made the beach in better shape than when they had left the ziggurat.

What they found at the beach was worse than what they had left at the ziggurat.

There had been two lean-tos constructed from sail canvas and mangrove roots. Of the Chess's Blight, there was no sign. The derelict hull of the storm and battle weary Flamerunner still held its lonely vigil over the mouth of the bay.

They were greeted by Tandi's squat dwarven frame rushing over towards them, along with Wanda, who's gait belied a great deal of fatigue.

"By all that's holy! Ye made it! I was suren' you all died when the Blight went up inna' ball o' black lightning." She sniffled, "Kilt' everyone aboard."

Crallick's eyes darkened. "Everyone?"

"Aye," Tandi nodded.

Wanda got to them. Huffing lightly, she added, "Tandi and Argent were taking their watch ashore when it happened. We were housing the sick and injured on the beach. It made life a little easier for Syllethra." She glanced back at the battered team. "You all look like you've seen better days too. Syll is in the farther tent." She looked at Crallick curiously, unsure whether he had heard her. His eyes didn't look focused.

He thought he could hear the dark goddess laughing.

"Wanda!" squealed Amalae.

"Oh my goddess, how you've grown. I'm so glad to see you, my dear. Let's all get you cleaned up," Wanda exclaimed.

"Excuse me?" A dawven maid tugged at Wanda's arm. "Is my father here? My name is Bekka Ironforge."

Smiling for the first time in quite a while, Wanda gestured and said, "First tent." Then she watched joyfully as the young dwarf ran off calling, "Papa! Papa!

Epilogue

"With a cloak of drake wing, Crallick soon departed
Carnage-born, Drakeslayer, and Crallick the cruel,
All titles to him, the bards justly imparted.
He used each as a badge for retirement's fuel."
Verse 17: Ballad of Ser Crallick Carnage-born

It had taken them nearly two tenday, and the help of the Halfling tribe, to make the Flamerunner seaworthy again. This was accomplished after they made a monument to their fallen with the names of those lost etched into a stone upon the beach.

Crallick's grim sensibilities convinced Vlados as the founding captain to name the bay Bloodbath Bay. Begrudgingly, Vlados relented and did so, perhaps half thinking they'd never survive the trip back to civilization to have to report it to anyone.

Under the combined care of Wanda's divine healing and Syllethra's chichurgical skills, all of their casualties made remarkably swift, and for the most part, complete recoveries. Those who had permanent failings were made comfortable.

Crallick's ribs had healed perfectly. Other than that, he remained unscathed, except for his liver and his peace of mind. When Amalae confronted him about owning a slave, and having a bride, and a tiger? What kind of man was he turning into? She was almost sixteen now. No, Crallick was fairly certain his peace of mind was a casualty, never to be regained.

Other than her prosthetic hand, Kittalae was completely healthy.

Erik was projected to make a complete recovery. So were Vlados Ironforge, Brom Corr, Hullaboo, and Wanda Swells

Syllethra, Tandi Burrowwell, and Argent Quinthee were all likewise healthy.

Bargress Trothe was stable and occasionally became conscious. His recovery would be both long, and in the hands of the gods.

Armon Faulk lost his eyesight. His hands recovered except for the missing fingers on his right hand.

Finally, Lawrence Marley felt happy and peaceful. He never realized he was a shadow of the man he used to be. His eyes were as good as ever, and he loved to patiently play eye-spy.

It was some time in the early high winter months that they decreed themselves ready to brave the trip back home. The thirteen rescuers, nearly two months after landing on the beach of Bloodbath Bay, were finally leaving the newly discovered lands.

The thirteen surviving rescuers bolstered their ranks with the seven surviving maidens, ten pygmies, and one now three-foot-long tiger.

Vlados found Crallick on deck the morning they decided to leave. "Hey there. How are you doing? You haven't been very talkative since your foray into the jungle."

"Hmmph," Crallick agreed.

"Your daughter and your slave seem to be hitting it off really well," Vlados offered.

Sparing him a sidelong glance, Crallick growled, "Pushing your luck."

"Humph," Vlados snorted. "Maybe I am. But you have to remember that girl loves you, my friend. Really she does."

"I know, she's my daughter."

"I was talking about the other one," Vlados corrected.

"Oh," Crallick grumbled. "I guess. But what can I do? I'm apparently married. And besides, she's too young."

"Fah!" Vlados spat in contempt. "My arse! Bend over and ye may find some more excuses hiding up that skirt o' yers. I thought it 'twer the hill dwarves who wore kilts, not the Bannathyr Vitani."

Crallick let the slurs roll off his back as he scratched the ears of his tiger.

"What I'm saying, my friend, is that you've suffered enough. Jyslin knows you deserve to enjoy some things for a change. What do you say? Shall we get home so you can finally relax and enjoy some peace and female company?"

Crallick felt himself begin a smile at his friend's shenanigans. "How about you get me home before we run out of rum and I kill everyone on the ship."

Vlados laughed good-naturedly. "There you go! I knew you had some mirth left in you somewhere. Let's away then." Walking off, he bellowed. "Weigh anchor, my lads! Mr. Hullaboo set course east, by northeast!"

"Who was joking?" asked Crallick as he looked down at his feline companion.

THE END

Made in the USA
Columbia, SC
29 October 2017